SEX EDUCATION
THE ROAD TRIP

Running Press Teens
Hachette Book Group
1290 Avenue of the Americas, New York, NY 10104
www.runningpress.com/rpkids
@RP_Kids

Printed in the United States of America

Originally published in 2021 by Hodder & Stoughton Limited
in Great Britain
First U.S. Edition: September 2021

Published by Running Press Teens, an imprint of Perseus Books, LLC,
a subsidiary of Hachette Book Group, Inc. The Running Press Teens name
and logo is a trademark of the Hachette Book Group.

The Hachette Speakers Bureau provides a wide range of authors for
speaking events. To find out more, go to www.hachettespeakersbureau.com
r call (866) 376-6591.

The publisher is not responsible for websites (or their content)
that are not owned by the publisher.

Print book cover and interior design by Alison Padley

Library of Congress Control Number: 2021942449

ISBNs: 978-0-7624-8028-9 (paperback), 978-0-7624-8029-6 (ebook),
978-1-5491-9379-8 (audio)

LSC-C

Printing 1, 2021

SEX EDUCATION
THE ROAD TRIP

KATY BIRCHALL

**Based on the series SEX EDUCATION,
created by Laurie Nunn**

RP | TEENS
PHILADELPHIA

ONE

Maeve closed her book and sighed.

Resting her head back on the sofa, she squinted at the sunlight streaming in through a gap in the caravan curtains. She lifted her right hand to chew her thumbnail, while tapping impatiently on the book cover with her left.

She'd read *Jane Eyre* a few times, but this bit still annoyed her. She hated Jane's cousin John Reed, and every time she read it he seemed to get worse. Bullying Jane just because he had everything and she had nothing and no one.

'Arrogant dickhead,' Maeve said out loud to the empty room.

She stopped chewing her nail and let her hands rest on her stomach, staring up at the ceiling. She could hear faint music coming from a caravan down the way and people in the distance chatting and laughing. She felt a stab of loneliness.

'This is what you get for reading the Brontës,' she reminded herself, running a hand through her hair and moving to sit upright.

Putting the book aside, she spotted her pack of cigarettes poking out from under the bag next to her and reached for it, pulling one out and grabbing the lighter from the table. She pushed herself up off the sofa and headed towards the door, swinging it open and stepping out into the sunshine.

'Morning, love.'

Maeve looked up from lighting her cigarette to see Cynthia, the caravan park owner, hanging some washing up on the line and smiling at her.

'Hi, Cynthia,' Maeve replied, exhaling and folding her arms across her chest.

'Lovely day,' Cynthia mused, pegging a denim skirt to the line that was exactly the same as the one she had on. 'You all right? Up to anything nice?'

'Just some reading.'

'Ah, lovely. Anything good?'

'*Jane Eyre.*'

'I think I've read it.' Cynthia looked pensive for a moment. 'That the one with the badger?'

Before Maeve could answer, Cynthia's caravan door swung open and her husband, Jeffrey, appeared in the doorway wearing a faded white sleeveless vest, a neon-green headband and very tight, tiny gym shorts. He put his hands on his hips and inhaled deeply. Maeve tried and failed to hide a snigger.

'What are you *doing*, Jeffrey?' Cynthia asked him, wrinkling her nose in disgust.

'Zumba,' he sniffed, clicking his neck as he moved his head from side to side. 'Thought I'd do it out here where there's more space to move.'

'Since when do you do *Zumba*?'

'Since today. I'm going to get into it.'

He reached to turn up the volume on the pop music the radio was playing inside the caravan. Under the scrutinizing gaze of his wife, he stepped down on to the grass, checked his headband was in the right position and then launched into a lunge.

'Just warming up,' he informed Maeve.

'Great,' she said, trying not to look.

Cynthia shook her head at him in disappointment. 'You look like an idiot, Jeffrey.'

'I once came second in a Latin dancing competition,' he declared, ignoring her. He tripped a bit coming out of the lunge, before enthusiastically rolling his hips in circles. 'I was told I had a lot of potential.'

'Who told you that? Your grandmother?' Cynthia muttered.

Amused, Maeve took one last drag, while Jeffrey began side-stepping back and forth, completely out of time to the beat, clapping his hands as he went.

'See you later,' she said, putting her cigarette out. 'Have fun, Jeffrey. Try not to pull a muscle.'

'Thanks,' he said, giving her a thumbs up while bopping his shoulders.

'Don't forget the rent this week, love, will you,' Cynthia said with a thin-lipped smile, tilting her head at Maeve. 'Only last time, you were a day late and I wish I could make exceptions, but it wouldn't be very fair on the others.'

'I'll get it to you.'

'Thanks, love.'

A couple of kids ran by, dodging past Jeffrey and almost getting hit in the face as he counted his star jumps. He lost his balance as they swerved around him and he stumbled, his headband slipping down over his eyes.

'Oi!' he yelled out after them as they ran off laughing,

and wrestled the headband back up to his forehead. 'Watch it!'

'I remember you at that age,' Cynthia said to Maeve with a drawn-out sigh. 'You were always getting into trouble around here. And your brother. No one to keep an eye on you both back then, what with your mother and her troubles. How is your brother? He all right?'

'Great, thanks. Yeah, he's really well actually.'

'Ah, that's nice.'

Maeve pointed awkwardly at her door. 'Better get back to reading.'

'Yes, nice story that one. Cheeky little badger.'

Jeffrey suddenly stopped running on the spot. 'What badger? It didn't go in the caravan, did it?'

'There is no badger, Jeffrey,' Cynthia replied, narrowing her eyes at him in disgust. 'I said it was a cheeky little badger in the book Maeve's reading.'

'See you,' Maeve said, giving them a small wave.

'See you, love.'

Stepping back up into her caravan, Maeve smiled to herself as she heard Cynthia hiss, '*Twat,*' at her husband, just before the door shut.

Pulling her phone out of her pocket to check for messages, she felt a pang of disappointment that there were none. She'd lied to Cynthia about her brother, Sean. She hadn't heard from him in a while, and every time she checked her phone she hoped by some miracle there might be a message from him, letting her know he was OK or revealing where he was. She supposed she should be used to it by now. Her idiot brother disappearing for months wasn't exactly a new

4

phenomenon. And it wasn't like she couldn't look after herself.

But she missed him.

Whatever. Shoving her phone back in her pocket, her eyes flickered to the table at the application form that she'd filled out last night. She stood there for a moment until a voice in her head went, *just do it.*

She went into her bedroom determinedly, grabbing her makeup bag and checking her reflection in the mirror. Reapplying her black kohl eyeliner, she thought about the sign in that bookshop window: *Part-time bookseller wanted, apply inside.*

Yesterday she was walking past the shop with her school friend, Otis, and as she spotted it, she'd done a double-take, stopping still on the pavement to read it properly. Her heart started racing. When she thought about getting a summer job, she assumed she'd end up working in the shopping center at the milkshake place or the waffle stand. She hadn't considered that she might get a job doing something she'd actually enjoy. Something she could be passionate about.

'Maeve, you can't stop suddenly like that,' Otis had said, scurrying back to her side as she stared at the sign, enraptured. 'I just carried on walking and chatting, and almost walked into the lamp post when I looked around to see where you'd gone.'

When she just started chewing her thumbnail without looking up at him in response, he took a moment to read the notice.

'Why don't you apply? You'd be great!' he said enthusiastically.

'Don't be a dickhead.'

'Come on, let's go in. You can fill out an application form.'

'I can't.'

Maeve's eyes dropped to the ground, before she shook her head and marched away down the road. She had made it quite far before Otis caught up with her.

'Why not?' Otis pestered. 'Why can't you apply for that job?'

'Because they wouldn't want someone like me working in their bookshop.'

'You mean someone super smart and really good at books?'

The corner of her lips twitched into a smile. '*Good at books?*'

'Yeah, OK,' he said, rolling his eyes and shoving his hands in his pockets. 'I realized as I said it that it sounded wrong. You know what I mean. Look, I really think you should apply. You could spend your days telling customers about brilliant feminist literature. It's your dream job.'

'They won't want me, Otis.'

'Why not?'

'Because' – she threw her hands up in the air in exasperation – 'look at me! I'm not the sort of person who lands a nice job at a bookshop. I've got a nose ring and dyed hair.'

'Oh right. Sorry. I didn't realize you were applying for a job in the nineteen fifties.'

She sighed, before stubbornly pursing her lips.

'You should at least think about it,' Otis said, nudging her arm with his elbow. 'Maybe apply tomorrow.'

'Fine.'

'Good.' He passed her a folded piece of paper from his pocket. 'Here's the application form.'

'What the—'

6

'I went in and got one from the counter. It's really nice in there. Smells like . . . books.'

'It's a bookshop, Otis.'

He continued to hold the form out to her, shaking it in front of her face until she eventually took it, frowning at his smug expression.

'You're so annoying.'

'No, I'm encouraging. You know who is annoying though? My mum. She started her vagina workshop at eight this morning and made me get up to make tea for everyone.'

As Otis launched into a rant about Jean, his sex-therapist mother, Maeve found herself reluctantly laughing, her mood instantly lifted. After saying goodbye to him yesterday afternoon she'd come home, sat down and filled out the form, weirdly full of hope.

Perfecting her eyeliner now in the caravan, she realized she'd been absent-mindedly smiling while thinking about her day yesterday with Otis.

There was a time when Maeve had thought Otis liked her. Like, *really* liked her. And, yes, there were times when she considered telling him how she felt. How he made her feel. But it was complicated; too risky. If anything went wrong, if she messed things up like she always did, and then she lost Otis . . .

The point is, it wasn't worth it. They were friends. Good friends. It worked that way. And who knew how he felt about her now? He'd moved on, she was certain of it.

They both had. Hadn't they?

She quickly snapped out of it and put her eye pencil down, looking for her lipstick. She checked her outfit: a dark-red top and short black skirt with fishnet tights and black, heeled lace-up boots. It was a hot day, but she grabbed her leather jacket and put it on anyway.

Checking her reflection one last time, she grabbed her phone and texted Otis.

> Going to go apply for that job

It vibrated with a reply straight away.

> Which job?

> The one in the bookshop
> Dickhead

> I was joking
> That's brilliant
> Want me to come with you?

> If you want

> Give me 20 mins
> Meet you at yours
> I'll leave my bike there and we
> can walk into town together

Maeve smiled, leaving her phone on the table as she went to put the kettle on while she waited for him. She fiddled with her necklace and imagined walking into the bookshop and handing in her application form. Her bag on the sofa caught her eye. She needed to check the contents of her purse. She grimaced and steeled herself as she picked it up, trying to remember how much was in there.

Opening it, she sighed in relief. There was enough for rent. She needed a job if she was going to pay next month's though. It's not like she was making any extra cash now that school was out and the sex clinic was on pause.

Running the secret clinic with Otis for fellow school students had been a brilliant idea, if she did say so herself. She handled the business side of things, bookings and payments, and he got to do what he was good at – offering sex and relationship advice. He had a gift, a natural talent for therapizing. It was as though by living with his mother he'd soaked up her knowledge and therapy skills. And it turned out the people they went to school with REALLY needed help. The clinic was a huge success.

But they weren't doing that right now, so summer job it was.

Maeve jumped as her phone started vibrating on the table, jolting her from her bookshop daydream. It was probably Otis calling to say he couldn't make it. Trying not to be prematurely disappointed, she went to answer it but didn't recognize the number. She frowned in confusion, deliberating over answering. She picked up just before it rang out.

'Hello?'

'Heeeey, Frog-face.'

She inhaled sharply at the sound of her brother's voice. *Finally.*

'Where the fuck have you been?' she asked angrily.

'You missed me then?'

'You left without saying goodbye,' she seethed. 'Again.'

'Look, I know you're angry, but I need your help.'

She closed her eyes, her heart sinking. His voice was strained and tired. Something was wrong. He wouldn't bother calling otherwise.

'Froggy?' he prompted. 'Come on. I'm in trouble. Speak to me.'

She asked quietly, 'What do you need?'

'I need *you.*'

'What do you mean, you need me?'

'I need you to come here and help me figure something out.' He hesitated. 'I was arrested.'

'You *what?*'

'I swear I didn't do anything wrong. I *swear*, Maeve. They've got it all wrong. They think I've stolen a diamond necklace. I was seeing this girl and ... Look, I didn't do it, Maeve. I need your help to prove it.'

'Are you calling from prison?'

'No, I was held for twenty-four hours and I've been released on bail. I'm crashing at my friend's house in the city. The police came by with a warrant to search his place while I was in custody, and they didn't find anything – because I *didn't take it* – but I know they're looking to pin this on me. It's only a matter of time before they come for me again.'

'A diamond necklace,' Maeve repeated, pacing around the room and trying not to panic. 'What do you mean, like actual diamonds?'

'Yeah. You should see it. Worth a shedload.'

'This sounds like a joke.'

'It's not.'

'Why do they think you've taken it?'

'It's complicated, but the most important thing for you to know is that I didn't do it. I need you to come here and help me prove it.'

'What the hell can I do about it? Shit, Sean! This is really bad!'

'Yeah, that's why I'm calling *you*. You know you're the clever one. No one is on my side here. They're not even trying to look for any other suspects, but if we could somehow work out who did take it, then I'd be completely off the hook. I don't have anyone else to help me. Please. Will you come here and help me figure it out?'

Maeve paused, her brain overloaded with all this information, busily trying to map out the best thing to do.

'Please, Frog-face,' Sean pleaded, adding hopefully, 'if you come, I'll make you pancakes with smiley faces and whipped cream.'

'This isn't really the time for pancakes, Sean.'

'Aw, it's always the time for pancakes.' He chuckled. After a moment he spoke again, but his tone was different this time. Serious and afraid. 'Please, I need your help. These people, they're powerful. I think I'm in a lot of trouble. And if I don't get out now, I won't ever get out. I don't have anyone else.'

Maeve bit her lip. 'All right.'

'You'll come?'

'Yes.'

'*Thank you*,' he breathed, sounding relieved. 'You've given me hope, Frog-face. I know if anyone can work this mess out, it's you.'

'Where will I find you?'

'I'll text you the details. Maybe pack for a few days. It's a bit of a journey. You know someone with a car you can borrow?'

'I'll work it out.'

He thanked her again, promising he'd make it up to her, and hung up. Not wasting any time, Maeve messaged Aimee, the only friend she could think of who had a car, asking her if it was all right to come over. Waiting for a reply, she saw the bookshop application lying on the table. She slid it towards her, glancing over what she'd written. Her phone vibrated with a message from Aimee.

Maeve picked up the application form, screwed it up into a ball and dropped it on the table.

She had to go and pack.

TWO

'Hey, where are you going?'

Maeve turned the key in the lock of the caravan door before spinning around to see Otis leading his bike towards her with a confused expression. She was pleased that Jeffrey had clearly given up on his Zumba and that neither he nor Cynthia were lingering outside.

'I'm pretty sure you don't need to sleep over at the bookshop to prove your dedication,' Otis continued, suspiciously eyeing the overnight bag slung over her shoulder.

'Change of plan,' she replied simply, coming down the steps. 'Sorry, I should have messaged. I have to go.'

'OK. Go where?' he asked, turning his bike around and following her as she walked off.

'Aimee's.'

'Is she having a sleepover or something?'

'No, we're not eight years old. I need to borrow her car.'

'Why?'

'Too many questions, Otis.'

'Not enough answers, Maeve.'

She ignored him, marching on.

'Hey, come on,' he said, his helmet wiggling about on his head as he hurried to keep up with her. 'What's going on?'

He reached out for her arm and she turned to face him. He took the opportunity to undo his helmet and take it off. If Maeve wasn't so annoyed and angry about everything right now, she'd take the piss out of his hair, which was sticking up in all directions.

'Talk to me,' he said gently, as she brought her eyes up to meet his.

This was the thing about Otis. He had this way of looking at you that made you want to tell him stuff, as though he would magically make it all OK. Yes, he wasn't a qualified therapist, being a teenager and all that, but he really did have a gift. Maeve couldn't quite put her finger on it, but you just . . . trusted him.

Tall and waiflike, Otis Milburn was smart, kind and incredibly awkward, seemingly uncomfortable in his own skin. It was as though he was constantly apologizing through his body language just for being there. He was an unlikely sex guru and an even unlikelier friend for Maeve Wiley. When they first started hanging out together, Maeve couldn't quite work him out and he seemed to be terrified of her. But in the end, they clicked. There was no explaining it.

'All right,' she said, kicking a clump of loose grass from under her foot. 'I heard from Sean.'

'Your brother?' Otis's eyes lit up. 'That's great! I mean . . . is it?'

Maeve's jaw clenched. 'He's in trouble.'

'What kind of trouble?' he asked, his eyebrows knitting together in concern.

'The police think he stole this really precious necklace,'

Maeve explained. 'He doesn't know what to do. He wants me to go and help him clear his name and argue he's innocent or something.'

'Is he?' Otis asked carefully.

Maeve hesitated. 'I don't know.'

She felt guilty saying it out loud. She *wanted* to believe her brother, but she'd been down this road before. He was very good at making promises and not so good at keeping them. He also had a habit of covering his tracks with his easy-going charm and convincing lies. To be honest, Maeve wasn't sure how far he'd go to make money if he was desperate.

And a diamond necklace would make someone a lot of money.

'I don't know,' Maeve repeated, annoyed at herself for being unsure. 'But I have to do something. I can't leave him in this on his own.'

'OK.' Otis nodded slowly. 'I'll come with you.'

'What?'

'I'll come with you,' he repeated.

'No. No way.'

'I'm not letting you go on your own,' he said firmly. 'This sounds like a big deal. You might need a friend.'

Maeve faltered. 'I can't ask you to do that.'

'You're not.' He shrugged. 'I'm insisting. It sounds like a scenario that could be stressful and personal for you, and you might need someone to help keep things in perspective. Let me be there for you.'

Maeve raised her eyebrows at him. 'Fine. But this is serious, Otis. We're talking my brother potentially going to prison.'

'I know.'

'It's not a holiday.'

'I didn't think it was. I'll go home and pack a bag and then meet you at Aimee's.'

She nodded and he veered off in another direction, getting on his bike and cycling back home. Maeve watched him go, pleased that she wouldn't be doing this alone.

Things always seemed a bit better when he was there.

*

'Oh my God,' Aimee gasped, her eyes widening. 'It's FATE!'

Maeve was taken aback by her friend's reaction. 'What?'

'Not the bit about your brother, obviously. That's bad,' Aimee said hurriedly, sitting cross-legged in the middle of her bed as Maeve perched on the end. 'But I was just about to ask you if you wanted to head that way with me! There's a baking convention there, in an arena, and I thought we could go together. You know, it's a big city, not much fun on my own. But now, you need to go there anyway, we can travel together! It's *fate*.'

Maeve blinked at her. 'A baking convention?'

'I know, cool, right? Perfect for a future professional baker like myself. And apparently there's, like, loads of free scones and stuff.'

'That is cool,' Maeve replied, deciding not to dwell on the fact that Aimee's last attempt at baking a cake resulted in the kitchen almost going up in flames, and her sponge was so rock-hard, Maeve almost broke her tooth on it. 'So we can take your car?'

'No problem!' Aimee beamed, flicking her thick, curly blond hair back behind her shoulder. 'I'll get some things together now and we can set off. How long do you think we'll go for?'

'Not sure. Depends, I guess.'

'I'll pack for a few nights then, just in case,' Aimee declared, scrambling off the bed and skipping over to her wardrobe. 'What do you wear to a baking convention, do you think?'

Maeve smiled and shrugged in reply. Aimee's sunny mood was infectious and Maeve found it oddly comforting compared to her deep-seated worry over Sean. She was relieved that Aimee could drive them, and not all that surprised. It was entirely like Aimee to decide on the spur of the moment to head off on a trip, and her less-than-interested mum was unlikely to stop her.

Sweet and naive, Aimee was one of Maeve's favorite people. She had this way of finding the good in everybody and everything, a ray of sparkling hope in an often gloomy world. She was also thoughtful and understanding, and frequently hilarious without always meaning to be. She had recently made the decision to become a baker, even though she'd never baked anything before. It was obvious to everyone that Aimee wasn't exactly a natural, but Maeve had to admire her commitment.

'Do you think I need to bring my own apron?' Aimee asked, pulling some bright, colorful tops off their hangers and putting them on the bed. 'Oooh, I can't forget knickers. Definitely will be needing some of those.'

'Definitely.'

'Don't worry, I'll pack fast. You must be really worried about Sean.'

Maeve glanced down at the floor. 'A bit.'

'We'll get it sorted,' Aimee said firmly. 'Promise.'

'Thanks, Aimee.'

'One of my cousins once escaped from prison by bribing the guards with some pot and a bag of Werther's Originals. So, if it comes to it, we have a backup plan.'

Maeve looked at her to check if she was joking. She wasn't.

'Great,' Maeve said. 'Comforting.'

The buzzer went for the driveway gate and Maeve offered to run downstairs and get it while Aimee finished packing. As she let Otis in and watched him make his way up the gravel towards the house, Maeve took a moment to appreciate how incredible Aimee's house was.

It was a countryside mansion with manicured lawns and black iron gates at the top of its sweeping driveway. Inside was a maze of spacious, tastefully decorated rooms with grand fireplaces, expensive Persian rugs, and old paintings of country scenes dotted about the walls. Every side table and mantelpiece seemed to have a priceless china vase sitting atop it, and the windows were framed by heavy, patterned curtains that looked like they belonged in a palace. Down the hallway from the front door, there was a beautiful dining room with a long table in the middle, with carved legs and about twelve chairs around it.

Maeve thought about the tiny table in the caravan in comparison and snorted.

'Hey,' she said, opening the front door for Otis. 'Why are you so sweaty?'

'Um, I walked here and it's a hot day?' he replied, dropping his backpack on the floor of the hallway. 'I'm going to get some water.'

'Your mum OK with you coming?' Maeve asked, following him into the kitchen.

They'd both been to Aimee's house a few times now and knew their way around. They also always assumed her parents weren't in and, so far, they hadn't been wrong.

'Define "OK."' Otis turned on the cold tap and filled a glass. 'She'll be fine. I told her it was important.'

Otis and Jean had been at odds lately – she felt that he was shutting her out; he felt that she was smothering him. And try as they might, neither of them could avoid analyzing the other.

Otis knew he was keeping his mum at a distance, but that's because he was growing up. He couldn't tell her absolutely *everything* about his life. He knew that he was all she had, and that maybe she had a fear of abandonment after his dad left, and was struggling to come to terms with Otis having his own life away from her. But she had to find a way to deal with it.

Jean worried that Otis was struggling with aspects of growing up and developing healthy relationships with his peers, and desperately wanted to let him know that their home was a safe space to divulge and discuss any issues, whether they be friend- or sex-related. She could help him navigate these tumultuous teenage years. Why wouldn't he let her in?

The start of the summer holidays had been a disaster in the Milburn household. Otis tried to be out as much as possible and when he was in, he shut himself away in his room, put a record on and pointedly turned the volume up, trying to block out Jean's polite but incessant knocks on the door, inviting him to come down for 'a chat.'

Otis was sorry that Sean was in trouble, but thankful for the opportunity to get away.

'It's good for her to get some space from me,' Otis continued. 'She can't know what I'm doing *all* the time. As much as she likes to try. I imagine she's going through my room as we speak, trying to find clues as to why I've left.'

'She goes through your stuff?' Maeve asked, noticing a strange toad statue on the side of the kitchen counter and wondering what it must be like to have the money to buy random ugly shit like that.

'Yep.' He sighed. 'She thinks I don't know, but I do.'

'Wow.'

Maeve didn't say anything more about it. She leaned against the kitchen counter and chewed her nails, while Otis drank his water. She wanted to tell him that he was lucky to have someone who was so protective and cared so much about him that they wanted to know every little detail of every aspect of his life. But it was none of her business.

It was hard not to think about her own mum when others complained about theirs. She wished she had the chance to be annoyed about stuff like her mum being worried about her. She had no idea where her mum was right now. But that was OK. Maeve could take care of herself.

And she didn't have time to wallow. What she had to do was find out the truth about Sean and this necklace. She didn't want him wrecking his life like their mum had, or even landing himself in prison. And she wouldn't desert him like their dad did either. Sean was convinced that they were on their own – but Maeve didn't want him to feel like that. They had each other at least, didn't they?

Maeve realized the skin around her nail was bleeding. She quickly pulled her hand away from her mouth. Draining the last of his water, Otis slammed the glass on the side and then screwed up his face in pain.

'You all right?' she frowned as he scrunched his eyes tight shut and pinched his nose.

'Brain freeze,' he squeaked. 'Shouldn't have downed a glass of ice-cold water.'

'You really do live on the edge, Otis,' Maeve teased, amused at his range of anguished expressions.

'Can Aimee lend us the car?' he asked once he felt better.

'She's coming with us. She was heading that way anyway, for a baking convention.'

'Oh right. Good.'

Starting to fidget, Otis cleared his throat and looked as though he was about to say something else, but then seemed to think better of it. Maeve watched him curiously.

'What is it, Otis?'

'Mm?'

'You seem . . . agitated.'

'I'm not agitated,' he said innocently. He went to nonchalantly lean on the kitchen counter, but his elbow slipped and he jolted forward before steadying himself again.

'Come on,' Maeve prompted impatiently. 'Spit it out.'

'Well, Eric called when I was getting my stuff,' he began.

Maeve stared him down. 'And?'

'And I mentioned to him where we were going.'

'Did you say why?'

'No!' Otis looked insulted she'd have to ask. 'But I said we were going there for a few nights and it turns out that on one of those nights there's this famous drag show at somewhere called The Courtyard that he's always wanted to go to . . .'

Otis trailed off, looking at Maeve expectantly, as though he hoped she would guess where he was going with this and jump in to say it was all fine, no problem. Her scowl didn't budge.

'And so,' he continued reluctantly in a quiet voice, 'I said maybe he could join us.'

Maeve folded her arms.

'It might be good to have more people to help,' Otis justified anxiously. 'He won't get in the way and . . . I couldn't say no.'

'This isn't a group of pals going on a bloody *road trip*, Otis.'

'I know!'

'My brother is in deep shit. Like, real life trouble.'

'I know. I know that,' he said, taking a step towards her. 'I promise I'm taking it seriously. But we're heading there anyway, and now that Aimee's coming . . . we might as well let Eric come too. But only if you're OK with it,' he added, quickly trying to read her expression.

She sighed. 'Fine.'

Otis smiled gratefully at her, and Maeve turned to head back to the hall, hearing Aimee coming down the stairs. Maeve liked Eric, but she'd meant what she said. They were making this journey for a serious reason and they had to stay focused.

'There you are,' Aimee said, dragging a suitcase across the hall to the door. 'I need your help.'

'With what?'

'Do you think I need to bring my own cooking things? Like a whisk? I only have an electric one and it seems a bit bulky. I don't want it bouncing about in my bag, getting all caught up in my bra straps.' Aimee's face brightened, looking over Maeve's shoulder. 'Hi, Otis!'

'Hello, Aimee,' Otis said, giving her an awkward wave.

'You don't need to bring your own cooking utensils,' Maeve informed her. 'You're not doing any of the baking demonstrations. Professional bakers will be doing that bit. And why have you packed a whole suitcase?'

'You said you didn't know how long we were going for! Who knows what we'll need? This way, I'm prepared for anything. Are you both ready? I'll grab the car keys. Not sure where I left them, but I think they're in the downstairs loo.'

Maeve and Otis shared a confused look as Aimee brushed past them to go and find the keys, before picking up their bags and heading out on to the drive to wait by the car. They soon noticed Eric approaching the gate. They couldn't miss him – he was dressed in a bright-green and orange geometric-patterned matching shirt and shorts combination. He gave them an enthusiastic wave.

'Hey, I'm here!' he called out, grinning at them. 'Can you let me in, please?'

'I'll go,' Otis offered, scurrying back to the house.

As the gates opened, Eric strode through, giving Maeve another smaller, but just as excited wave. Clutching the straps

23

of his backpack with one hand, he used the other to lead a large wheelie case.

'Hey, Maeve,' he said, reaching her. 'How's your summer going?'

'Disappointing. Yours?'

'Yeah, good, thanks.'

Eric was both intimidated by and in awe of Maeve. She was so *cool*. Naturally chatty, Eric often found himself nervously yabbering away to her before realizing she hadn't said a word the entire conversation.

Once at school he overheard her mention humpback whales and he rambled on about how he'd seen this amazing documentary on them. He talked about whales for a full four minutes while she just fixed him with a hard stare. When he came to the end of his passionate speech, she went, 'I said *hardbacks*. As in hardback books?'

He styled it out by insisting he knew that, but she hadn't looked convinced.

Eric glanced up at Aimee's house. 'Where's Otis gone?'

'He went to open the gates to let you in and now he's probably helping Aimee find the car keys,' she explained. 'Apparently, they're somewhere in the loo.'

While they waited, she got a cigarette out and lit it. Eric stood tensely next to her, attempting to look at ease in her company.

'I am so excited to be doing this,' he informed her. 'Otis and I have talked about going to this show *forever*. It's on once a month at The Courtyard. I've never seen a drag show live before, so when Otis mentioned you were heading that way,

I thought it would be the perfect chance to see it. Are you going to come too?'

She exhaled. 'Not sure I'll have time.'

'Hopefully you can. It's meant to be *spectacular*. Apparently, someone in the audience was so amazed he had a heart attack and had to be rushed to hospital. I think I read that he died. That's how good this show is. People die.'

Maeve raised her eyebrows but didn't say anything, watching Eric in amusement as he shifted his weight from one leg to the other, before kicking some gravel out of one of his espadrilles. She took another drag of her cigarette, pleased to see Aimee and Otis emerge from the house at last. She wanted to get on the road as soon as possible.

Otis smiled to himself as he approached his two closest friends standing at odds next to each other: Eric a burst of eye-catching colors; Maeve in her signature black.

Otis had never dared tell either of them, but he often considered Eric and Maeve quite similar, in a strange way. Yeah, they were complete opposites in that Eric was ebullient, animated and full of positivity, always dressed in bold, bright colors and with the most infectious roaring laugh anyone on the planet had ever heard, while Maeve was sarcastic, cynical, brilliantly pessimistic with a bone-dry sense of humor and a wardrobe that consisted of dark colors matched with other dark colors.

But they were both more courageous than anyone Otis had ever met. Maeve had been abandoned by her whole family – her mum, her dad, her brother – but she relied on herself, and, even though she had been let down by those closest to her, she was so instinctively caring that she put everyone else first.

And then there was Eric, his brilliant, brave best friend. Eric was confident, proud and hilarious. Otis knew that Eric's religious Nigerian-Ghanaian father was worried for, and protective of, his gay teenage son, concerned that it might be easier for Eric if he blended in a bit more. But blending in just wasn't Eric, and, without realizing it, he inspired his parents and his friend by embracing exactly who he was, no matter the pain and ignorance his father was so terrified he'd face.

Otis wondered if he should tell the two of them how much he admired their strength and courage, but he just never quite knew how to say it.

Aimee held up the car keys and jangled them triumphantly, calling out as she dragged her suitcase across the gravel. 'Guess where I found them?'

'The toilet?'

'Nope! In the dog bowl! Don't know how they got in there.'

'I didn't know you had a dog, Aimee,' Eric said.

'We don't,' she told him cheerily. 'Shall we get everything in the car?'

She opened the boot and heaved her suitcase into it, the others piling their stuff on top. Aimee nabbed Maeve's cigarette from her and had the last couple of drags, while Eric and Otis moved the bags around to fit in Eric's case.

'Thanks for driving us, Aimee,' Eric beamed, as they managed to get the boot shut.

'Sure! You know, my grandfather drove backward into a lake

once,' Aimee said, putting out the cigarette and holding the stub to put in the car, rather than risk leaving it on the drive for her parents to find. 'Apparently, he drove out of the water and there was an eel in the back seat! So funny, isn't it? Anyway –' she turned to Maeve – 'shall we go now?'

'Let's,' Maeve said, suppressing a smile.

'An *eel*?' Eric whispered to Otis in horror.

Maeve noticed Aimee prodding at her stomach with a confused expression before getting in the driver's seat.

'What are you doing, Aimes? Are you OK?'

'I'm just checking if I need a wee,' she replied, pressing again on her bladder. 'I think I'm all right for a bit though. Let's get going.'

'Yeah!' Eric cried excitedly, sliding into the back seat. 'ROAD TRIP!'

Otis winced and Maeve shot him a dirty look before getting into the front and slamming the door shut. Aimee turned the key in the ignition and they set off, Maeve staring out of the window, her stomach fluttering with nerves.

This was going to be a long drive.

THREE

'So how are you going to prove your brother didn't do it then?' Aimee asked, driving down a winding country lane towards a main road.

'No idea,' Maeve replied, gripping the door handle so hard her knuckles went white as Aimee sped around the corners.

There was a collective 'oof' from the passengers as the car hit a pothole at full speed. Aimee didn't seem to notice or care, with one hand on the wheel and using the other to pick up the stick of lip salve sitting in the cup holder next to the gearstick, before applying it liberally.

'Driving gives me such dry lips,' she sighed, clicking the lid back on. 'It's so weird.'

'I think it's the air con, Aimes,' Maeve pointed out.

'No, it's the driving,' Aimee insisted. 'It doesn't happen if I'm in the back seat.'

'What's going on with your brother, Maeve?' Eric asked, trying to distract himself from the feeling he might die at any moment from this erratic driving.

'Oh shit, you didn't know?' Aimee grimaced, glancing apologetically at Maeve. 'Sorry, I assumed they did.'

'Otis does,' she murmured.

'You don't have to say if you don't want to,' Eric offered,

knowing he'd be devastated if she didn't.

'It's nothing.' She stared out of the window. 'My brother's been accused of stealing. But he says he didn't do it.'

'Oh goodness.' Eric dramatically placed a hand on his heart. 'Such injustice.'

'The plan is to find out who really committed the crime,' Otis explained, his palms clammy as they hit another pothole and slammed forward against their seat belts.

'Sorry about that!' Aimee chirped, shaking her head. 'These holes in the road keep coming out of nowhere!'

'So you're going to see Sean to prove his innocence then.' Eric nodded. 'That's amazing. What do they think he stole?'

'A diamond necklace. Very expensive apparently,' Maeve muttered.

'Wow!' Eric turned to look at Otis wide-eyed. 'That's like in a film!'

'Yeah, it is,' Aimee agreed. 'A real-life puzzle. Like a murder mystery. You know, that famous detective. What's his name? Oh yeah, Pharaoh!'

Maeve looked confused. 'You mean *Poirot*?'

'Yeah.' Aimee nodded. 'That's what I said.'

'Why would Sean be accused of stealing a diamond necklace?' Otis wondered out loud. 'And who would he have stolen it from?'

Maeve sighed. 'Guess he'll tell us details when we get there.'

'Does he live in the city?' Eric asked excitedly. 'So cool. Are we staying with him?'

'No. I haven't thought that far ahead yet.'

Eric blinked at Otis, who shrugged in reply. 'Wait. We don't have anywhere to stay? Otis. I thought you said you had everything under control.'

'I said we'd sort everything,' Otis assured him. 'And I meant it. As soon as we get there.'

'What, we're going to just *show up* somewhere?' Eric shook his head, looking out of the window. 'Literally every murder mystery starts out this way, but we're the ones who get murdered.'

'I once watched this documentary, yeah,' Aimee began, 'where this guy got framed for a big jewelry heist and then the people framing him ended up killing him with a steamroller.'

The car fell into stunned silence. Eventually Eric cleared his throat.

'Although one might see some similarities there to Sean's current predicament, I don't think that's going to happen to him, Maeve,' he said in his most sophisticated, sincere tone. 'I'm sure he won't be murdered with a steamroller. Or murdered at all. He'll probably be fine.'

Maeve continued to look out of the window, not saying anything. Otis frowned at Eric, who held up his hands and mouthed back, '*What?*'

As Otis shook his head, his phone started ringing. He took it out of his pocket, saw it was his mum and put it down on the middle seat to let it ring out.

'Why are you ignoring Jean?' Eric asked him, glancing down at the screen. 'Have you had another fight?'

'No, she keeps calling to check I'm all right. I've only been gone an hour and I've got three missed calls.'

Aimee smiled. 'Aw, that's sweet.'

'No, it's not sweet,' Otis said through gritted teeth as his phone started ringing again. He put it on silent. 'It's maddening. My mum is a nightmare.'

'Jean is a goddess,' Eric corrected, more at ease now that they had turned on to a main road with no potholes or deadly blind corners.

'Last weekend my mum said I shouldn't smile so much otherwise I'll get wrinkles around my mouth,' Aimee said matter-of-factly. 'But at Christmas she told me I shouldn't frown too much as I'll get forehead lines. So apparently I've got to strike a neutral face expression.'

'I don't think you should smile less, Aimee,' Maeve offered.

'I agree,' Otis said. 'Studies have shown that smiling releases endorphins and serotonin, natural chemicals that elevate the mood and relax the body.'

Maeve glanced at the dashboard.

'Shit. Aimee, I think we may need to fill up on petrol soon.'

Aimee gasped. 'How do you know that, babes?'

'The petrol gauge,' Maeve said slowly. 'It's pointing at the red bit. That means we're dangerously low. We should stop soon.'

'Good idea. We can stock up on Werther's Originals too,' she said solemnly. 'Always handy to have some on you, just in case.'

'What, in case you have a toffee-related emergency?' Otis laughed.

'You never know, Otis,' Aimee said, holding eye contact with him in the rearview mirror until he felt suitably unnerved. 'You *never know*.'

Luckily they soon passed a sign for a petrol station and Aimee pulled in, coming to a sudden stop and throwing everyone against their seat belts again.

'We're here!' she announced chirpily, opening the door and hopping out.

'I need the toilet,' Eric muttered, rubbing his neck from the seat belt scrape. 'And maybe a sedative to get through the rest of the journey.'

'I'll get some snacks,' Otis volunteered.

Leaving Aimee humming to herself as she filled up the car, Maeve followed Otis and Eric into the shop, helping Otis with the snack selection.

She snorted as he picked up four bags of Haribo. 'What are you doing?'

'What do you mean?'

'Why are you choosing four packs of the same sweet? Don't you want to mix it up a bit?'

'Um, Haribo is already mixed? There's lots of different types of sweet in one bag.'

'They all taste the same and they have the same . . . gummy texture.'

He blinked at her. 'They do *not* all taste the same.'

'I think you need to be a bit more adventurous with your choice.'

'Oh really? And what would you pick, oh, confectionery guru?' Otis asked, giving her jazz hands.

She shrugged. 'No preference. Sweets aren't really my thing. I don't care.'

'Ah, but you do care, Maeve Wiley.' Otis nodded gravely.

'Otherwise you never would have commented on my choice of Haribo. I reckon I can work out what you would pick.'

Maeve folded her arms stubbornly. 'Go on then.'

'Love Hearts,' Otis said, pointing his finger at her. 'You're a Love Hearts person.'

Maeve narrowed her eyes at him.

'Or . . . Dip Dab?' He stroked his chin thoughtfully. 'Maybe Curly Wurly?' He clicked his fingers. 'No, wait, I've got it. Gobstopper. That's got to be your thing. At least, it should be.'

Maeve tried not to laugh, snatching one of the Haribo bags out of his hands and whacking him over the head with it. 'Shut up, dickhead.'

'Don't hit me with the Haribo!' He laughed as she wielded it again. 'Maeve! Put the Haribo down! Or I will retaliate.'

'I'd like to see you try.'

'You will awaken the beast,' Otis warned, causing Maeve to snigger. 'You don't know what I'm capable of.'

Eric suddenly ran up to them looking frazzled. 'I hate using public toilets. I've washed my hands eight hundred times and I still feel dirty.' He took a moment to notice what Otis was holding. 'Why are you only buying Haribo?'

'You like Haribo!'

'Yes, but there are other products on offer, Oatcake.' Eric shook his head at him in disappointment, grabbing a bag of Haribo from him, opening it and shoving some in his mouth. 'Broaden your horizons for once. Am I right, Maeve?'

Maeve nodded in agreement as Eric stalked out of the petrol station, scoffing from the bag. They watched him through the window as he approached Aimee and offered her a sweet.

She didn't take one. She was too busy staring at the fuel nozzle she'd just put back with a puzzled expression.

'I haven't paid for those yet!' Otis called out after Eric, but rolled his eyes when he was ignored. 'Guess I'll have to just tell them at the till.'

'I'll meet you out there,' Maeve said, distracted, still watching Aimee carefully. 'Get some other stuff too, yeah?'

'Like what?' Otis asked in a panic, but she had already left. He sighed, frowning at the rows and rows of colorful packs in front of him, whispering to himself, 'I'm *really* not ready for this kind of responsibility.'

Maeve reached Aimee just as Eric gasped in reaction to something she was telling him.

'What's going on?' Maeve asked Aimee bluntly.

'I filled the car with petrol.'

'That's a good thing.'

'No, it's not,' Aimee said. 'This car is diesel.'

'What?'

'It's diesel,' she repeated, gesturing at the car. 'I've filled it with the petrol one. Which is strange, because I literally had a dream about this the other day, except instead of it being a car, it was a camel.'

'You filled a camel up with petrol?' Eric asked, wrinkling his nose.

'No, I had to get on the camel, but when I looked closer, it wasn't a camel, it was a kangaroo. Do you think I'm one of those people who can tell the future? A psycho!'

'I think it's psychic,' Eric said slowly, glancing at Maeve, whose jaw was clenched.

'Yeah, that's what I said.'

'Aimee, this is bad,' Maeve jumped in. 'We need to sort this out. You can't drive the car with petrol in. It will ruin the engine.'

'Don't worry, I have a gold AA membership,' Aimee revealed cheerfully. 'I'll give them a call and they'll be here in a jiffy. Just got to find the card with the number to phone. I think it's in the car somewhere or maybe at home in that drawer in my dressing table. That's where I keep all the important things.'

As Aimee set about looking for her membership card in the glove compartment, Maeve closed her eyes in despair.

'I'm sure it will all be fine,' Eric said with a big smile, attempting to be optimistic. 'This happened to my dad once.'

'Yeah?' Maeve stuck out her chin. 'Was it quick to sort?'

'Um . . .' Eric looked down at his feet. 'No. It took quite a long time. I remember because my sister and I played hopscotch for two hours while we waited. Made my legs hurt actually. Put me off hopscotch forever. And someone who drove past threw a half-eaten burger out the window and it hit me in the face.'

Maeve stared at him. 'What a precious memory.'

'It was really quite traumatic.' Eric frowned.

'Found it!' Aimee cried, waving the AA card around. 'I'll give them a call now!'

'What's going on?' Otis asked, walking up to the car with two shopping bags full of snacks.

'Otis, did you buy the whole shop?' Eric laughed.

'I couldn't decide what to get!' Otis said, putting the bags down. 'You both got in my head. Everything I decided on seemed too boring or too out there. I needed to hit the right balance. So I got a wide selection. That way, everyone can be happy.'

'They're on their way!' Aimee beamed, hanging up the phone. 'We just need to sit and wait now.'

'Who are we waiting for?' Otis asked, putting his hands on his hips.

'Slight mix-up with the petrol and diesel,' Eric explained, nodding his head towards Aimee. 'She's called the AA though.'

'Ah. I see.'

'I'm going to go use the loo,' Aimee said brightly. 'Anyone want anything?'

'I don't think Otis has left anything in there for anyone else to buy,' Eric replied, pointing at the chocolate spilling out of the overfull bags on the ground.

'Did they say how long they'd take to get here, Aimee?' Maeve asked.

'Within half an hour, they said. I think. Maybe it was an hour.' She shrugged. 'But soon. Anyway, I really have to pee.'

As she wandered off, Maeve leaned against the car, disheartened.

'You OK?' Otis asked, coming to stand next to her while Eric rooted about in the shopping bags.

'I just want to get there,' she replied, chewing her thumbnail and looking out at the road as the cars zipped by.

'I know. But we will. And maybe it's a good thing if we see your brother tomorrow morning, rather than late tonight,' he reasoned. 'Fresh mind and all that.'

'I guess. We'll have to find a place to sleep.'

'We'll find somewhere.'

'It has to be cheap. I don't have much cash on me,' she admitted, trying not to think too much about how she promised she'd pay Cynthia her rent on time.

Maeve hadn't hesitated to bring all she had with her in case she'd need it to help Sean. She'd have to think of another way of getting Cynthia the money when she got back.

'Maybe we can go to a karaoke bar and sing for money,' Eric suggested, joining the conversation. 'Like Britney Spears in that movie she did, *Crossroads*. She got enough tips to stay in a posh suite of a hotel.'

Otis smiled. 'It's an option.'

'I'm shit at singing.' Eric sighed.

'I thought you were musical,' Maeve said.

'Aw, thank you, Maeve!' He smiled smugly at her. 'I'm actually in swing band. I play the French horn. You may remember when I performed in school assembly?' He hesitated, his eyes flickering to Otis, who looked as though he was about to speak. 'DON'T SAY IT, OTIS.'

'He got an erection on stage.'

'Oh yeah.' Maeve nodded slowly. 'I remember now.'

'It was a semi!' Eric protested, glaring at Otis. 'And erections are natural! Isn't that what you're always saying, Otis? When you get them at the supermarket around the pineapple section?'

Otis flushed furiously. 'I don't get—'

'Anyway, the point is I *am* musical, Maeve, yes,' Eric said haughtily as Maeve couldn't help but laugh. 'Are you any good at singing? Bet you're fierce with a microphone.'

'That looks like an AA van,' Otis said, suddenly straightening. 'That was quick.'

'Course they were,' Eric said, waving it over. 'Aimee's family would only have the best, right?'

'I'm here!' Aimee said, hurrying over as the AA man parked up. 'Shall I go and speak to him, do you think? Or let him come to me?'

'It's not a guy in a bar, Aimee,' Maeve said.

'Suppose you're right. Hello!' Aimee waved as he approached them. 'I'm Aimee and this is the car we need you to fix, please.'

The others got out of the way and went to sit on the pavement next to a little area of grassy mounds to the side of the petrol station car park. After a chat with the AA guy, Aimee came over to join them and together they sat and waited, eating their way through the sweets, as he moved the car and then began to start the process of draining the tank.

Digging around the shopping bag, Aimee pulled out a pack of Polos and her face lit up. 'I know what we can do while we wait!'

'Ensure we have fresh breath?' Eric guessed, looking confused as she held up the mints triumphantly.

'We can play the Polo Mint Game,' she enthused, unwrapping the tube and encouraging them all to take one. 'You have to suck on the Polo and then whoever can make theirs last the longest and get the thinnest mint ring without it snapping wins!'

'I've never heard of this game,' Maeve admitted, taking a Polo.

'My parents used to play it with me on car journeys,'

Aimee explained. 'I think they actually did it so I wouldn't talk so much, but it is also really fun. Everyone ready? Pop in your Polo!'

They each placed the mint with the hole on their tongue. After a while, Maeve could see why it was a good car journey game – they'd been silent for ages as they concentrated on carefully sucking at their Polo, thinning it down but making sure it didn't snap.

'Damn it!' Eric exclaimed, crunching on his. 'Mine snapped.'

Maeve gave up with a shrug and started crunching hers. 'Mine too.'

Otis suddenly gasped and began coughing, before saying through splutters, 'I swallowed mine by accident.'

Aimee stuck her tongue out and displayed the perfect, thin round mint resting on it, before crunching away happily. 'I'm the winner then! I'm weirdly good at games like this.'

'There are other games in this genre?' Otis asked, catching Maeve's eye and smiling.

'Yeah!' Aimee assured him. 'There's the Polo Fruits Game, which is quite hard because they're not so powdery a texture, so they take longer to suck. Then there's the Polo Spearmint Game, the Sugar-Free Polo Mint Game—'

'Excuse me,' the AA man interrupted, approaching them. 'Your car's ready to go.'

'Thank God,' Maeve muttered, as they all scrambled to their feet, relieved that they wouldn't be forced to play Polo Mint Games for the next few hours.

'Is it fixed?' Aimee asked hopefully.

'Yeah,' he answered. 'The tank is drained and refilled,

everything else looks fine and you can get on your way. The thing is . . . Well . . . I think it was correctly filled with diesel in the first place.'

Maeve blinked at him. 'What?'

'I'm pretty sure it didn't need to be drained,' he informed them, putting his hands on his hips. 'It was filled correctly with diesel.'

Otis buried his head in his hands. Maeve closed her eyes and inhaled deeply, trying to remain calm. Eric's jaw dropped to the floor as he faced Aimee expectantly.

'But that's *great*!' Aimee clapped her hands. 'Did you hear that, everyone? I didn't fill it wrong! I filled it with diesel! We can get going!'

Aimee headed back to the car happily. Eric followed her with the shopping bags, muttering about how they should probably stock up on more snacks. Otis put a hand on Maeve's shoulder and squeezed it.

'I know it doesn't feel like it, but I promise you,' he said quietly as they watched Aimee natter away to the AA man like they were old friends, 'one day – maybe not today, maybe not tomorrow, but one day in the future – we'll look back on this and laugh.'

FOUR

It was dark by the time they reached the hotel on the outskirts of the city.

Otis had started searching places on his phone where they might be able to stay as they neared their destination, trying to find somewhere cheap with rooms available last minute. Eric was no help since he'd fallen asleep a while ago with his head lolling back, his mouth wide open. Aimee had offered to help, but Otis and Maeve agreed she should keep her eyes firmly on the road. When this two-star hotel came up on the search, Otis consulted Maeve and they both agreed it was a good option. It was cheap and right next to public transport to get around the city.

They parked up – taking two spaces, but no one could be bothered to point it out to Aimee and wait for her to correct it – and while Otis got out of the car to stretch, Maeve and Aimee went to go and speak to someone at reception. At least, they assumed it was the reception. The wonky sign above the door actually read 'RE-EP-ION,' and someone had decorated it with delightful graffiti of a giant penis with very small balls.

'We only have one room available, I'm afraid,' the woman behind the desk said.

She didn't look much older than them and seemed bored out

of her mind. When they first walked in, she'd been slumped back in her chair, her feet up on the desk, scrolling through her phone with a glazed expression.

'This place is that full? Seriously' – Maeve glanced down at the name badge pinned to the receptionist's blouse – 'Helen?'

'Yeah,' she replied bluntly. 'Do you want the room?'

They didn't really have a choice. It was late and the room was cheap. They'd been traveling for hours and the idea of driving around finding somewhere else was not particularly tempting.

'Yeah, we'll take it,' Maeve confirmed, after consulting with Aimee.

'How many nights?'

'We're not sure at the moment,' Maeve replied, biting her lip. 'Can we let you know?'

'We have it booked from next Monday.'

'Hopefully we'll be gone by then.'

'All right.'

Maeve was surprised at her agreeing. 'Do we need to give you notice for when we're checking out or anything?'

'You can just tell us on the morning,' she replied wearily.

'OK. Great. And you'll let us know if any more rooms become available while we're here?'

Helen shrugged. 'You can ask and we'll tell you.'

'Fair enough.'

She typed something into the computer and then reached for a set of keys underneath the desk, sliding them across the counter.

'I'll need a card to take the deposit,' she informed them. 'We'll deduct it from your total when you've finished your stay.'

'Here, take mine,' Aimee offered.

Maeve smiled at her gratefully as Aimee passed her credit card over. They both knew Maeve didn't have one.

'That's all sorted,' Helen informed them, giving the card back. 'You need to go out the door and around the back to get to your room. Oh, and we don't supply kettles.'

'Sorry?'

'People sometimes ask if they can have a kettle,' she said, picking up her phone. 'But they can't. We don't have any. And if you hear a clattering sound in the night and some screaming, it's the resident fox who comes to pick through the bins.'

Maeve raised her eyebrows. 'The resident fox?'

Helen didn't look up. 'I call him Lewis. He pops by about midnight.'

'Awww,' Aimee said. 'I love foxes. They're like little orange wolves.'

'How do you know it's the same one that comes by every night?' Maeve asked Helen.

'His whiskers are quite pronounced.'

Maeve nodded. 'Right. OK then, thanks for all your help.'

She grabbed the keys and headed out, leaving Helen to her mindless scrolling. Eric had been rudely woken up by Otis and they were waiting in the car park with the bags at their feet. Maeve held up the room key.

'There's only one room left.'

'One room. For the four of us?'

'Yes, Otis. That's what I said.'

'I wonder if they'll be bunk beds,' Aimee said, tilting her head. 'Shotgun the top bunk! I don't like being on the bottom.

I'm always scared the top bed will fall and squish me flat. I just lie awake all night on the bottom bunk with my hands above my head in case I need to protect my face from the bed above collapsing. I did that at a summer camp once and lost all the feeling in my arms. It was so weird, like my arms had turned into blobs.'

Eric and Otis shared a look, not sure how to respond. Maeve cleared her throat.

'I think it will be just one double bed, Aimee. But it will be fine. I don't really fancy driving around finding somewhere else, do you? This place is cheap. Between the four of us, even cheaper. We can always ask for another room tomorrow, right?'

'It's better than nothing,' Otis agreed, picking up his bag and holding out Maeve's for her.

They traipsed along the pathway to room 22. Maeve turned on the light and they piled in. The room looked as though it hadn't been touched in decades. Almost everything was a muddy brown, from the carpet to the curtains. The double bed was covered by a brown and orange floral duvet and there was a small mustard-yellow moth-eaten sofa under the window. The bare light bulb hanging from the middle of the ceiling blinked incessantly.

Eric surveyed the room and wrinkled his nose.

'What's that smell?'

'I think someone may have died in here,' Aimee said solemnly.

'It isn't that bad,' Otis reasoned, attempting optimism, but the high-pitched tone of his voice gave him away. 'This is fine! Aimee and Maeve, you should have the bed. Aimee drove all this way, so you deserve it. And I'm guessing you'd rather share it with Maeve than either of us.'

'Great, thanks!' Aimee said brightly.

'I wouldn't thank him yet,' Maeve cautioned, going over to inspect the sheets. 'Let's just check these are clean and that there are no bed bugs.'

Aimee gasped, spotting the door on the other side of the room. 'There's an en suite bathroom! Amazing!' She pushed open the door and hesitated. 'Oh. It's a bit gross. Did anyone else bring shower shoes?'

'And where am I supposed to sleep?' Eric asked Otis, putting his hands on his hips.

'You can take the sofa.'

Eric glanced at it and then turned back to Otis in disgust. 'How generous.'

'Would you rather have the floor?'

'Who knows what's happened on this sofa?' Eric asked, going over to examine the cushions. 'There's a stain here that looks like the blood of a murder victim.'

'I'm going to go and ask for more blankets,' Otis sighed, ignoring his friend's dramatics.

'Yes, please, and get lots,' Eric instructed. 'My skin cannot touch these cushions, Otis. I'm going to need layers of blankets to lie on. You hear me? *Layers*.'

'Good luck with the receptionist,' Maeve said, slumping down on the mattress. 'She's not exactly employee of the year.'

'I once went on a date with a guy who was the pencil employee of the year,' Aimee told Eric and Maeve once Otis had left.

Maeve's forehead furrowed. 'What, like, in a stationery shop?'

'No,' Aimee replied, shaking her head. 'He was a *pencil* expert.'

As Maeve and Eric shared a look of bewilderment, Aimee disappeared into the bathroom to brush her teeth. Much to Maeve's surprise, Otis returned with a pile of blankets and a couple of pillows for him and Eric, reporting that Helen had actually been quite helpful. When they'd all got themselves tucked up in their blankets, Otis locating a suitable spot on the floor, Maeve suddenly remembered something.

'Oh yeah, if you hear screaming in the night, that's probably the local fox, Lewis,' she announced into the darkness. 'Apparently he likes to help himself to the bins.'

'Perfect,' Eric replied drily, trying to get comfortable on the stiff, narrow sofa. 'Have we double-locked the door?'

'Yep, I did,' Otis assured him.

Eric shivered. 'I wonder if we'll make it through the night alive.'

'Only one way to find out,' Maeve replied, turning over and making the bed creak. 'Night, everyone.'

*

Otis had an erection.

It wasn't that uncommon an occurrence; it was just sort of there sometimes when he woke up. He knew it was normal and, in case he ever forgot that fact, he could always refer back to the desperately unwelcome nuggets of information that were imparted by his mother during an incident he'd really like to forget.

One morning last year, she barged into his room without knocking.

'Nothing to be ashamed of, darling,' Jean said in all sincerity, when she flung open the door and noticed the pyramid effect of the duvet. 'Even in the absence of stimulation, the increase in testosterone that is thought to occur after your rapid eye movement sleep stage is enough to cause an erection. It all links to the parasympathetic nervous system, which is active when you're asleep. This is probably one of many erections you've had during the night.'

'MUM!' Otis cried, curling into a ball and pulling the duvet over his head. 'GET OUT!'

'All right, darling, I'll leave. No need to snap,' she replied calmly. 'Oh, and I've been meaning to say don't forget to give the floor of the shower a swill of water after you've used it, just to make sure any hair from your head – or otherwise – goes down the drain. Now, would you like me to bring you a cup of tea?'

It had been a truly traumatic morning for Otis.

But this one was worse.

Not only had he woken up with an erection, but he'd happened to wake up just as Maeve emerged from the shower wearing only a towel.

'You're awake,' she observed, droplets of water dripping down her neck from her wet hair. Her eyes glanced down at his blanket and she couldn't help but smirk. 'Good night, was it?'

'Morn—' he began and then noticed. 'ARGH!'

He quickly rolled over on to his side, holding the blanket around him. Eric, who had also just woken up to witness the exchange, burst into hysterical laughter.

'It isn't because of you!' Otis squeaked to Maeve, curling up even smaller as his face reddened. 'It definitely is NOT because you're there in a towel. I mean, not that you don't look good in a towel. You do! You do look good in a towel. You look great in a towel! I mean, in a respectful way. I'm not objectifying you. But what I mean to say is I don't have an erection because of you in a towel. It's because it's the *morning*.'

'OK.' Maeve shrugged, going to get some clothes out of her bag.

'Oh my God, please can this not have happened,' Otis whined, shutting his eyes in mortification.

'God can't help you now, my friend,' Eric laughed from the sofa.

Otis's phone started ringing from where he'd left it on the floor and Maeve glanced at the screen.

'It's your mum,' she informed him, before going back into the bathroom and shutting the door to get changed.

'You should really message Jean,' Eric advised with a yawn. 'Tell her you're here safely.'

'I messaged her last night,' Otis said, his voice muffled by the blanket that he'd pulled over his head, hoping to disappear completely.

'What are you doing?' Eric chuckled, propping himself up on his elbows. 'It's normal, you know, Oatcake.'

'Leave me alone,' Otis groaned.

The door opened and Aimee appeared with a tray of four polystyrene cups. She scurried in and shut the door behind her.

'Morning!' she said brightly, putting the tray down. 'I bought us some tea!'

'What time were you up?' Maeve asked, towel-drying her hair and opening the bathroom door now that she was dressed. 'I didn't hear you leave.'

'Oh, I'm an early riser,' Aimee said, brushing off the question. 'You know what they say, the early bird gets the bug.'

'I think it's "the early bird catches the worm,"' Eric mentioned.

'That's the one.' Aimee held out one of the cups for him. 'Here you go! They didn't have any milk, so I just put loads of sugar in.'

'Um. Thanks,' Eric said with a fixed smile, taking the cup. He tried a sip and winced, placing it on the floor and shaking his head at Otis in warning as she passed one to him.

'We can go to the cafe down the road for breakfast,' Aimee said. 'They can fit us in easy. It's empty in there!'

'Always a good sign,' Maeve commented, hanging up her towel.

'I checked and they do crumpets!'

'I like crumpets,' Eric announced.

'Me too. Then I had better get off to the baking convention and you lot can go and see Sean. Are you going with them, Eric, or do you want to come with me?'

'I think I'm sticking with Otis and Maeve,' Eric said, glancing at Maeve for confirmation, but she was busy rummaging about in her bag for makeup. 'The show isn't until tomorrow evening. In the meantime, I'll help in whatever way I can.'

'We should get going soon. I'll call Sean now,' Maeve said, picking up her phone from the bedside table and heading out of the room.

'You shouldn't go outside with wet hair,' Aimee warned her, but the door swung closed. She sighed, shaking her head at Eric.

'What, because she'll get a bad cold?' Eric asked.

'That, and once this girl I knew went out with wet hair and she got chased by an alpaca.'

Eric blinked at her. 'An alpaca?'

'Yeah.' Aimee nodded solemnly. 'Apparently it was really into her honey shampoo. It didn't hurt her or anything, but I never go outside with wet hair now, just in case.'

'Wow. Anyway, I'll . . . um . . . I'll get in the shower,' Otis said, standing up carefully and holding the blanket tight around his waist.

'Why are you bringing the blanket to the bathroom?' Aimee asked curiously.

'He's got an erection,' Eric informed her.

'Oh, right.' Aimee nodded.

'Thanks, Eric,' Otis seethed, scampering into the bathroom and slamming the door behind him.

'I've told him it's normal,' Eric said, before picking up the cup next to him without thinking and taking a sip. He quickly spat it out, spraying it all over the floor.

He wiped his chin and apologized, but they both ended up agreeing that the hotel carpet actually looked better that way.

FIVE

Maeve stopped to double-check the map on her phone, before turning right down a quiet residential road.

'We're almost there,' she said over her shoulder to Eric and Otis.

'How are you feeling?' Otis asked.

'Fine. Why?'

'Because you hardly said a word at breakfast,' he pointed out.

'I'm fine, Otis. I just want to get there. You don't need to analyze me.'

'Yeah, Otis, stop analyzing her,' Eric said, before darting to the side and gasping, pointing accusingly at the pavement. 'Dog poo! I almost stepped in it! That owner is *very* irresponsible. They should not own a dog if they do not clear up its POO!'

'All right, maybe keep your voice down,' Otis muttered, his eyes darting up at the windows of the houses they were passing.

'Why? The residents of this street agree with me, I'm sure,' Eric said haughtily. 'I'm wearing espadrilles. Do you know how difficult it is to get dog poo out of the soles of espadrilles? Very difficult, Otis. There are lots of grooves.'

Maeve found Eric's theatrics strangely comforting in that

they distracted her from the chaos of her brain. Otis was right – she had been quiet in the cafe this morning, feeling too nervous to eat, no matter how much Aimee encouraged her to dig in to a couple of crumpets.

She wasn't sure what to expect when she saw Sean. She was scared that she wouldn't be able to help him. The journey here was one thing, but actually seeing him and everything being real, that was another. What if it was all hopeless? What if his future was genuinely ruined? What if he ended up going to prison, just like their mum?

What if he was lying to her? What if . . . he really did steal the necklace?

Maeve shook her head. She didn't want to think like that. Not until she'd spoken to Sean properly and heard the full story. She focused instead on reading the door numbers of this row of houses and listening to Eric's passionate ranting about the hazard of neglected dog poo.

'This is it,' she said, stopping in front of number 113 and suddenly feeling sick.

Otis stood next to her and nudged her. 'Are you ready?'

She looked up at him and nodded, before pressing the buzzer of Flat B. She stood back and took a deep breath as they heard a door open and shut inside upstairs, followed by footsteps approaching. The front door swung open and a tall man she didn't recognize stood in the doorway. He was, at a guess, in his thirties with dark, wavy hair, pronounced stubble across his chin, dark-brown eyes and strong, broad shoulders. He was wearing a white T-shirt and black jeans and there was a date tattooed across his left wrist.

Otis gulped. He looked like the kind of guy who could kill you with his thumb.

'You must be Maeve,' he said bluntly. His eyes drifted over to Otis and Eric.

'These are my friends,' she said, gesturing behind her. 'Is Sean here? Sorry, he gave this address.'

'Yeah. Come in.' He stood back and gestured into the hallway. 'I'm Amit. Sean's crashing with me until all this is sorted out.'

The three of them apprehensively entered the building, standing awkwardly in the hall until Amit closed the door behind Eric and then led the way up the stairs. The door to the flat had been left on the latch, so he pushed it open and ushered them all in.

He led them down the hall and through a door at the end which opened into the lounge. Sean was sat on the sofa, rolling a cigarette. He looked up at Maeve and grinned, little crinkles forming around the corners of his mouth. He'd always had a cheeky smile, right from when he was little. Their mum used to say it all the time: *Sean can get out of anything with that smile.* He looked tired though, his eyes bloodshot, as though he hadn't slept properly in a while, and his dark hair was messy and unkempt from the many times he'd run his fingers through it.

'Frog-face,' he said as she came in. He stood up and held out his arms. 'Here we are, back together again.'

'Hello, Sean,' she replied coldly.

'Come here,' he sighed, stepping towards her and gesturing for a hug. 'I know you're cross, but after what I've been through, I deserve a friendly hello, don't I?'

'Not sure that is what you deserve.'

'What did I tell you, Amit?' Sean chuckled, looking over her shoulder at his friend. 'Didn't I say she was warm and cuddly? Like a teddy bear, this one.'

Before she could protest, he wrapped his arms around her. She didn't hug him back, but she softened a little at his familiar, comforting smell. He pulled away and put his hands on her shoulders.

'You look good.'

'Wish I could say the same.'

'Yeah, well, I've had a fun couple of days. Twenty-four hours in prison is great for your zen,' he said, before gesturing to Otis and Eric. 'Who are your mates?'

Eric stepped forward confidently and held out his hand. 'Hello, Sean, I'm Eric. And this is Otis.'

Otis held up his hand to wave gingerly.

'Nice to meet you,' Sean said, bemused, shaking Eric's hand. 'I wasn't expecting a whole team of you.'

'They were coming this way anyway,' Maeve said.

'Oh yeah? Why?'

'I want to go to a drag show at The Courtyard tomorrow,' Eric announced enthusiastically. 'Apparently it's brilliant. I've wanted to go for ages.'

'It's great,' Amit confirmed, much to Eric's delight. 'Make sure you get tickets beforehand online though; you won't get any on the door. It sells out.'

Eric beamed at him. 'I will. Thanks for the tip!'

'Why don't you all sit down?' Amit suggested. 'Anyone want anything?'

'Just a glass of water, please,' Maeve said, sitting next to Sean on the sofa as Eric perched on the armchair under the window and Otis remained standing awkwardly, leaning back against the wall.

Sean took a moment to look Otis and Eric up and down, curious at his little sister's choice of friends. They weren't exactly who he'd expect her to hang around with. They were just so . . . harmless. The one standing didn't stop fidgeting. He was very tense. Sean thought about telling him to chill and relax, but didn't think his candid observations about Maeve's friends would go down too well right now. She was giving him that hard look of hers. The one where she expected him to explain himself.

'Sorry I haven't been in touch before now, Froggy,' he began, sliding the rolled cigarette behind his ear.

'I'm used to it.'

'Yeah, well, I had a plan, right? I was going to get a job in the club where Amit works – he'd got the ball rolling, spoken to his boss and everything – and then, once I'd saved up a bit of money, I was going to come see you and work out moving back. I'd get a job nearby and we could get a place together – I'd get a good job reference from here, you see? Had it all worked out.'

'Sure.'

'I wanted to be in a good place. Show off to my sister that I'd got my life together. Things have veered a little off course, obviously,' he added.

'Obviously,' she snapped. 'Nice of Amit to let you stay here.'

'Yeah, well, he's a good friend and he trusts me.' He slumped back against the sofa, watching her. 'I do appreciate you being here, Frog-face. Knew I could count on you.'

Maeve didn't say anything, her jaw clenching. Otis shifted uncomfortably. Amit came back in and handed her a glass of water before lingering by the door with a cup of tea.

'I ... uh ... I like those drawings,' Eric said, his voice cutting through the silence as he gestured to the framed sketches on the wall.

'My better half drew those,' Amit informed them. 'He's an artist. That one there in the top left is me.'

Eric looked up at the sketch, which was a squiggle of lines and then two eyes diagonally opposite each other.

'Wow. Right. Amazing.'

'I had to sit for hours,' Amit said, gazing up at it. 'He really captured me. It's abstract, of course, but I think you can really see my soul.'

Eric looked up again at the squiggles, before managing to simply say, 'Sure.'

'Come on then, Sean,' Maeve blurted out impatiently. 'You need to tell us everything if we're going to work out a way to help you.'

'Right, well, as you know,' he said, sitting upright and addressing the room, determined to make the story as entertaining as possible, 'I was arrested for allegedly stealing something I didn't steal. I'm being framed.'

'Have they found the necklace?'

'No, but they found the necklace box in my jacket pocket. It was empty. I'm a little concerned as to why someone has planted it on me, and if they have another step in their plan, what that might be.' He paused, shaking his head. 'It's obvious why I would be suspected first before anyone else.'

'Because you had the jewelry box in your pocket,' Maeve muttered.

'Because I'm the outcast of the group,' Sean corrected, rolling his eyes at her. 'The obvious fall guy. You know me, Frog-face' – he put on a playful tone – 'always attracting trouble.'

Maeve inhaled deeply, trying not to lose her temper. He had a habit of turning everything into a joke. But this wasn't funny.

'Start at the beginning,' she demanded. 'What's this group?'

'All right, fine,' he sniffed, shifting forward to perch on the edge of the sofa so he could properly hold the attention of the room. He cleared his throat dramatically and put on a grand storyteller voice. 'Once upon a time, I went to Amit's club—'

'You own a club?' Eric interrupted, much to Sean's irritation.

'No,' Amit replied, sipping his tea. 'I work on the door of one. I got Sean in.'

'Exactly.' Sean nodded. 'Amit works on the door of the club and one night a few weeks ago, I go in, see some mates and they introduce me to' – he paused for effect – '*Tabitha*.'

'Tabitha Pearce, daughter of Ralph Pearce. He's a wealthy businessman, owns some properties in the city,' Amit explained.

'Tabitha Pearce.' Sean chuckled, shaking his head. 'Smart, cutthroat, an unbelievable narcissist. I found her . . . *captivating*. No, seriously, she was actually quite interesting to talk to and I got sucked in. The thing is, she was looking to score some stuff and I just so happened to have some on me.'

'You sold her drugs,' Maeve said bluntly. 'I thought you didn't do that any more.'

'I don't, sis! Like I said, it was a happy coincidence that night. I only do it here and there, just until I got the job at the club. That was the plan.'

'Let me guess, you stayed in touch with Tabitha and there just happened to be a few more happy coincidences.'

'You are very cynical, Froggy, did you know that?' Sean gestured to her, looking from Otis to Eric. 'You know, she was like this as a baby too. Always putting a negative spin on things. I'd build her a little tower from building blocks, what would she do? Smack it down.'

Maeve scowled. 'You met Tabitha. What happened next?'

'She kept buying, I kept selling,' he explained with a shrug. 'Any time she and her friends needed a little pick-me-up, she'd give me a call. We started seeing each other a bit too.'

'What does that mean?'

'What do you think it means?' he snorted, taking the cigarette from behind his ear and rolling it back and forth between his fingers. 'There was a spark between us. A flirtation. A wild romance of epic proportions.'

'Shut up.'

He grinned at his sister. 'It was harmless fun, all right?'

'Sure. Really harmless.' Maeve bristled. 'Look where it's landed you.'

He looked down at his hands, unable to come back to that one. Otis cleared his throat, eager to get the full story before tensions ran too high.

58

'So you and Tabitha started seeing each other often,' Otis prompted, gesturing for Sean to continue.

'Quite a bit, yeah,' Sean confirmed. 'Then the other night I got a phone call from her. She'd been at a fancy event – some ball or something that her dad had hosted – and she was having a little after-party at her place. Just a select group of friends and she invited me to go.'

'To supply them,' Maeve assumed.

'Well, why not?' Sean sighed. 'I had been out with Amit at the time, so he came with me to join in the fun.'

'Not my scene,' Amit commented, wrinkling his nose. 'They're pieces of work, those kids. Arrogant, boring wankers, most of them.'

'You were at the party with Sean the whole time?' Otis asked hopefully. 'That's a good thing, isn't it? You have a witness.'

'I only stayed about ten minutes,' Amit revealed with an apologetic expression. 'Like I said, it wasn't really my scene. I shouldn't have let Sean persuade me to go in the first place. And anyway, I had yoga the next morning. I didn't want to be out late.'

'You should see this man do the locust pose.' Sean nodded at him in respect. 'Majestic.'

'What happened after Amit left?' Maeve asked.

'I stayed a couple of hours at the party. I was hanging out with Tabitha quite a bit, but we couldn't do anything because her dickhead boyfriend was there.'

'She has a boyfriend.' Maeve rolled her eyes. 'You didn't mention that little detail.'

'I didn't think it was very important. I don't know him, do I?

It's not my business.' He shrugged. 'Anyway, I had a good time and then I came back here in the early hours, no harm done. Next thing we know, the police come knocking, asking if I'd mind coming down to the station for a few questions. Apparently a very expensive diamond necklace had gone missing from Miss Pearce's room. And then guess what they found in the pocket of my jacket during a little standard search?'

'The empty necklace box,' Otis answered quietly.

'Exactly. Look, there were only a few people at the party, all of them Tabitha's nearest and dearest. I'm the outsider. Easy to pin it on me, isn't it? As soon as she noticed it was missing, Tabitha pointed the finger right in my direction and her pals all agreed I was the likeliest suspect. I left my jacket on a sofa downstairs the whole night and grabbed it before I left. Anyone could have put the box in there. Now they won't let me near them, so I can't ask them any questions or work out how the hell it ended up in my pocket.'

'Tabitha won't speak to you?' Eric asked, his forehead furrowed in concentration.

Sean shook his head. 'Unsurprisingly, no. I've tried messaging her, but she doesn't believe a word I say.'

'She doesn't believe a word her dealer says? Shocking,' Maeve said drily.

'You think someone else put the jewelry box in your pocket on purpose,' Otis commented.

'There's no other explanation as to how it got there.' Sean threw up his hands in exasperation. 'I don't know what to do. Who knows where that necklace is? I have no idea who took it or why they'd want me to look guilty. All her other friends are as wealthy as she is; it's not like any of them needed the money. I'm stuck. And no one will help me. The police think I'm guilty. I don't know if they're bothering to question anyone else. My lawyer keeps telling me how it looks bad, and if I admit my guilt it will go down favorably. But I'm not guilty. I didn't do it.' He held up three fingers. 'Scout's honor.'

'You weren't a Scout,' Maeve said sharply.

He sighed, swiveling on the sofa to face her front on. 'Do you remember when Mum was arrested?'

She stared at him angrily. 'How could I forget?'

'You asked me what was going on and I looked you in the eyes and told you that, when it came to the important things in life, I wasn't going to lie to you, even though you were a kid. Even if the truth wasn't very nice.'

Maeve didn't say anything.

'I told you the truth about Mum then and I'm telling you the truth now. Whoever took that necklace, it wasn't me.'

'How are we going to find out who really did it?' Eric asked, enraptured. 'We need to work out a plan. Get a list of everyone at the party.'

'Yeah, that sounds good. Can we go and do that wherever you lot are staying?' Sean asked. 'Only Amit has family coming over for lunch.'

'My sister's just had a baby,' Amit explained with a wide grin. 'A little boy.'

'That's great, congratulations!' Otis exclaimed, as Amit thanked him profusely, getting out his phone to show them pictures.

'We'll get out of your way,' Maeve said, standing up. 'Let's go back to the hotel.'

'You think we have a genuine shot at sorting this mess out?' Sean asked, getting to his feet and sticking his hands in his pockets, his front of confidence faltering.

'Absolutely!' Eric declared, slapping him on the back. 'There won't be any injustice on our watch, isn't that right, Otis?'

Otis gave an awkward thumbs up. 'That's right.'

As Eric and Otis declared their allegiance to her brother, Maeve felt an instinctive urge to protect her friends from Sean and his lies. She was then hit by a consequent wave of guilt for not believing him herself. She wished she could blindly trust that he was telling the truth and that he wouldn't risk getting her and her friends into trouble unless he really was innocent. But, as horrible as she felt about it, she just didn't believe him.

They never should have come.

'Great. Thanks,' Sean replied, shooting a confident thumbs up back at Otis, who wasn't sure if he was being mocked or not. 'Glad I've got you lot on my side.'

'Don't you worry, I have seen a LOT of detective dramas,' Eric proclaimed, putting his hands on his hips. 'We can map it all out, suss out the motives. Otis is good with people, aren't you, Otis? So he can get them talking. And Maeve is very clever, which is great because this is basically like solving a puzzle. And I'm a very good motivator.' He clapped his hands together. 'I'll whip you all into shape.'

'That all sounds great,' Sean said, glancing to Maeve. 'What a team.'

'Come on then! No time to lose!' Eric cried, punching his fist in the air as he led the way out of the room towards the front door, much to Sean's amusement. 'We have some detective work to do. Thank you so much for your hospitality, Amit.'

'Wow,' Sean whispered to Maeve. 'This is quite the motley crew, eh, sis?'

'I suggest you get used to them,' Maeve replied, as she followed Otis and Eric out of the room. 'Looks like we're all you've got.'

SIX

'How about those pancakes I promised you?' Sean proposed, rubbing his hands together as he walked into the supermarket. 'We can buy chocolate chips, whipped cream, the works. I'll make them just how you like them, Froggy.'

'There's no kitchen at the hotel,' Maeve said, following him as he marched away down the first aisle. 'We can't cook anything.'

'Then we'll buy premade pancakes,' he said, refusing to be beaten. 'And we can add the chocolate chips and whipped cream. There, you see? Problem solved.'

Maeve shook her head as Sean snatched a pack of pancakes from the bakery aisle and tossed it in the air triumphantly, catching it and heading off to hunt down the whipped cream. They were supposed to be getting lunch for everyone that they could eat at the hotel while coming up with the grand plan to prove Sean's innocence.

It had been Otis's suggestion that Maeve and Sean grab some food and meet him and Eric back at the hotel. He hadn't said anything else, but Maeve could tell he thought she should have some bonding time with her brother and resolve any tension.

But so far she'd stayed quiet, mulling things over, and Sean had sauntered along next to her, rambling about anything and everything. He never did like silence.

She was wondering whether to call the whole thing off. She could tell him here and now that it was a mistake to come.

She opened her mouth to speak, a lump rising in her throat. 'Sean—'

'Can you see the chocolate chips anywhere?' he called out, examining the row in front of him. 'They should be in the baking section, shouldn't they? Come here, I need a second pair of eyes.'

She sighed. 'We can't just get stuff for pancakes, Sean.'

'Why not?' he asked, genuinely baffled. 'Everyone loves pancakes.'

'It's hardly lunch food, is it?'

'Yeah, but we need *brain* food. You were basically raised on pancakes and you're the brainiest person I know. Shall we get some beers too?'

'What? No. Look—'

'Why not?' He glanced over her shoulder and rolled his eyes. 'Uh-oh, we're being watched. Doesn't this guy already know I'm headed to prison?'

Maeve looked back to see the security guard eyeing them suspiciously, before she turned back to her brother. 'For fuck's sake, this isn't all a big joke, Sean!'

'What do you mean?'

'You keep acting like it's a joke. But it's serious.'

'Aha, but that's why I should joke about it,' he insisted, shaking the pack of pancakes at her. 'What else am I going to do? Sit around and feel sorry for myself? That gloomy attitude

65

working out well for you, is it? No. You have to relax a bit, Frog-face. Things happen. It's life.'

'Yeah, well, maybe things wouldn't happen so often if you took a bit of responsibility.'

He raised his eyebrows at her. 'You think this is my fault then, do you?'

'I just think—'

'Don't worry, mate,' Sean suddenly called out over her head to the security guard, making other customers look curiously in their direction. 'We're just having a heart-to-heart, we're not stealing anything.'

Blushing, the security guard cleared his throat and then moved away to linger elsewhere. Sean shook his head.

'Sorry, what were you saying before I rudely interrupted?'

Maeve took a deep breath. 'I think . . . It's just . . . Well, clearly this group of people you've been hanging around with don't sound like they were good for you.'

'Well, yeah, doesn't take a genius to work that one out.' He snorted. 'I didn't see them as my friends. I saw them as a way of making a bit of extra cash, which I needed. But before you get all judgmental, it was temporary.'

Maeve looked down at her feet. 'You said you'd stop selling.'

'Yeah, I did.' He held up his hands. 'But sometimes things aren't that simple. It's not like jobs land at my feet. In case you haven't noticed, me and you, we don't get any help. We're in this *alone*. We have to do what we can to get by.'

'There are other ways of getting by.'

He laughed. 'Like what? Some of us didn't get the chance to finish school and get qualifications that we'd need to secure good jobs, because we were too busy raising our little sister when our mum got arrested and our dad buggered off.'

'I'm not the reason you didn't finish school,' Maeve snapped.

'Yes, yes, I know.' Sean sighed. 'I'm sorry. I messed up. Trusted the wrong people, but it's not fair that I go down for something I didn't do. Even I know that. Look, I'll change things. I'll make things right. I just need that fighting *chance*. You know that and that's why you're here, isn't it?'

She didn't believe him. She *couldn't* believe him. But maybe he was right. Maybe, no matter what he'd done, a part of her still wanted him to have the chance to do better.

Maeve reluctantly nodded.

'So, the way I see it, with you here with me, fighting my corner, there's hope. Right? Enough of this bleak attitude; we want positivity. Now, where were we? Oh yes.' He shook the pack of pancakes in her face. 'Brain food. Now, are you going to track down the chocolate chips or not? Because if I'm honest, Maeve, you haven't been the best assistant so far in this lunch mission. In fact, you've been a bit crap.'

Maeve tried to suppress a smile. 'What makes you think, between the two of us, I would be the assistant?'

'Touché.' He grinned. 'All right then, what do *you* want for lunch? You can pick.'

She pretended to think for a moment and then reached out, snatching the pancakes from his grip. 'Let's find the chocolate chips.'

*

67

By the time Maeve and Sean arrived at the hotel room, Eric and Otis had attempted to tidy things a bit by piling everyone's bags on top of Aimee's huge suitcase in one corner, so they had a bit more floor space. They had also written some questions on the notes app in Eric's phone that they believed would help to get the ball rolling.

'First things first,' Eric said, inviting Sean to have a seat on the sofa. 'Who else was at the party the night the necklace went missing?'

'Can I actually sit on the bed?' he asked, grimacing as he inspected the stains on the cushions. 'The sofa looks like someone wanked all over it.'

'I had to sleep on that,' Eric said, looking haunted.

'That's awful, mate.' Sean patted him on the arm and then took a seat on the end of the bed, getting his phone out his pocket. 'Right, here you go. Here's the lot of them.'

He held up his screen to show them a photo of a group of friends. 'This is Tabitha's Instagram. She mostly posts pictures of herself, but this one features the others. There's Tabitha and then you've got Casper, Grace, Noah and Cece. They were the only people at the party.'

'Our suspects,' Eric announced.

'Can you screenshot that and send me the picture?' Otis asked. 'I have an idea about how to make this easier.'

Sean did as he asked and then Otis left the room to go to reception, promising to be back in a minute, Eric volunteering to accompany him. In the meantime, Sean was asking Maeve questions about how she was doing at school when the door flung open and Aimee bustled in.

'What are you doing here?' Maeve asked, brightening at seeing her friend. 'You're supposed to be at the baking convention.'

'Get this,' Aimee said, a little out of breath from walking all morning. She'd got VERY lost on the way to the arena. 'The baking convention is next year!'

'What?'

'It's next year, not this one,' Aimee explained, amazed. 'Isn't that strange? I must have read the date wrong on the advert. There I was at the arena and do you know what's on there?'

'Not a baking convention?' Sean guessed.

'No! Exactly! A twitter event!'

Maeve frowned in confusion. 'Twitter?'

'Yeah! Can you imagine? A whole arena full of bird-watchers!'

'You mean a *twitcher* event, Aimee,' Maeve corrected with a knowing smile.

'Yeah, that's what I said. There were LOADS of them. Wandering around with their notebooks, comparing rare birds they'd seen. So many stands for binoculars! A woman tried to sell me a pair that were filled with nitrogen, she said, to prevent fogging.' Aimee put her hands on her hips. 'I can't believe the baking convention is next year.'

'Sorry, Aimes,' Maeve offered.

'Should have checked the date,' she reflected, before her expression lit up. 'But now I can help you solve the mystery! Hi, Sean, I'm Aimee.'

'Hello, Aimee.' Sean waved. 'I'm sorry too, about the baking convention.'

'Don't be! In a way it's a good thing, because now I can help work out how to clear your name! So it was lucky, really, that I got the wrong date.'

'Great,' he said unenthusiastically. 'So lucky to have someone so observant on the case.'

'I won't let you down. Together we'll work out who really did this.' She looked at him wide-eyed. 'Have you ever tried a mind map?'

'A what?'

'Aimee loves mind maps,' Maeve told him.

Aimee nodded vigorously. 'They're brilliant. It's a fun way of engaging your brain.'

'Sounds . . . epic,' Sean said.

'I need a pen and paper,' she announced. 'Then we can get started.'

Before she could start hunting down the materials she needed, Otis and Eric returned, carrying some pieces of paper.

'Great! You've got paper for the mind map!' Aimee exclaimed.

'No, these are photos printed out,' Eric told her, looking confused. 'What are you doing here? Why aren't you at the baking convention?'

'It's actually next year,' Sean informed him, leaning back on his hands. 'This year it's the twitcher convention.'

Eric blinked at him. 'Sorry?'

'What have you got there?' Maeve asked Otis as he began pulling blobs off the slab of Blu Tack he was holding.

'I thought we'd stick up pictures of the other people at the party, so we have a clear idea of who's who,' Otis explained, as Eric began helping him tack the various pictures up on the wall. 'We printed out the group photo that you showed us, Sean, and then cut it up so we have individual faces.'

'Where did you find a printer?' Maeve asked, impressed.

'I just asked Helen,' Otis answered with a shrug. 'She lent us some scissors too, and the Blu Tack. She asked if we were model scouts needing to inspect potential client photos.'

'I think she has a crush on Otis,' Eric divulged, winking at them.

'No, she doesn't,' Otis sighed wearily. 'We just got chatting and she needed a bit of advice.'

'She was stalking her ex-boyfriend on social media—'

'She wasn't stalking him,' Otis interrupted disapprovingly. 'She was obsessively checking his photos and updates, which is a natural thing to want to do when you're suddenly cut out of someone's life.'

'But Otis asked her why she was doing that and whether it was benefitting her,' Eric said wisely. 'He reminded her that we lose context on social media – things look better than they may be – and she should be directing her energy instead into new things.'

'Poor Helen,' Aimee sighed, downcast. 'Breakups are horrible.'

'Anyway, back to the matter at hand,' Otis said, keen to get the ball rolling on Sean's predicament.

'OK, so here is everyone who was at the party,' Eric said, gesturing to the completed line of individual pictures. 'Sean, please will you come up here and take us through them all? I will write their names underneath the pictures.'

'Don't write on the wall though,' Aimee advised. 'I did that once when I was younger and my parents were furious. I did use a permanent red marker pen though. And also, instead of the wall, it was a painting by someone old and famous. A French guy, I think. His name sounded a bit like Suzanne.'

Maeve's jaw dropped. 'Not . . . Cézanne?'

'That's the one!'

'Thanks for the tip, Aimee,' Eric said, laughing at Maeve's shocked expression. 'We got some extra paper from Helen, so I'll just tear some off and stick it up underneath. Sean, when you're ready.'

'OK, let's do this,' Sean said, jumping on the bed.

He stood next to the pictures, beginning with the one on the far left. It showed a striking girl with black curly hair, bold eyebrows, sharp cheekbones and intense dark eyes framed by long eyelashes.

'This is Tabitha Pearce,' he said, pointing at her. 'She's the one who owns the necklace that has gone missing. She was hosting the party that night. As you know, we were having a bit of a . . . fling, shall we say.'

He moved along to the picture next to her of a guy with slicked-back fair hair, freckles across his nose and a strong jaw line. 'This is her boyfriend, Casper.'

'I thought you just said you were having a fling with Tabitha,' Aimee pointed out.

'That's correct.'

'But she has a boyfriend. Casper.'

'Also correct.'

'Oh.' Aimee looked confused and then her eyes widened. 'Ooooooh.'

'Let's keep things moving,' Sean said, gesturing to the next three photos. 'The one with flaming-red hair is Grace, Tabitha's best friend; one along is their other friend, Noah, and at the end there is Cece, full name, Cecily Pearce. She is Tabitha's little sister.'

'So we've got Tabitha, who is the victim of the theft,' Otis said, as Sean nodded along and Eric frantically finished writing the names to match the pictures. 'Then we have her boyfriend, Casper; her friends, Grace and Noah; and her little sister, Cece.'

'You got it,' Sean said.

'One of these people here took the diamond necklace.' Aimee bit her lip. 'But they all look so nice and smiley! Just goes to show, pictures can be so misleading. Also, Noah is a total babe.'

'He's a model. And will tell you that several times when you meet him.'

'All right,' Maeve began, studying the pictures up on the wall. 'Say you have been framed, Sean—'

'I *have* been framed,' Sean said, his eyes flashing with anger.

'Who up here would have a motive?' Maeve continued, brushing his comment aside.

'Very good place to start, Maeve,' Eric said, nodding his approval as he finished sticking up Cece's name. 'Sean, take us through motives.'

'Well, Casper, I guess, if he found out about me and Tabitha.' He grimaced. 'Could also be Grace though. Considering what I saw that night at the party.'

'The best friend? Why?' Otis asked. 'What did you see?'

73

'Grace and Casper shagging in Cece's room. I was looking for Tabitha and didn't realize they were in there.'

'Oh my God, scandal,' Eric gasped. 'The best friend and the boyfriend?'

'OK, this is a great start,' Otis said optimistically. 'We have two suspects. Casper could be out to get you because you slept with his girlfriend, or both Casper and Grace wanted to frame you because you saw the affair.'

'Might have been Noah, actually,' Sean added, stroking the stubble on his chin as he examined the photos. 'He owes me quite a lot of money. Maybe he wanted to clear his debts, so to speak.'

'Well. At least we can take Cece down then,' Eric said, reaching for the last picture.

'I wouldn't,' Sean said, holding up his hand. 'She was very angry with me that night.'

'Please don't tell me you were sleeping with Tabitha's younger sister,' Maeve groaned.

'No!' Sean looked insulted. 'I'll have you know I turned her down. That's why she was cross. She was drunk and hitting on me. I told her I wasn't interested and she wasn't happy about it. Don't think anyone from the Pearce family has ever experienced not getting something they want. She didn't take it well.'

'Technically, then, *everyone* up on the wall had a motive to frame you,' Aimee considered, her forehead furrowed in concentration.

They all turned to look at Sean in anticipation. He stood thoughtfully for a moment, his eyes drifting back and forth over the line of photos.

'Yeah,' he confessed eventually with a shrug. 'Yeah, that's right.'

Otis slumped down on the bed, disheartened. 'No clear leads then.'

'We need to speak to them,' Maeve stated.

'They'll probably be at the club tonight,' Sean said confidently. 'The one where Amit works. He can get you through the door. Tabitha loves the DJ playing there.'

'We don't have ID,' Otis pointed out.

'Like I said, Amit can get you in. I'll make sure he knows. But if you're going to speak to them, you need to pretend you don't know me, yeah? They'll never tell you anything if they think you do,' Sean warned.

'So what you're saying,' Aimee began slowly, 'is we need to go undercover.'

'Essentially. And this place is nice, so you can't go dressed like that.' He gestured at Maeve specifically, who scowled. 'And if you're going to infiltrate this group enough to get some answers, then you need to stand out. Get them to notice you.'

'How are we going to do that?' Otis asked, aghast.

'We need to dress to catch the eye, you say,' Eric said, looking euphoric. 'You leave that to me, my friends. You leave ALL of that to me.' Suddenly exhilarated, he clapped his hands. 'Aimee?'

She stepped forward. 'Yes?'

He flashed her a wide grin. 'We're going to need your suitcase.'

SEVEN

It was the challenge of a lifetime.

Eric had four people to transform, including himself, and just a pared-down wardrobe to work with. Thank goodness he and Aimee had taken the trip seriously enough to bring a selection of outfits. The other two weren't much help, but there was nothing he could do about that now. After a bizarre but admittedly delicious pancake lunch, Eric requested that everyone lay their clothes across the bed and he inspected his options.

Sean left soon after eating, hoping to meet a mate of his who might have some work for him that paid in cash. As Maeve raised her eyebrows, he reassured her that it wasn't anything illegal, just some heavy lifting. He thanked the others profusely for helping him out and promised to stay in touch to get updates.

'I honestly don't know how to thank you, but I'm forever in your debt,' he said, giving them a dramatic bow with a flourish of his hands.

'We haven't done anything yet,' Maeve reminded him. 'Just keep your head down and don't get into any more trouble, would you?'

'Scout's honor.' He grinned, holding up his three fingers and putting his other hand on his heart, before thanking them again and heading off.

'We have a while until we need to get ready,' Otis observed, as Eric walked up and down the bed, picking up various items of clothing and examining them. 'We could go for a walk, check out the area.'

'Sorry, Otis, but if this evening is going to be a success, I'm going to need as much time as possible to focus,' Eric informed him, gesturing to the pile of clothes. 'I have my work cut out, as you can see.'

'I'll come with you,' Maeve said to Otis, heading for the door. 'I could do with some fresh air.'

'I'll stay here with Eric,' Aimee volunteered. 'He might need someone to bounce ideas off. Like a human mind map.'

'Great.' Otis nodded, following Maeve out of the room. 'See you in a bit.'

He hurried to catch up with Maeve and they strolled along together out of the hotel car park, Otis with his hands in his pockets, glancing at Maeve every so often while she chewed her fingernails, barely paying attention to where they were going.

'You OK?' he asked eventually.

'I'm fine.'

'If you're worried about Sean, then I promise we'll do everything we can to—'

'I said I'm fine, Otis,' she snapped, before feeling guilty and softening her expression as she looked up at him. 'Sorry. It's . . . a lot. With Sean and everything.'

'It is,' he said, nodding, before giving her a gentle nudge. 'But you're an amazing sister. He's lucky to have you.'

Acknowledging that Maeve clearly did not want to talk about it, Otis changed the subject and started chatting about the squirrel he could see on a tree they were passing. Maeve appreciated his efforts and nodded along, pretending to listen.

His comment was well meant, but it only made her feel worse. She wasn't an amazing sister, because then she'd have her brother's back. Nothing he'd done so far had convinced her he was innocent – brushing off serious issues with playful jokes, his revelation that he was still mixed up in selling drugs, his hurrying off now after a phone call about a cash-paying job with a vague description. She'd seen it all before.

She wasn't sure what she'd been expecting. That there was a chance he might have changed his life around, magically transformed into a responsible, trustworthy, honest person, and had found himself in trouble through no fault of his own, just an unfortunate stroke of luck?

She didn't believe in miracles.

This was the same Sean who stuck around long enough to cause a disaster, before disappearing without a trace, leaving everyone behind to sort out his mess. She had a responsibility to her friends and she wasn't going to let them fall into a trap she knew all too well.

Trusting Sean only led to anger and disappointment.

By the time they got back to the hotel room, Eric and Aimee had separated the clothes into four separate piles. Eric greeted Maeve by enthusiastically picking up a fitted black mini dress with a sweetheart neckline from the top of Aimee's pile and holding it up to her.

Aimee nodded in approval. 'That would look so good on

you, Maeve. I wore it once to a tree-planting ceremony. I got quite cold in it, but it went really well with the spade.'

'Yes, this is *it*,' Eric agreed. 'I will create a look around this for you, Maeve. Leave it to me. They'll have NO idea you're really Sean's sister. We've discussed it and we were thinking that you could be a glamorous punk rock star on the rise?'

'What do you think?' Aimee asked eagerly.

'I don't know,' Maeve admitted. 'I don't know about any of this.'

'You haven't seen it on yet,' Eric pointed out. 'Once you do, I think that—'

'I'm not talking about the dress,' she said, slumping back against the wall. 'I don't think this plan is going to work.'

'Why not?' Aimee asked, frowning.

'Because for it to work, Sean would have to be telling the truth.'

Her statement was met with silence. Aimee and Eric shared a stunned look, while Otis watched her carefully, moving to sit down on the bed.

'Why do you think he's not being honest?' Otis asked.

She shrugged, leaving one arm across her body and lifting the other to bite her nails. 'Because he doesn't think. He's not very good at dealing with consequences.'

Otis nodded in understanding. 'He's let you down before. How do you know he won't let you down this time? Trust is one of the most crucial things in a relationship. When it's broken, it takes time to rebuild. It also takes risk. You're risking being hurt again. And that can be frightening.'

'I don't need therapizing, Otis.'

'All I'm saying is it's understandable that you're feeling scared.'

'You don't know him like I do.' She scowled, feeling angry at Otis for thinking he understood. 'He's been in trouble before and his way of handling it is to escape. Get as far away as possible from the problem.'

'Maybe it's a good sign that he's stuck around then,' Eric said cautiously, his eyes darting to Otis nervously. 'If he was guilty, wouldn't he have run off by now?'

'Look.' Maeve pursed her lips, her eyes fixed to the floor. 'I don't want you lot involved with this.'

'You have to let us help you,' Otis insisted. 'Maybe the way to look at it is, if there's any chance he's innocent in all this, it's worth checking it out, right? Then at least we'll know the truth either way. And we're not going to let you go it alone.'

'That's right,' Aimee said, nodding vigorously. 'We're in this together.'

'We might as well try,' Eric added with a warm smile. 'If it doesn't work or if it all comes to nothing, then at least we can say we gave it a shot. Sometimes it's worth taking a leap of faith.'

Maeve sighed, lifting her eyes. Their determined, hopeful expressions caused her anger to subside, giving way to an overwhelming sense of appreciation towards them. It seemed pointless to attempt to dissuade them.

'All right,' she said, giving in. 'Fine. We might as well give it a try.'

'Any time you want us to take a step back, you just say,' Otis told her sternly. 'Whatever you feel comfortable with.'

She nodded gratefully.

'So,' Eric began tentatively, 'what do you want to do about tonight?'

'I think Sean is probably right that these people won't talk to us if they know who we are and what we're up to,' she admitted, putting her hands on her hips. 'So come on, Eric. Turn me into a punk rock star.'

'Yes!' Eric cried, punching the air. 'I was hoping that would be your answer. Now, show me all the jewelry everyone has on them.'

Maeve set about looking for her makeup bag that doubled as her jewelry case, before Eric asked her to try on Aimee's black dress. She pulled it on in the bathroom and felt instantly different. You could tell it was expensive, from a really nice label, and the fit and material made her feel glamorous, as though she really could be someone important.

Aimee began lining outfits up for Otis on the bed, chatting him through the pieces Eric had set aside for him, while Eric sat Maeve down on the sofa next to him to do her makeup once she was dressed.

'I'm thinking heavy eye makeup and bold lips,' Eric said, prepping their combined makeup options. 'Then I think we should style your hair curled and up in a loose do.'

'Sure,' Maeve replied, deciding to just go with the flow.

He started with some primer and foundation before moving on to bronzer. She liked the feel of the soft brush against her skin. It was strangely comforting having someone else do her makeup.

'My mum used to paint my nails sometimes,' she blurted out.

'Yeah?' Eric smiled, softly running some blusher on her cheekbones.

'It was such a peaceful moment. Like, I remember so much chaos around my mum when I was little, but then I remember it being so quiet and calm when she painted my nails. Because she had to concentrate, I suppose. So it didn't smudge.'

'Sounds nice.'

'It was.'

'Close your eyes,' he instructed, reaching for the eyeshadow. She did as she was told and he gently brushed an electric-blue shade across her eyelids.

'Did your mum teach you how to do makeup?' she asked.

'I taught myself. It was frustrating at first, I was so bad at it. But now I love it. It's kind of therapeutic. The focus and harmony of it. Like you say, it's calming.' He chuckled, blending the eyeshadow with his finger. 'My mum's not the person to go to for makeup tips. She's amazing though. Really loving and caring. Very religious. Family is everything to her, you know. I think she misses her own family in Lagos, so we do a lot of stuff together. Open your eyes.'

She did so. Eric smiled at her.

'You look *fierce*.'

'All right, you two,' Aimee suddenly announced, bounding over to grab their attention. 'What do you think?'

She gestured at Otis. He was wearing a pair of Eric's bold red trousers, a black polo neck and a matching bright-red blazer. He'd also donned a pair of Aimee's Wayfarer sunglasses. Eric's jaw dropped and Maeve laughed in surprise.

'Well?' Otis asked, giving them a spin, before peering at them over the top of the sunglasses.

'You SLAY, Oatcake!' Eric confirmed.

'You look like a sleazy art dealer,' Maeve concluded.

'No,' Aimee said, admiring him. 'He looks like this guy who once came to the house and sold my mum this really weird statue of a toad smoking a pipe and holding an umbrella.'

'So . . . a sleazy art dealer,' Maeve repeated drily.

'Yeah, guess he was!' Aimee said, clicking her fingers. 'Dad was so mad about her buying that. It cost a fortune! And it's so ugly. He made her put it outside next to the pond where he couldn't see it, but she took it in the next day and put it in the kitchen, right on the side of the counter. You know, he's never even noticed.'

'What, never?'

Aimee shook her head. 'Never. Otis, you look great!'

'Yeah, it's perfect,' Eric agreed. 'We need to slick back your hair and smudge a little eyeliner on your bottom lash line to make your eyes look smoky and mysterious when you take off the sunglasses.'

Otis brushed down the lapels of the jacket. 'I feel very hot.'

'You look hot!' Aimee exclaimed.

'I mean *actually* hot.' He took off the sunglasses and pulled at his polo neck. 'I'm not sure I can wear this to a club. I'll sweat a lot.'

'Fashion knows no sweat, Otis,' Eric told him. 'You look brilliant in that outfit. Do not touch anything and wait in the queue for eyeliner.'

'What are you thinking for me, Eric?' Aimee asked, excited.

'The pink polka dot dress with hot-pink makeup,' he stated, concentrating on Maeve's mascara. 'And my silver glitter bomber jacket. Finished off with big hair.'

'Oh my God, I love it!' Aimee hugged the silver jacket to her chest before her eyes widened at the feather boas lying on top of Eric's case. She picked up the pink one and flung it around her neck. 'This is *amazing*!'

'Thanks!'

'You have so many nice clothes, Eric. You know,' Aimee said, wiggling her eyebrows, 'we do have time to try a few things on. Come on, Otis, what do you say?'

'What do you mean?' he replied, looking panicked.

'I mean, makeover montage!' she exclaimed, grabbing his arm and jumping up and down. 'You know, like they do in films when they try on lots of different clothes and it's all fun and happy and heartwarming.'

'Oh, I don't think we have time for—'

'We definitely do!' Aimee decided, wrapping the feather boa around his neck. 'I'll pump up the music; you pick your next look!'

'Yes, Otis!' Eric giggled, standing up and flinging some clothes at him. 'It's time for a catwalk!'

Otis looked at Maeve for help, but she just shrugged.

'I think Maeve could use some cheering up,' Aimee added, shimmying her shoulders. 'Let's give her a FASHION SHOW!'

'Fine,' Otis sighed, unable to argue. 'Makeover montage it is.'

Aimee squealed, grabbing her phone and selecting a song, before turning it up full volume.

'You take photos!' Aimee told Maeve, passing her the phone. 'Come on then, Otis! Take to the floor!'

Maeve nodded and then sat back to enjoy the spectacle of Otis strutting across the room, pretending he was on a catwalk, encouraged by whistles from Eric and whoops from Aimee.

Eric disappeared into the bathroom for a minute before sliding out wearing Otis's clothes, making them all burst out laughing as he shoved his hands in the pockets of Otis's statement blue, red and beige bomber jacket and yellow-framed round sunglasses. He pouted and posed for the camera while Otis shook his head at him. Aimee chose a leopard-print dress from Eric's collection, the pink feather boa around her neck and Maeve's black leather jacket draped over her shoulders.

They all did an outfit change, with Eric lobbing items of clothes at each person. Maeve couldn't stop laughing at how much fun it was to see them emerge from the bathroom in a different, bolder outfit each time and dance around to the music, putting on quite the show for her. She felt very honored to be the guest of honor at this bizarre, spontaneous event.

After a while they checked the time and realized they should get back to their final looks for the club tonight as they had to get dinner at some point. The three of them joined hands and did a bow for Maeve, who clapped and cheered, still giggling.

She would never have thought that makeovers or pretend catwalks in a shitty hotel room were really her thing, but she had to admit she'd loved every minute of this one. Sean, school, money, rent – all of the stress that constantly weighed down on her was forgotten in a whirlwind of hysterical laughter, stupid poses and colorful clothes. Even if she could lose herself in all this fun just for a bit, it meant a lot.

Eric came over to sit with her and finish her makeup, while Otis changed back into his red suit, laughing with Aimee as she set about teaching him how to shimmy properly. Eric chose a bright-red lipstick for Maeve, before brushing shimmering highlighter along her cheekbones. He finished with sticking on some long fake eyelashes, which felt strange for her. She could see them hovering above her own lashes but Eric promised she'd get used to them.

'You're done,' he told her, sitting back to admire his work.

'How do I look?' she asked. 'Ready for battle?'

'Maeve Wiley,' he grinned, his eyes twinkling at her, 'you look ready for anything.'

EIGHT

'Anyone else really need a poo?'

Everyone turned to stare at Aimee. She blinked back at them, unabashed. It was a peculiar time for her to pitch the question, having just arrived at the club. The four of them were standing on the pavement opposite, watching Amit across the way checking the ID of everyone in the long queue winding around the side of the building before waving them through the door.

'I always need to go when I get nervous,' Aimee continued with a gulp. 'What if I mess this up somehow and then, because of me, Sean goes to prison?'

'You won't mess this up,' Otis assured her. 'None of us will. Remember, we're just four friends having a fun night out. Hopefully, when we get their attention, we can get this group talking about things that have happened to them recently. The necklace incident has to come up naturally.'

'And we're looking out for anyone who is really angry at Sean,' Eric reminded them. 'Anyone who sounds as though they're really pleased he's been caught. Or anyone who acts a bit suspiciously or guiltily if it comes up.'

'Maybe even listening out for someone bragging about getting away with it,' Otis pointed out. 'Alcohol loosens the tongue and sometimes people get caught out because they're showing off and forget what they're supposed to be hiding.'

'And we should check to see if anyone is wearing a big diamond necklace,' Aimee added thoughtfully.

'Yes,' Eric said, with a side glance at Otis. 'That would be quite the giveaway.'

Maeve remained quiet, watching Amit on the door and wondering whether this mad plan was actually going to work or whether they'd somehow all completely lost their minds.

'Hey,' Otis said gently, nudging her arm, 'it's going to be OK.'

She looked up at him, amazed at how he seemed to read her mind like that. 'What if they don't want to talk to us? What if this has all been a waste of time?'

'Trying is never a waste of time. We go with this plan and if it doesn't work, we come up with another one.'

'I don't know if I can pull this off,' she admitted, tugging at the skirt of her dress.

'Are you kidding?' Otis grinned. 'You look like you're the new member of Bikini Kill, about to join them up on stage for a reunion tour.'

Maeve raised her eyebrows and broke a smile. 'Really?'

'Yeah. When you walk in there' – he pointed at the club door across the road – 'just imagine that that's who you are.'

'Shall we?' Eric asked the group, gesturing to cross.

'We shall.' Maeve nodded with a steely expression. 'Let's do this. Let's go and find the truth.'

'But not before I go to the loo,' Aimee added.

'Right. After Aimee goes to the loo, THEN we go and find the truth.'

Giving each other encouraging smiles, they waited for a gap in the traffic and then crossed the road, all of them feeling as though they were walking into their new characters. As they strode towards the club, Eric couldn't help thinking that if this was a film they'd be emerging out of billowing smoke in slow motion.

Maeve, in her black dress and bold makeup, was starring tonight as ROXIE, a punk rock musician on the edge of making it, recording her first EP and always looking for new inspiration for her soul-searching lyrics.

Otis was playing JEM, the red-suited son of an art-gallery owner, who dabbled in watercolors himself and wore sunglasses indoors.

Aimee was striking in her bright-pink dress and silver jacket, and stepping into the shoes of MOLLY, an ambitious actor with her heart set on drama school, refusing to let anyone get in her way.

And Eric, dressed in a velvet multicolored blazer, purple satin trousers with heeled boots, and glitter swirled around his eyes, was arriving as FINLEY, an eccentric writer and poet.

Eric was extremely proud of his four character creations. He had not had all the materials to hand that he would have liked and yet they all totally looked the part. There was no question that they would capture attention, and they'd created sufficiently vague personas that were sure to go down well with Tabitha and her friends. Eric had decided to stick to the arts because it made sense that they'd run in the same circle that way.

'Evening.' Amit greeted them with a sharp nod of his head

as they strutted up the pavement. He gestured for them to skip the queue. 'You lot can head on in.'

'Thanks so much,' Otis said, smiling at him before Eric gave him a prod in the back with his finger.

'What are you doing?' Eric hissed as Otis glanced around at him in confusion. 'You were not in character then!'

'I was just thanking him,' Otis argued, following Maeve and Aimee through another set of double doors, as they passed the cloakroom.

'You said "thanks so much," all bright and cheery like Otis.' Eric sighed. 'You're meant to be cool and collected, remember? You want to be a trendy famous artist like Banksy or someone.'

'Banksy might say things like "thanks so much" for all we know,' Otis pointed out. 'Considering Banksy is anonymous, there's no telling . . .'

Otis trailed off as they walked into the main room of the club. It was big and bright and loud and busy. Eric gasped in amazement. Otis froze in fear. He hated crowds and he hated noise. He'd never been a party kind of guy.

'This feels like it's over capacity,' he commented to Eric, as his friend gazed around in awe. 'I don't think Amit is doing a very good job of keeping the numbers to a safe limit.'

'There you are being Otis again,' Eric said, laughing and grabbing his arm. 'You're Jem now, remember? Jem is well up for this night of debauchery.'

Maeve took Aimee's hand and dragged her over to the back of the room behind a pillar, gesturing for Otis and Eric to join them.

'I can see Tabitha,' she informed them, raising her voice so they could hear her over the thumping bass, the vibrations of which Otis swore he could actually feel in his heart it was so loud. 'I think it's her anyway, with the rest of them too. They're in a booth at the side of the dance floor.'

'Of course they have a VIP booth,' Eric said, nodding in approval. 'We should really have one too.'

'I think we go and dance near them?' Maeve suggested, unsure. 'Then maybe they'll spot us and invite us over for a drink. That's the point of these characters, right? Attention grabbing.'

'Right,' Eric confirmed with a sharp nod. 'Let's go and break out some exquisite moves on the dance floor then.'

'I'll go to the loo first,' Aimee announced, pointing at the toilets just behind her. 'I'll meet you back here in a sec, then we can get in there.'

As Aimee hurried off, Otis wiped his forehead nervously. 'Do we have to go right on to the dance floor? Can't we keep to the edge? I don't think Jem is much of a dancer, so to be true to my character, maybe I'll just hang around here.'

'What, behind the pillar?' Eric asked. 'Jem does not hide away, Otis. He dances, swaying to the rhythm of the music, enjoying the heat of the spotlight on his skin. He's an *artist*.'

'Yeah, well, maybe he's an observant and introverted artist, who stands on the edge of a dance floor behind a pillar. You know, observing.'

'OK, I can see you're nervous,' Eric said in a calm, encouraging tone. 'I feel you. I have been there with swing band.'

'What?'

'The first time I performed in front of them, I was nervous. I wanted to hide away behind a pillar. But I took a deep breath and I went for it. And look at me now! I'm basically the star of the band.'

'Didn't swing band forget to tell you where and when practice was last term and you missed the first two sessions?'

'The point is, Otis, that I *overcame my fear*.' He placed a comforting hand on Otis's chest as Maeve hid a smile. 'You can do that too. Right? Believe in yourself.'

'Right.' Otis nodded, stealing a glance at Maeve, who was sniggering behind her hand. 'Thank you, Eric.'

'You're very welcome.'

'I'm back!' Aimee beamed, appearing at Eric's side. 'Luckily it was a quick one. It usually is when I'm nervous. Just goes right through me.'

'OK, let's get on the dance floor and try to catch their eye,' Maeve said with renewed enthusiasm, leading the way to the middle of the room.

Securing a space near the booth, the four began to dance to the music, Otis taking Eric's advice to just go for it, shrugging off his Otis inhibitions with a bop of his shoulders. The sunglasses were a great help, acting as a sort of shield between him and everyone else. Aimee and Eric threw themselves into their roles – Aimee actually managed to make their space wider, much to Otis's delight, due to the energy she was putting into her arm moves and jumping around in general.

'You are *slaying* this, Aimee,' Eric cried out above the music, shimmying next to her.

'I think Molly would have done loads of movement

workshops,' she revealed, to which he heartily agreed. 'She expresses herself on the dance floor!'

'Is it working?' Maeve asked Otis, as she danced next to him. 'Have they noticed us?'

Otis stealthily glanced in the direction of the booth. Tabitha and her friends were staring right at them. Tabitha looked intrigued.

'Yes,' Otis replied, before unleashing some 1960s-inspired moves, such as the mashed potato, which took him by surprise but must have been the spirit of Jem shining through.

Encouraged by the first stage of their plan seemingly working, they continued to dance as extravagantly as possible, waiting for someone in the group to make a move. But after a while, nothing had happened. They were still just being watched with curiosity.

'Why isn't anyone coming over?' Eric asked, as the song changed and the crowd around them went wild.

'Maybe we have to approach them,' Aimee suggested.

'Sean said they weren't that kind of people,' Maeve relayed.

Aimee was confused. 'Everyone's that kind of people.'

'According to Sean, Tabitha has to invite you to join her. You can't just walk up and say hi. Think of her like Ruby at school,' Eric said.

Ruby was one of the most popular girls at Moordale High and you couldn't just approach her. She selected those she deemed to be of suitable social status to hang out with her and her elite group.

Aimee had once been good friends with Ruby and, even though they'd fallen out since Aimee decided to hang out with

Maeve instead – someone definitely not considered worthy enough to even be in the same vicinity as Ruby – Aimee didn't see her as intimidating or someone to shy away from.

She didn't see Tabitha and her friends that way. And she didn't think her character, Molly, would either. If Molly was going to take on Hollywood, she could take on this lot.

'Leave this with me,' Aimee declared, making a beeline for the booth.

'What's she doing?' Otis asked, panicking.

'I don't know! Just keep dancing,' Eric instructed, craning his neck to see. 'Pretend you're not looking, like this is totally normal.'

While continuing to dance like she couldn't care less, Maeve carefully sneaked some glances at Aimee, watching her stop at the booth and start talking directly to Tabitha, who was sitting in the middle of the group. After a few moments Tabitha started laughing at something Aimee had said. The guy with his arm around Tabitha – her boyfriend, Casper – spoke animatedly back to Aimee and she replied, sending them all into hoots of laughter once more.

After a bit more conversation, she saw Tabitha say something to her sister Cece, who was sitting at the edge of the booth. Cece then nodded and moved up, allowing room for Aimee to join them. She sat down happily and then pointed over at the others and, on receiving a nod from Tabitha, waved them over.

'She just walked up to them and said hi,' Eric muttered in disbelief as they casually made their way over to the booth.

'Way to go, Aimee,' Otis said under his breath.

'These are my friends,' Aimee announced, perched next to Cece, who was giving them a look up and down in a similar way as to Tabitha across the table.

'Hi, I'm Tabitha.' She gave them a thin-lipped smile. 'This is my boyfriend, Casper; our friends, Grace and Noah; and that's my little sister, Cece, who was just about to get drinks in, weren't you, Cece?'

'Isn't that bottle full?' Cece asked, gesturing to the champagne in one of the two ice buckets on the table.

'I was thinking more like shots were in order,' Tabitha said, tilting her head at her. 'Would you mind?'

Cece looked as if she might mind, but then thought better of it. 'Of course. Coming right up.'

'Don't forget to get some for our new friends,' Tabitha instructed, as Cece slid out past Aimee, before turning her attention to Maeve, Eric and Otis. 'Come and sit down.'

'Here, I'll get up so there's space,' Noah offered, having been sitting next to Grace.

'There's really no need,' Eric began, but Noah insisted.

'Honestly, I've been on my arse all day,' he chuckled, sweeping his hair back from his face. 'I've been shooting an advert where I—'

'You already talking about your advert, Noah?' Casper laughed, slapping the table. 'That's got to be a record. One minute into meeting them and they're already up to date on your modeling career.'

'No harm in building a fan base,' Noah retorted, raising an eyebrow. 'Seriously, though, you sit down. I've got pins and needles.'

Hoping they looked a lot more confident than they felt, Eric slid in next to Grace, who was next to Tabitha on the other side, while Maeve went to perch next to Aimee. Otis remained standing, leaning against the side of the booth in what he hoped was a suave and sophisticated manner. Noah stood next to him, checking his reflection in the mirror on the wall behind the booth.

'We were just saying to your friend that we thought you must be new to the area,' Tabitha informed them, taking a sip of her drink. 'Love your style! We would have noticed you if you'd been in here before.'

'We're here on a city break,' Eric replied, puffing his chest out at the confirmation from Tabitha that his eye-catching ensemble had hit the mark. 'Just, like, hanging around, you know. Seeing the sights.'

'If you need any tips, we're all from around here,' Grace replied with a warm smile. 'There's some really cool—'

'Casper, be careful!' Tabitha cried, snatching up her bag from where it was sitting on the seat in between them. 'You almost crushed it!'

'Oh my God,' Aimee began, wide-eyed. 'I love handbags and I love orange! That's both!'

Tabitha glanced down at her bag. 'Yeah, it is. I actually love handbags too.'

'I once dropped mine in a restaurant and everything spilled out,' Aimee related, rolling her eyes. 'A waiter slipped on a tampon and dropped his tray of red wine glasses.'

Casper burst out laughing. 'A similar thing happened to Tabitha! Remember, babe, at that concert?'

'Oh my God, I'd forgotten about that!' Tabitha gasped, before leaning into Aimee. 'We were at a Fleetwood Mac concert and I got so into my dancing, I flung my bag around my head and it wasn't closed. My lip gloss went flying out and hit this old guy in the head.'

'I love concerts!' Aimee exclaimed, before linking her arm through Maeve's. 'And also my friend here is the most amazing singer, aren't you . . . uh . . .'

'Roxie,' Maeve uttered, hardly moving her lips.

'Roxie! My friend Roxie here is a singer,' Aimee said. 'She does punk rock music. Tell them all about that brilliant gig you just did, Roxie!'

'Well, I . . .' Maeve hesitated, suddenly feeling completely unprepared for any questions about her character. 'It was a gig. Underground. It was an underground gig.'

'That is so *cool*,' Tabitha said, fascinated.

'Yeah, the crowd was up on their feet, going wild,' Aimee said, elaborating on behalf of Maeve, who was extremely grateful. 'She's recording a song in a studio and everything.'

'Do you write your own songs?' Casper asked.

'Yes.'

'Whoa.' He nodded slowly in respect.

'I've always thought about singing in a band,' Tabitha declared after taking a swig from her glass. 'But then I thought maybe I'd try acting instead? Seems less . . . sweaty.'

'Oh my God.' Aimee reached over to grab Tabitha's hand as she put her glass down on the table. '*I'm* into acting!'

As Tabitha launched into conversation with Aimee, Maeve and Casper about her career trajectory, Grace leaned in to talk to Eric, nodding towards Aimee.

'Your friend is really lovely.'

'I know, right?'

'So genuine. You don't meet people like that so often.'

'Yeah,' Eric agreed, proudly watching Aimee chat away, Tabitha and Casper completely enraptured in her story.

'I'm so sorry, I don't think I actually got your name? In case you missed it when Tabitha reeled us off, I'm Grace.'

'I'm Finley,' Eric said, pleased that he remembered to say his character name.

'It's nice to meet you. Your glitter is amazing. It really sparkles under the lights on the dance floor, you know.'

'Was I like a human glitter ball over there?'

'You really were,' Grace laughed. 'And who wouldn't want to be a human glitter ball?'

'That's what I always say. It's the look I was going for.'

Grace smiled warmly, sitting back. 'So what sights do you have in mind?'

'I'm sorry?'

'You mentioned you were seeing the sights of the city. If you need any pointers, then I might be able to help. Depending on the stuff you like, of course.'

'Yeah? That would be amazing! Well, we're all very *arty*,' he said, trying to sound like he knew what he was talking about. 'I'm actually a poet AND a writer.'

'Seriously? That's great. How can I read your poetry?'

Eric faltered. 'Huh?'

'Do you have a website or anything? I'd love to read some.'

'Oh. Uh. No.' He searched for an excuse as to why a

confident, outrageous poet like himself wouldn't have his poetry up for the world to read. 'I don't like it being read . . . online. Yeah. The medium of the screen is very . . . bright. I like my words to be against the dull background of paper.'

Grace nodded. 'That's an interesting viewpoint.'

'Are you a writer too then?' Eric asked, keen to move the topic of conversation along.

'No, but actually' – Grace looked down modestly – 'I have this photography exhibition on this week. Not to plug my own stuff, but if you wanted to come then you'd be really welcome, but don't feel—'

'Grace, we are SO on the same wavelength!' Tabitha interrupted, looking up from her phone. 'I just told Molly and Roxie about Casper's pool party tomorrow afternoon! You should all definitely come. Right, Casper? It's *decided*.'

'Uh . . . she was actually talking about her photography exhibition,' Eric explained, but neither Tabitha nor Casper were listening.

'My pronouns are they/them, but no worries,' Grace told Eric with a grin. 'And I can tell you all about the exhibition when I see you tomorrow, if you're interested, since you'll be at the pool party whether you like it or not. Apparently, it's decided.'

Eric laughed. 'Sounds like fun to me.'

'And you can maybe bring some of your poetry if you like.'

'Yes, I shall,' he said robotically, panicking inside. 'Marvelous.'

Tabitha checked her phone screen and then knocked the last of her drink back. 'Right. We're leaving.'

'You sure you don't want to stay a bit longer, babe? It's your favorite DJ,' Casper said on autopilot, checking his phone.

'Not any more. We have to go,' Tabitha said apologetically to Aimee and Maeve. 'There's a new club opening down the road and I booked a table. Also, this place kind of has bad memories for me right now and I thought I'd be fine, but it just annoys me thinking about . . . what went down.'

Maeve sat upright. 'Something went down?'

'Ugh, yes.' Tabitha rolled her eyes. 'Not here in the club exactly, but because of someone we met here. Supposed to be a friend. Anyway, it's boring.'

'No, it's not,' Maeve said, leaning forward. 'Sounds . . . interesting!'

'Trust me, it's boring.' Tabitha stood up to get out of the booth. 'So nice to meet you all though!'

Noah snorted next to Otis. 'Definitely not boring. Bloody scandalous.'

Otis had been less entertained than his friends so far, as Noah had filled him in on his modeling career, from his very first photo-shoot experience to his current fitness routine. It had been easy to keep him happily talking by asking questions about himself, and Otis had not had to answer one question in the guise of Jem the artist, which he was quite happy about. From their conversation, Otis had learned that Noah was vain, self-involved and career-driven, but hadn't had much luck finding out anything relevant.

But that had suddenly just changed.

'Scandalous? What happened?' Otis asked him, trying to sound like he was being naturally curious and not overly interested in his answer.

'Basically, Tabitha had this—'

'I'm BACK!'

Cece suddenly appeared next to them with the shots. Otis was furious at the unfortunately timed interruption, but plastered on a grin as she proudly held the tray aloft for everyone to appreciate.

'Sorry, the queue for the bar took FOREVER. And then I got chatting to the barman.'

'Thanks, Cece,' Tabitha smiled, grabbing a shot, downing it and then popping the empty glass back on the tray. 'We're leaving.'

'What?' Cece looked crestfallen, sliding the tray on to the table. 'But I only just—'

'Don't worry, we're going somewhere else.' Tabitha sighed, rolling her eyes at her sister. 'Come on, let's go.' She swiveled back to face Aimee. 'I have your number. I'll message you the details for the pool party at Casper's tomorrow. You can bring friends, as long as they're as cool as you are. And feel free to take this booth for the rest of the night.'

'Thanks, babes!' Aimee replied, waving at her as she stalked away.

Tabitha's group loyally followed her out, all saying their goodbyes and that they'd see them tomorrow. Otis apologized to Cece about all the shots, but she brushed it off with a laugh, before hurrying to catch up with Grace.

Otis slumped down into the booth next to Eric and the four of them sat in a silent daze for a moment, the club buzzing all around them.

'That went well,' Eric said eventually. 'Really, really well. We've got an invite to the party tomorrow!'

'Aimee, you were brilliant!' Maeve exclaimed. 'Genuinely brilliant. It's all thanks to you that we got talking to them in the first place AND that we've got an invitation to the party tomorrow. They *loved* you.'

'They loved all of us,' Aimee said brightly. 'Eric, the outfits worked! They spotted us the minute we walked in, they said! They were wondering why we were hiding behind the pillar, so I explained that I had to go poo.'

Eric's jaw dropped. 'You WHAT?'

'Hang on,' Maeve said, holding up her hands. 'Is that why they were all laughing when you first walked over to start chatting with them?'

'Yeah,' Aimee nodded. 'I just said it and they thought it was hilarious. You know, they seem quite guarded, so I think it surprised them that someone was being so honest.'

Maeve giggled, throwing her arms around her and pulling her in for a hug.

'We should do a toast,' Eric announced, passing around a shot to each of them. 'A successful beginning to the plan.'

'Such a fun night,' Aimee agreed, taking the shot glass he gave her. 'And you know, I think we have a good chance of finding out what happened. Tabitha almost told us about it then.'

'I agree. I think Noah was about to spill all the "scandalous" details,' Otis said. 'But the group setting won't work if we want to find out the real truth. I think tomorrow we need to get them on their own. See what each of them *really* knows. Divide and conquer.'

'To tomorrow then,' Eric declared, holding up his glass. 'When we divide and conquer!'

'Divide and conquer!' they chorused, clinking their glasses with his.

They downed their shots, winced at the burning sensation in their throats, and slammed their glasses back on the table.

'What now?' Aimee asked, her eyes watering from the alcohol.

'We go back to the hotel room?' Otis suggested.

'No, we do not! We have a VIP booth to ourselves!' Eric pointed out.

'That's true,' Maeve said, shrugging to Otis. 'The night is young.'

'Yes, Maeve, the night is young,' Eric repeated, a smile spreading across his face as Otis groaned. 'And it's time for dancing.'

NINE

The next morning Maeve woke up to find Aimee already awake and dressed, lying next to her, scrolling through her phone.

'Yay, you're awake!' Aimee whispered as Maeve rubbed her eyes. 'I hope you don't mind, I just used your hairspray that you left in the bathroom.'

'I didn't bring any hairspray.'

'Huh.' Aimee looked confused. 'I swear it's there. I just sprayed it all over my hair. The can on the floor, next to the sink.'

Maeve paused. 'I think that's Eric's deodorant.'

'Oh. Oh well! Does the job.' She shrugged, putting down her phone. 'Shall I go and get tea for everyone? It's such a nice sunny day!'

Maeve wished she could be as enthusiastic as Aimee at this time of the morning. How did she keep getting up so early? Maeve told Aimee not to bother with the teas because they might as well head to the cafe for breakfast once everyone was ready, and then reached for her phone. She had messaged Sean last night when they got back late to say they'd managed to get in with Tabitha, and saw now she had a missed call from him. Reluctantly pulling the duvet away, she swung her legs out of bed and headed into the bathroom to get ready for the day, deciding to call him back on the way to the cafe.

'A party at Casper's, eh? You did well to bag an invite to that,' he said down the phone, once she'd filled him in on the night before.

'I can't take the credit. It was mostly down to Aimee,' Maeve admitted, hanging back outside as the others piled into the cafe to get a table. 'We're going to the shopping center this morning to get some stuff for the pool party.'

'I'll come and join you.'

'No need,' Maeve said sharply.

The less time Sean spent with her friends, the better. She wanted to keep them as distanced from the situation as possible. But Sean insisted he'd see her there, despite any protests, arguing that it would be nice to hear about last night's events in full. She hung up and pushed through the cafe door to join the others for lukewarm crumpets and weak tea.

'One advantage to going to a club where the drinks are really expensive is no hangover,' Eric pointed out, tearing off a chunk of crumpet.

'I know a really good trick to not getting a hangover,' Aimee claimed. 'A soap star once told me it. You eat an avocado before you go out.'

'An avocado,' Eric repeated.

'Wait a second.' Aimee frowned in concentration. 'Maybe the tip was you had to eat an avocado *while* you were drinking.' She hesitated. 'Or was it afterwards?'

'But it definitely involves eating avocado,' Otis said, sharing a smile with Maeve.

'Yes, definitely avocado.' Aimee nodded, before biting her lip. 'Or was it asparagus?'

'Oh my God,' Eric suddenly gasped at the table, getting his phone out and typing into it furiously. 'We need to get tickets for the show tonight! I was so caught up in everything I almost forgot to buy them in advance and Amit said it was essential. PHEW!' His shoulders physically relaxed as he clicked on the website. 'There's still some left. Am I getting four?'

Otis and Aimee both looked at Maeve hopefully.

'Yeah,' she said, deciding that they had plenty of time to talk to the 'suspects' all day at the pool party, and she didn't want Eric to miss out. 'You're getting four.'

When they got to the shopping center later that day, Maeve realized that she hadn't actually thought properly about what she was going to *wear* to this party and felt a bit panicked about it.

'Ah, but it's not you, is it, Maeve,' Eric said, gripping her shoulders as he ushered her into a clothing shop behind Aimee and Otis. 'It's what *Roxie* is going to wear.'

'I don't think punk rock musicians hang out at pool parties.'

'Um, hello! What do you think they all do in LA?'

Maeve smiled. 'Hadn't thought of that.'

'You're in good hands, Maeve. You look through this rail,' he instructed, drifting off to the back of the shop. 'Tell me if anything pops out at you.'

She was waiting for something to pop out at her when Sean appeared at her side, making her jump.

'I'm curious,' he said, leaning on the clothes rail that Maeve was sifting through. 'What will you be like at a pool party?'

She glared at him. 'You really didn't need to come.'

'I'm just saying,' he continued breezily, ignoring her, 'I can't really imagine you chilling by the pool. No offense.'

'Shouldn't you be busy thanking my friends and me for going on your behalf?'

He sighed, taking a step back. 'All right, all right. I remember now. No jokes allowed.'

'It's still not that funny.'

'I am very grateful to you and your friends,' he said sincerely. 'What do you want me to do? Stand here thanking you over and over again?'

'Sounds better than you standing there being a dickhead.'

He smiled. 'Fair enough. How about I ask more questions about how last night went? I take it from the pool party invite that it went *swimmingly*.'

She sighed, leaving him to chuckle at his own joke.

'Come on then, how was it?' Sean encouraged, as Maeve wandered over to another rail. 'What did they talk about? Did they say anything useful?'

'No one admitted stealing the necklace if that's what you're asking.'

'One of them has it, Frog-face, that's what's so . . .' He trailed off, biting his lip, before taking a deep breath. 'It's frustrating.'

'We're going to speak to each of them today,' Maeve said, watching him carefully. 'If one of them has it, maybe someone will let something slip.'

'*If?*' He looked at her warily. 'Curious language.'

She shrugged. 'Maybe it's just lost.'

'And the box jumped into my pocket of its own accord, did it?' He shook his head. 'One of them put it there.'

'Yeah, well, if they did, we'll find out,' she snapped, wanting to move the conversation on.

'Right.' He clapped his hands together, his expression brightening. 'So are you thinking like a big sunhat or what? Because I can see you in one of those huge ones that flops right down over your face.'

Maeve watched him as he selected a pair of sunglasses from a stand and tried them on.

'You know what,' he said, admiring his reflection in the mirror. 'I think Tabitha would like these on me. I look . . . mysterious.'

'What is it exactly about Tabitha that you like?' she asked curiously. 'She doesn't seem like the sort of person you'd spend time with.'

He shrugged. 'She's fun.'

'That's it? She's *fun*.' Maeve snorted. 'Fuck's sake, Sean, all this for someone who's fun.'

'Better than all this for someone who's boring,' Sean retorted, taking off the sunglasses and trying on a different pair. 'Was Casper there last night?'

'Yes.'

'What did you make of him?'

'Not sure yet,' Maeve answered honestly. 'He didn't say much. Tabitha's the talker.'

'She cares a lot about him.'

'Funny way of showing it. They've both cheated on each other.'

Sean took the sunglasses off, carefully slotted them into the stand and then moved to examine the row of T-shirts hanging up in front of them. 'You know those people who try to be apart but end up coming back together again.'

'What do you mean?'

'You know.' He sighed, gesturing with his hand as he tried to explain. 'People who are drawn to each other. They keep finding their way back to one another.'

Maeve glanced over his shoulder at Otis, who was admiring a pair of plain blue swim shorts, much to Eric's disdain.

'What about them?' she said, regaining focus.

'Well, that's like Tabitha and Casper. They're suited. So they end up together. But' – he held up his finger – 'they're only suited on paper, those two.'

'Do you think Casper feels strongly enough about Tabitha to frame you?' Maeve asked. 'If they're only right on paper and not in real life, would he go to all this trouble?'

'Maybe.' Sean shrugged. 'It might be a pride thing. And Casper has plenty of that.'

'But we're not sure if he even knew about you two. And it would be disgustingly hypocritical of him, when he cheated on Tabitha.'

'That's what you have to find out today,' Sean reminded her. 'Get him riled up and maybe he'll admit something.'

'He has a temper?'

'Oh yeah. So does Tabitha. When they argue, it gets loud.'

'OK. This is helpful to know.'

Otis approached them, holding a few pairs of swim shorts. 'Sorry to interrupt. I think I need your opinion.'

'Eric's in charge of wardrobe,' Maeve stated, as Sean drifted off to join Eric and Aimee.

'Yeah, but he reckons Jem the artist would look good in these.' He held up a pair of salmon-pink shorts with toucans all over them. 'But I have a feeling that Jem would look very washed out wearing this color. I think these blue ones are more Jem's vibe.'

'My advice would be to go with Eric on this one. He seems to know what he's doing. We can always buy you some fake tan if you'd like?'

'I'm all right, thanks.' He sighed. 'Fine. Toucans it is.'

As he folded up the blue pair to put them back on the shelf, his phone started ringing. He checked the screen and rolled his eyes, sliding the phone back into his pocket.

'Have you found anything yet?' he asked Maeve. 'Want some help looking?'

'Was that your mum?'

'Yeah.' He brushed it off with a wave of his hand. 'I think this rail isn't cool enough for a punk rock musician. We should look—'

'You should tell her you're OK.'

He rolled his eyes. 'Honestly, Maeve, it's fine. She knows I got to the hotel safely.'

'Maybe at least send her a message. She wouldn't keep calling if you picked up once in a while.'

'Trust me, she would. You don't know what she's like.'

'It's nice that she calls.'

'It's smothering. Anyway, let's please stop talking about my mum,' he said with a heavy sigh, before fishing out a pair of leopard-print shorts from the rail. 'These are *very* you.'

Maeve did her best not to smile as he wiggled them in

front of her face.

'Or how about' – he grabbed a neon-pink and purple skirt with a swirled diamanté pattern around the hem – 'this. To me, this *screams* Maeve Wiley.'

'Piss off,' she muttered, trying and failing to suppress a laugh as she swiped it from his hands.

'Otis!' Eric called from the other side of the shop, where Sean was holding up several pair of bright printed swimming shorts. 'We have more of a selection for you!'

'Better get back,' Otis said. 'Shout if you need any help.'

'Will do,' Maeve said, watching him go. She smiled as he got to Eric and buried his head in his hands at the sight of a pair of bright-yellow Speedos being offered to him.

Aimee suddenly appeared over her shoulder. 'I saw that.'

'Saw what?'

'The way you were looking at Otis,' she replied smugly.

Maeve started busying herself with riffling through the clothes in front of her. 'I wasn't looking at him in any way.'

'You had that look in your eye.'

'What look?'

'That longing look. I totally recognize it.'

'I was not giving him a longing look,' Maeve replied, her cheeks growing hot.

'You two are like that couple in the Shakespeare play. You know, the one with the fish tank.'

Maeve frowned. 'I don't think there's a fish tank in any Shakespeare play.'

'Yeah!' Aimee nodded vigorously. 'You know, the one where they both die in the end because that priest forgot to post the letter next-day delivery or something.'

'Are you talking about *Romeo and Juliet*?'

'That's the one.'

'You know the bit with the fish tank is from a movie version of the play. It's not the actual play itself.'

'You need to tell Otis how you feel. Otherwise you both might end up dead, like Romeo and Juliet, and you can't tell people you like them when you're dead, Maeve. Oooh!' She picked out a rainbow-striped swimsuit, while Maeve stared at her, not quite sure what to say. 'I hope they've got this in my size!'

*

As they neared Casper's address Eric couldn't help but notice Aimee putting her hand down the back of her shorts.

'Are you all right, Aimee?'

'I've got a wedgie,' she explained. 'It's this swimsuit. It keeps riding up.'

'Remember, everyone,' Maeve said, trying not to feel intimidated as they strolled down a road of the poshest town houses she'd ever seen, 'the plan is to get each person on their own. Try to draw out what they know. I might try and take a peek around the house while you all distract them.'

'Whoa, whoa, whoa,' Otis said, surprised. 'What do you mean "a peek around the house"?'

'You know, look for clues.'

'You mean, look for the necklace?'

'That, and anything that might show something about

Casper we don't already know.'

'You should look in his bathroom cabinet!' Aimee chipped in eagerly. 'When my parents used to take me to posh parties and then ignore me for the night, I used to go around checking out the hosts' bathroom cabinets. I'd always find some weird shit in there. Once I found a recording device, and then that person went to prison a few months later for fraud.'

'OK,' Maeve said. 'Good tip, I guess.'

'I don't know, Maeve. That sounds risky to go through his stuff,' Otis pointed out. 'What if he finds you and then kicks us out?'

'I'll make sure he doesn't find me then.'

'I think this is it,' Eric announced, stopping in front of some black iron gates through which they could see a beautiful house with tall white pillars. 'Oh my God. This looks like the house in *The Parent Trap*. The one Lindsey Lohan lives in when she's being British!'

Maeve rang the buzzer and they stood waiting in the sunshine. They were all dressed in bright standout colors, except for Maeve. She was in high-waisted denim shorts, a tucked-in loose white T-shirt and lots of jewelry with black sunglasses, having made the decision she probably wouldn't be going in the pool.

'If I go in, I'll go in fully clothed.' She had shrugged earlier in the shop, leaving the swimwear to everyone else.

Eric had to admit it was a rock-star attitude.

Aimee was channeling old-school Hollywood glamour in a retro-style blue polka dot swimsuit with a statement white-buckle belt around the waist, and a full-length white sheer cover-up that billowed out behind her as she walked. Her hair was swept to the side, curling over one shoulder, and she was wearing bright-pink lipstick with big bug-eye sunglasses. She'd also brought her phone, purse and makeup along in a giant beach bag, which she'd surprised the others with earlier when she'd pulled it out of the bottom of her suitcase.

'I like to have this on summer trips,' she'd explained, after Maeve asked her why on earth she'd packed a beach bag for a baking convention and a few days in the city. 'Once I had to carry some watermelons and I was so grateful for it! Ever since that, I always try to make sure I pack this trusty bag.'

Eric was in one of Aimee's oversized mustard-yellow shirts with large daisies printed on it, wearing it buttoned down and the sleeves rolled up, with a pair of lime-green swim shorts. He'd accessorised with a statement beaded necklace and matching beaded bangles. Otis had given in to the salmon-pink toucan shorts and Eric had paired them with a white shirt that had ruffles down the middle.

'Well, hello,' Casper's voice crackled down the intercom. 'You made it! Come on in.'

The gate creaked open and they headed down the short drive and up to the front door. It swung open and Casper ushered them in. He was wearing a pink linen shirt, designer navy swim shorts and Wayfarer sunglasses, and was holding a large cocktail with an umbrella in his hand.

'Head on through to the party, people,' he instructed, waving for them to follow him through the house.

Maeve gazed around the grand interiors. Everything seemed

to be marble, from the floor to the stairs, and sparkling chandeliers dangled from the high ceilings. It all looked so clean and new and cold, kind of like a museum. The sort of place where you're afraid to touch anything. It was stunning, but not exactly homely.

It needed some character, Maeve determined. Like an ugly statue of a toad smoking a pipe.

They walked down the hallway and through a vast kitchen with two islands, before stepping out through the sliding doors at the back into the garden.

'Wow,' Eric breathed, speaking for all of them as they took in the view.

There was a DJ to one side and booming speakers set up in all corners of the garden, in the middle of which was a turquoise-blue swimming pool. Guests were dancing around it holding bright, colorful cocktails, or sunbathing on the loungers. A bar was stocked with drinks and manned by smartly dressed staff.

'Make yourselves at home,' Casper said, patting Otis on the back before dancing over to a group of people clustered next to the DJ.

'I feel like I've walked into an episode of *90210*,' Eric commented, before noticing Tabitha on one of the sun loungers. She was peering at Casper over the top of her sunglasses with a thunderous expression as he twirled around another girl, who stumbled and fell into his arms, giggling. 'And I have a feeling this could be just as dramatic.'

TEN

'Hey!' Cece said brightly, coming over to them as they remained standing in a line, taking in the pool party scene. 'Why do you all look like you've seen a ghost?'

'Oh, no reason,' Eric said, remembering that they were supposed to be people who went to parties like this all the time. 'This reminded me of . . . the time I was in LA. Total déjà vu. You know how it is.'

'I don't know if this is quite LA standard.' She laughed. 'And don't tell Casper you were thinking that. The moment you do, he'll tell you about the time he spent the summer in California with the Kardashians and all the wild parties he went to.'

Eric's jaw dropped. 'You're joking.'

'Not joking.' She rolled her eyes. 'They're, like, family friends or something, but it still rubs Tabitha up the wrong way whenever he bangs on about it. I mean, you can see why she'd be worried, but he says they're all just friends. So anyway, how was the rest of your night?'

'It was good, thanks,' Maeve answered, noticing Tabitha's eyes still locked on Casper. 'How was yours?'

'The club we went to after was so amazing, and the VIP area was really nice. Way less crowded than out in the main bit with everyone else.'

Eric noticed Grace standing next to a giant inflatable flamingo by the side of the pool. They spotted him and waved him over.

'I'm going to go have a chat with Grace,' he said, waving back. 'I'll see you lot in a bit.'

'O— I mean, Jem,' Maeve said to Otis, as Eric strolled off. 'I think Tabitha is waving at you.'

They turned around to see Tabitha signaling in their direction, but Cece sighed and shook her head. 'No, she's waving at me. She wants me to reapply her sun lotion. But I'll do it in a minute. I really want one of those neon-blue cocktails that everyone else seems to have.'

'Jem, why don't you go and help Tabitha with her sun lotion?' Maeve suggested pointedly.

Otis raised his eyebrows above the top of his sunglasses. 'Huh?'

'You go and help Tabitha with her lotion and, you know, maybe have a *chat*,' Maeve emphasized. 'Cece, I'll come with you to the bar. Those cocktails do look nice.'

'I'll come with you,' Aimee said to Otis, as he stood panicking while Maeve led Cece away.

'What do we say?'

'Don't overthink it.' She shrugged. 'Come on.'

Prodding him in the back with a sharp fingernail, Aimee forced Otis to move, dodging around the other guests chatting and laughing by the pool and stopping awkwardly at Tabitha's sun lounger. She was wearing a shimmering gold bikini and designer sunglasses. She smiled up at Aimee.

'Molly, hey,' she said, pushing herself up on her elbows and gesturing for them to perch on the lounger next to her, which had a towel and some bottles of sun cream on it.

'Isn't someone sitting here?' Otis said, glancing down nervously, while Aimee just plonked herself down. 'I don't want to steal their seat.'

'Oh, don't worry, it's Cece's stuff, but she's over by the bar with your friend. So how are you two today? Glad you came!'

'Thanks for inviting us! Casper's house is really nice,' Aimee said. 'It's all so . . . shiny.'

Tabitha smiled politely and then yelped as someone in a small pair of Speedos doing lengths splashed her with their clumsy front stroke as they passed.

'UGH!' she huffed, before turning to Otis. 'Can I have your flip-flop, please?'

'Excuse me?'

She clicked her fingers impatiently. 'Your flip-flop. I would use mine, but they're Gucci.'

'Use it for what?' Otis asked warily, sliding it off his foot and handing it over.

She snatched it from him and then took aim before lobbing it at the swimmer's head as they came back the other way. It struck them and they bobbed their head up in confusion, treading water. As they lifted their goggles up on to their forehead, Otis and Aimee realized it was Noah.

'You splashed me!' Tabitha yelled as he turned to see her scowling at her from her lounger.

'Sorry, Tabby,' Noah laughed, retrieving Otis's flip-flop and chucking it back out of the pool. He came to lean on the side.

'And sorry to your friends. Hey, we haven't met. I'm Noah.'

'We actually we met last night,' Otis corrected him, shaking water off his shoe.

'Oh yeah! You were the guy up in the DJ booth. Good to see you again.'

Otis shook his head. 'No, no, that wasn't me. I'm Jem.'

'And this is Molly,' Tabitha said impatiently, gesturing to Aimee. 'Don't call me Tabby, Noah. You know I hate it. Do you have to do lengths? This is a party, not an Olympics heat.'

'You know I have to get in my workout every day, no exceptions, and swimming is great exercise,' Noah explained. He addressed Aimee and Otis as he pushed himself away from the ledge and adjusted his goggles back over his eyes. 'Staying in shape is pretty important in my line of work.'

'Oh my God, just go back to your swimming and don't splash so much,' Tabitha grumbled as he gave her a salute and then started his lengths again. 'He is so self-involved.'

Casper came sauntering over, sucking the last dregs of his drink through his straw. 'Anyone over here keen for a game of table tennis? I'm the undefeated champion and looking for a worthy challenger.'

'I am well good at table tennis!' Aimee exclaimed, jumping to her feet.

'Oh yeah?'

'Yeah! When I was younger I'd put one side of the table up and play against myself,' she informed him with a beaming smile. 'I won every time!'

'Challenge accepted,' Casper declared, before heading across the grass to the table.

Tabitha stared as Casper walked away and then seemed to collect herself, shaking her head and picking up her bottle of sun cream. She held it out to Otis.

'Would you mind putting some on my back? I would normally ask Cece, but she's taking her time getting a drink.'

'No problem! I can handle sun cream,' Otis croaked, grappling with the slippery bottle and wondering why he told her he can *handle sun cream*. This was not the cool, confident Jem he was supposed to be.

She turned on to her front and he took a deep breath, squeezing some out into his palm, spreading it over his hands and then leaning forward to rub it into her shoulders.

'So,' he said, clearing his throat, 'last night was fun.'

She gave a noncommittal 'Mmm' in response.

'Noah mentioned you've been having a hard time recently,' he said carefully.

'Did he?'

'Well, you were saying something about a bad incident . . .'

'Oh that. Yeah. This guy stole something from me.' She sighed as Otis carefully squeezed more sun cream into his hands for her lower back.

'That's horrible.' Otis finished with the sun cream and wiped his hands down his legs. 'Was it something expensive?'

'Yes. But, more importantly, it was sentimental. Dad gave it to me for my eighteenth. It was my mum's jewelry.' She hesitated. 'She died when I was little.'

'I'm sorry.'

She waved her hand. 'It's a long time ago. Anyway, hopefully I'll get it back soon if they can find it.'

'Does anyone know who may have taken it?'

'He was . . . a friend. I thought he was, anyway.'

'Must be hard, that betrayal of trust.'

'Yeah. It was actually. I didn't know him long,' she admitted. 'But he was really funny and nice, such a joker. I didn't think he would do that. He just . . . I don't know. I guess people will always surprise you. That's what my dad says all the time. I shouldn't have trusted him.'

'Are you sure it was him who stole from you?'

'It looks that way. There weren't many others there that night. I don't *think* it would have been anyone else.'

She hesitated and Otis latched on to the opportunity.

'But you're not sure?' he prompted in a hushed voice.

'I don't know.' She propped herself up on her forearms and lowered her voice. 'Don't tell anyone I told you this, but it's been playing on my mind. Noah has a past, if you know what I mean.'

Otis frowned. 'What kind of past?'

'He stole from a shop when we were about fifteen.'

'Like, chocolate bars?'

She snorted. 'I said fifteen, not five. No, he didn't steal chocolate bars. He stole designer clothes. Which was so weird, because it's not like he couldn't afford them. Anyway, I know he was going through something and he stopped all that, but, you know, does a leopard ever change its spots? Once you get that thrill . . .'

Otis watched Noah as he reached the end of a length at the shallow end and stood up, whipping his hair back dramatically.

'Can't be easy for you to spend time with someone you think

may have done that to you,' Otis pointed out, returning his attention to her.

She shrugged. 'I'm used to it.'

'Used to . . . people betraying your trust?'

'Yeah.' She nodded, glancing over at Casper as he lost another point to Aimee and cursed loudly. 'I guess that's about right.'

'Are you talking about your relationship?' Otis asked gently. 'You and Casper . . .'

She didn't say anything at first but then, narrowing her eyes at Casper, she muttered dismally, 'Things are a little tense.'

'Why?'

'Not sure. Something has changed. He's being distant.' She hesitated, shaking her head. 'Sorry, we've only just met. You don't need to know any of this.'

'No, no, I do!' he protested, perhaps a little more enthusiastically then he should have. Tabitha frowned at his reaction and he quickly explained himself. 'I mean, I don't *need* to know anything, but it's good to talk about things. And I'm happy to listen. If you want.'

'OK,' she said slowly, looking unconvinced, but then became distracted by Casper punching the air in celebration of scoring a point off Aimee. Her expression softened watching him, and she began to talk as though her barriers were lowering in spite of herself.

'I've tried so many things to make it work with him. But no matter how much I try to get his attention, he doesn't care. I can do anything, and he shrugs it off as though it's nothing. Even bad stuff. I wish he'd get angry or mad at me, but he's just indifferent. He doesn't care any more.'

'Bad stuff,' Otis repeated, nodding in understanding. 'This funny guy you mentioned earlier, the one who may have stolen from you, did you . . .'

She raised her eyebrows. 'Shag him?'

'I was actually going to say, did you like him?' Otis insisted.

'Yes, I did. He gave me attention, made me feel special.' She pursed her lips. 'But it wasn't serious.'

'Did Casper find out about you two?'

She shrugged. 'I don't know. I was hoping it would spark something in him. Jealousy, anger, anything. But like I said, he doesn't care.'

'Have you tried talking to Casper about how you feel?'

'What good would that do?'

'Well, a relationship is about connection and fulfilment. Sometimes it's not enough to be loved, you have to *feel* loved. And I don't think Casper is making you feel that way. I think there's a lack of emotional connection, and doing things to get his attention, that's not making you happy and it's not fair on either of you. Expressing your feelings to your partner is important – it gives them the chance to listen and make changes. Sometimes it can help build that trust back and strengthen relationships.'

Tabitha blinked at him. 'Who talks like that? Who *are* you?'

'Uh . . . it doesn't matter who I am,' Otis said hurriedly, as she looked him up and down, bewildered. 'All I'm saying is, you should speak to him. I just said it in a really long-winded, pretentious way.' He held up his hands and gave a nervous laugh. 'Classic artist. Sorry.'

'Whatever. Look, if I talk to him it becomes real. What if he's waiting for me to say it out loud and then he'll just break up with me?'

'It's difficult to be honest and vulnerable, and, yes, sometimes confronting a problem can lead to the realization that the relationship isn't working, and that can be frightening.' Otis paused, taking a deep breath. 'But it's the right thing to do.'

'Maybe.' She sighed, looking sad as she glanced over at Casper. 'I'm starting university at the end of the summer. I feel like I'm clinging on to something that's not there any more.'

'Change is daunting. It's natural to fear it; we can't anticipate the outcome and we feel like we're not in control. Maybe that's why you're reluctant to risk what you have with Casper.'

She nodded, giving Otis a weak smile. 'You know you talk strangely, right? Like, really deep.'

'I've been told that before,' he said, before realizing he was dangerously close to blowing his cover. 'My mum owns an art gallery, so I know loads of artists. Being deep is second nature to me.'

'Right. Well, thanks for the chat, Jem. It's nice to speak to someone who actually listens. If I were you, I'd reconsider the art career and think about one in therapy.'

'HA! Therapy!' Otis cried, going a little overboard and surprising Tabitha with his loud reaction. 'I'm into *art*, not therapy. Ha ha! Funny one!'

Over by the bar, Maeve noticed Otis's terrible acting and forced laughter and wondered whether she needed to intervene, but up until now he'd seemed as though he'd been having a really good talk with Tabitha. She'd noticed he'd been leaning forward on the lounger with his hands clasped together resting on his legs, as he tended to do when he was in therapist mode.

She wasn't doing very well getting any useful information out of Cece. It's safe to say that chatting to a stranger about their love life in a casual manner wasn't exactly one of her strengths.

'So, relationships,' Maeve began as soon as they'd reached the bar and ordered their drinks. 'They're tough.'

Urgh. Maeve had to turn away briefly to roll her eyes at herself.

Cece gave her a strange look. 'Um. Sure?'

'You in one?'

Cece looked taken aback, as Maeve tried to act as natural as possible. She kept her eyes fixed on the barman making their drinks, smiling at him, as though her question to Cece had been a throwaway one.

'Sort of,' Cece said, eyeing Maeve suspiciously.

Maeve could understand her reaction. It was a personal question and they barely knew each other, and it wasn't like Maeve had beaten around the bush. Still, at least Cece had answered. She couldn't lose her nerve now.

'Sounds complicated,' Maeve commented.

'It's not complicated. It's new,' Cece admitted, thanking the barman as he passed her a blue cocktail.

'Exciting. Are they here?' Maeve asked, trying to work out if she was talking about Sean.

Cece gave her an inquisitive smile. 'Why are you so interested in my love life?'

'I'm not,' Maeve said quickly. 'I was just wondering.'

'Has someone said something to you? Are you trying to find out if I'm single? Who said it? Oh my God, does someone here like me?'

'No, no one likes you. I mean, I'm sure everyone likes you,' she added quickly as Cece looked a bit wounded. 'Just no one has said anything to me.'

'You're being very suspicious, Roxie,' Cece said curiously. 'You're hiding something.'

'I'm really not.'

Cece pestered her a bit longer, pleading with her to tell her who'd said what, but Maeve batted away her questions. She eventually managed to move the conversation on by steering it back towards Cece's interests, which then transitioned into a discussion about her hopes to work with her dad in his property business.

What Maeve needed was to go and have a look around Casper's house for some clues. If anyone had framed Sean, Casper was a strong suspect. There was a small chance the necklace could be upstairs right this minute. If she found it, then that would be that. Case closed. But there were so many people at this party and some of them were milling about inside. She couldn't risk being seen sneaking into his room on her own. She could pretend to be looking for the toilet maybe.

It wasn't the strongest excuse to have up her sleeve, but it was all she had.

'I've interned quite a bit for other property companies, you know, because it's important to see what else is out there,'

Cece informed Maeve, stirring her cocktail with the umbrella and jolting her from her thoughts. 'I've been told I have an eye for it.'

'That's great,' Maeve replied. 'Anyway, I need—'

'It's a real talent, it's not easy. Properties are all so . . . different. You have to know what you're looking for and I am so all over that. Am I as confident as Tabitha? Not exactly. But I can spot a good deal a mile off. I've studied the business a lot. I'm very dedicated. Hopefully I'll do some work experience with Dad this summer and he can show me the ropes, just like he did with Tabitha last year.'

'I really need—'

'Oh, here's your friend,' Cece said brightly as Eric approached. 'Are you having a good time?'

'Really good, thanks,' Eric replied, noticing Maeve looked relieved at his arrival. 'Grace has invited me to their photography exhibition tomorrow.'

'Yes, you *have* to come.' Her eyes flickered over to the pool. 'Do you think Noah looks like he needs a top-up? He's done so many lengths, I don't know how he's not exhausted.'

'He looks like he needs a top-up,' Maeve said firmly.

'I think you're right. I'll take one to him and see you in a bit.' She wiggled her fingers at them, grabbed a bottle from the bar and went towards the pool to fill up Noah's glass.

'She's nice,' Eric commented.

'She's talkative,' Maeve hissed, making him chuckle. 'I've been wanting to escape for a while. Good going on the photography exhibition. Any luck with getting details about Grace and Casper?'

He shook his head. 'Sadly not. I tried to ask stealthily but I think it was *too* stealthy, because somehow Casper wasn't mentioned at all and then we got on to a conversation about bees.' He paused, adding in a serious voice, 'Bees are so important.'

'Don't worry about it.'

'If we go to the exhibition, I'm going to need to be a bit more prepared, poetry-wise.' He grimaced. 'I forgot Grace asked if they could read some of my work and then, when I said I didn't bring any, they persuaded me to spout a few lines.'

Maeve looked impressed. 'You ad-libbed poetry?'

'I said a couple of rhyming lines that *may* have been from a Kelly Clarkson song,' he admitted guiltily. 'Grace said they could tell my poetry came from the heart.'

'I'm sure you pulled it off,' Maeve said comfortingly, before checking to make sure no one could hear her. 'Look, I've had an idea. Can you cause a distraction?'

'Why?'

'I need to find Casper's room and do a bit of searching.'

Eric gasped, his eyes widening with excitement. 'Do you really think the diamond necklace is upstairs?'

'Could be, but to find out I need to get into his room without anyone seeing.'

'Shit, this is so cool, like you're Sherlock Holmes and you have three Watsons!' Eric squealed, clasping her hands before calming immediately at her deadpan expression. 'What I mean is, yes, Maeve, I will cause a distraction.'

'Great. What are you going to do?'

Eric put his hands on his hips and surveyed the party, looking for inspiration. His eyes fell on the pool, which was nearly empty, with Noah climbing out having achieved his exercise goal, and just a few other people drinking on the steps with their feet in the water. On the grass next to the pool were several inflatables and some foam noodles. He glanced over to the DJ, a smile spreading across his face.

'Maeve, you came to the right person. Get ready for a big distraction.'

She didn't doubt it as she watched him march over to the DJ and ask to borrow the microphone.

'Hello, everyone! Hello, can I have your attention, please!' Eric's voice boomed around the garden, causing everyone to look over in his direction. 'I would like to propose a tournament of POOL NOODLE JOUSTING! Select your inflatable, grab your noodle, last one floating WINS!'

There was a moment of silence, but then from across the garden near the table-tennis table, Aimee's voice came floating through the air.

'OH YES!' she cried, throwing down her bat. 'SHOTGUN THE FLAMINGO!'

As she bolted across the grass towards the inflatables, Casper jumped into action, chanting, 'NOODLE JOUST! NOODLE JOUST!' as he legged it after her.

Suddenly there was a rush of guests scrambling to get the noodles and Eric passed the microphone back to the DJ, who continued the noodle-joust chant while turning up the music.

'FIRST ROUND!' the DJ announced, playing a *ding, ding, ding* sound effect as Aimee popped the flamingo in the pool and then catapulted herself on to it holding a pink foam noodle, followed by others with their inflatables.

Anyone who wasn't able to get to an inflatable in time crowded around the pool to watch the tournament, cheering and clapping for their friends, laughing at the noodles swinging through the air, ready to jump on an inflatable when anyone in the pool was knocked off.

As people came spilling out of the house to see what all the noise was about, Maeve was certain that no one noticed her dart in through the doors and creep up the sweeping marble staircase.

But someone did.

ELEVEN

Maeve got to the top of the stairs and knocked on the door to the first room on her left, before slowly pushing it open.

She knew instantly it wasn't Casper's room. It looked like the master bedroom and was almost definitely his parents' room, considering the large framed wedding photo on the wall of a couple kissing under a canopy of fairy lights. It was also immaculately clean and tidy in there, with a photograph of Casper on the dressing table by the window.

Not wanting to waste any time, she shut the door firmly and checked the next room along, which was a bathroom. The one next to that, however, had its door slightly ajar and, walking in after no response to her knocking, Maeve realized that this could be Casper's bedroom. She wasn't sure if he had any siblings – she hadn't checked – but if he didn't then this had to be it.

It was painted a dark navy and smelled of deodorant and dirty socks. There was a slim computer monitor sitting on top of the desk, as well as a brand-new laptop next to the keyboard and a stack of books, and the wardrobe was open displaying a long row of ironed shirts and tailored jackets.

Maeve spotted some Polaroid photos on the desk scattered next to the books. She picked up the top one – a photo of

Casper and Tabitha. It couldn't have been taken too recently though, they both looked a lot younger. The photo underneath was of all the friends together. This had to be Casper's room. It was time to begin searching.

She started with the desk, which she finished quickly as it was a modern design with no drawers. It was unlikely that he'd leave the necklace lying underneath some papers on his desk but she wasn't taking any chances. She glanced over to the tables on either side of the bed. Both of them had drawers. Again, it would be stupid of him to leave it somewhere that his girlfriend might find it, but Maeve wouldn't put it past Casper to just shove it in a drawer until he knew what to do with it. She hurried over to one side, checked, and then made her way over to the other side, opening the drawer to just find a load of bits and bobs in there, like an old phone charger, some pens and a packet of cigarettes. She sat down on the bed and reached under the pillows, before patting them down to make sure there was nothing stashed away in there.

Getting down on her hands and knees, she lifted the edge of the duvet to look under the bed. That's when she saw it. Nothing else under there but an old shoebox. She reached for it, her fingertips touching the sides of the box.

'What are you doing?'

She gasped, scrambling to her feet and spinning around to see Casper watching her from the doorway. He was wet from the pool, his T-shirt sticking to his skin and a towel tied around his waist, his hair plastered across his forehead.

'Casper, hi,' she said, her brain clawing for a good enough

excuse. 'I thought you were playing the noodle tournament in the pool.'

'Yeah, I was, but your friend Molly is quite the opponent. She's got a bloody good aim and a powerful swing. She knocked me off the dolphin as soon as I got on.'

'She's very . . . enthusiastic.'

'Yeah. Also very good at table tennis.' He folded his arms, leaning on the doorframe. 'She took my crown there too.'

'Oh.' Maeve clasped her hands behind her back. 'Great. I should go and congratulate her.'

'You haven't answered my question about why you're in my room, snooping through my things and under my bed,' he pointed out. 'I saw you sneak into the house when everyone else was by the pool. Like you were on a mission.'

'I . . . I'm not on a mission.'

Casper frowned, stroking his chin thoughtfully. 'Tabitha's dad didn't hire you, did he?'

'What?'

'Just give me a straight answer: were you or were you not hired by Ralph Pearce?'

'I was not!' Maeve stated, stunned at the accusation. 'Why would Tabitha's dad hire someone to look through your stuff?'

'Because I'm hoping he'll give me a job and it seems like the kind of thing he might do before making me an offer, considering he's a terrifying control freak.' He hesitated. 'You're definitely not working for him, are you? If you are, don't tell him I said that.'

'I am *definitely* not working for Ralph Pearce.'

'Did Tabitha send you up here? I know she has trust issues but—'

'No! She didn't send me! Honestly, I was just . . . I . . .'

Maeve ran a hand through her hair, scrambling for a reasonable justification and not finding any that gave her a good reason to look under his bed. *Come on, Maeve, think!*

'I was looking for cigarettes.'

He blinked at her. 'What?'

'Cigarettes,' she repeated. It wasn't her best work, but there was nothing she could do now but go with it. 'I thought you might have some up here.'

He didn't look convinced. 'Why wouldn't you ask someone downstairs for one? There are a few people smoking outside.'

'Because I didn't want anyone to know I was smoking. I didn't want my friends to see me. They'd be angry. I quit and I promised them . . . I promised them I wouldn't smoke.'

Casper's eyes widened with understanding and he clicked his fingers. 'Of course. Because you're a singer!'

'Exactly.' Maeve nodded, her shoulders sinking with relief as he appeared to believe her story. 'Because I'm a singer.'

'You know, your friends are right to be strict with you,' he said solemnly. 'You really shouldn't smoke in your profession. Got to protect those vocal cords. Having said that' – his expression brightened – 'do you want one? We can smoke out of my window and I have a pack. Didn't you see it in the drawer?'

'No! No, I . . . I keep mine stashed under the bed, so I thought that would be a smart place to look.'

'Weird.' He grinned. 'I promise I won't tell your friends if you don't tell Tabitha.'

He shut the bedroom door behind him and went to his bedside table, pulling out the pack of cigarettes and a lighter, before throwing open his window. He grabbed a small dish that had ash stains in it from the side of his desk and balanced it on the windowsill.

'Tabitha doesn't like you smoking then.'

He shook his head, offering her one from the pack before taking one for himself.

'Sometimes I have one on a night out in front of her, throwing caution to the wind and all that after a few drinks. She gets really angry at me, and anyone else who smokes around her, like Grace. She's very health focused. Grace thinks it's quite sweet. Shows she cares.'

Maeve noticed his eyes drop to the floor as he finished the sentence.

'That not a good thing?' Maeve asked, exhaling through the window. 'That she cares, I mean.'

'Course it is,' he said, taking a drag, but it sounded like he was trying to persuade himself.

Maeve looked at Casper sideways while she tried to work out the right thing to say. This was a golden opportunity for a one-to-one with their main suspect. But how would she get him to talk about any of this deeply personal stuff when they barely knew each other? Where the hell was Otis when she needed him?

'You in a relationship then?' Casper asked, jolting her from her panicked thoughts.

'Uh . . .'

An idea suddenly struck her. This could be a way to make

him talk. She found that people were more inclined to admit their own sins when they heard someone else's. Knowing you're not the only one out there making mistakes; it helps you connect.

'Yes,' she said firmly. 'Yeah, I am.'

'A good one?' he asked with an easy smile. 'Or is it complicated?'

'Complicated,' she confirmed, exhaling a long stream of smoke through the window. 'I don't deserve him.'

He raised his eyebrows. 'Why do you say that?'

'I've made some big mistakes.'

'Like?'

'I cheated on him.'

'Oh.' Casper nodded, intrigued. 'Does he know?'

'I think so. We haven't talked about it, but when we're together it feels . . .' She paused, searching for the right word.

'Tense?' he offered. 'Yeah, I know the feeling.'

'Really? You do?'

'Yeah. The elephant in the room. You both know it's there, but you don't want to talk about it because then it's real.'

'What happened with you two?'

'You'll hate me if I tell you.'

She shrugged. 'I won't. Everyone's human. No judgment here.'

He took a long, slow drag, keeping the suspense lingering in the air. He didn't speak until he'd exhaled, avoiding eye contact with Maeve and looking straight ahead out of the window, as though almost forgetting she was there and he was talking to himself.

'I've known for a while that Tabitha and I aren't going to work out. It's, like, we're miserable together, but we don't want to acknowledge it because our lives are so intertwined. It seems impossible to break apart. Anyway, the two of us have "made big mistakes," as you put it.'

'You mean you've both cheated?'

He nodded. 'She did first. Then I did. Not that it makes it any better which way round it happened. I just want to put it out there that she did it first. Neither of us achieved anything. Oh, she doesn't know I cheated on her, by the way.' He lifted his eyes to meet Maeve's. 'And I'd prefer it stayed that way.'

Maeve mimicked zipping her lips up and throwing away the key. 'Was it someone you knew?'

'I had a stupid one-night stand with a friend.' He exhaled and looked down at the floor, shaking his head. 'I wasn't thinking. I'd had a few drinks, Tabitha and I had argued and I was pissed at her. She'd done it to me, so I got my revenge. Stupid, right? OK, come on. Your turn – did you know them?'

'Sorry?'

'The person you cheated on your partner with. Did you know them or was it a one-night stand?'

'Oh! I . . . I knew them. *We* know them, I mean. Both of us. That's what makes it quite awkward. The guy was new to the group. He was so different to my boyfriend. Always up for a good time, really funny, good-looking, smart . . .'

Casper sniggered. 'If that makes him different to your boyfriend, what's your boyfriend like? Sounds like a bore. No offense.'

'You know what I mean,' she said breezily, quite enjoying making up this fake love triangle.

'So you got taken in by his easy-going charm, did you?' Casper tapped the ash off the end of his cigarette into the dish. 'Sounds familiar.'

'Yeah?'

'Tabitha . . . she sort of liked this guy we met. He was very laid back. The sort of person who doesn't seem to give a shit about anything. She started sleeping with him.'

'That must have made you angry.'

'Not really. I wanted her to have some fun.'

Maeve frowned. 'Wait. It didn't bother you?'

Casper let out a long sigh. 'Look, no one likes being made a fool of, and she wasn't exactly being subtle, but as I say, Tabitha and I have been drifting apart and I knew she was lashing out at me. And if this guy meant she'd get off my back for a while, then great. I worked out pretty quickly that she was just doing it to get my attention. She didn't care about him properly. And unfortunately it turned out he was nothing more than a thief. As soon as I saw him I could tell he was a twat. As usual, I was right.'

He snorted. Maeve's jaw clenched, a wave of anger hitting her like a punch to the gut, but she had to keep it together and play her part. She took a drag on her cigarette.

'At the end of the day,' he continued, oblivious to her reaction, 'the guy was doing me a favor.'

'If you feel that way, why don't you just break up?' Maeve asked after exhaling.

'No can do.'

'But if you're miserable and cheating on her . . .'

'She doesn't want to break up with me. She loves me.'

'Doesn't it matter what *you* want? Or are you just scared?'

'It's complicated.'

'How?'

He jutted out his chin. 'Circle of trust, right? No judgment?'

'I told you my story,' she reminded him, plastering on a smile that she hoped looked convincing. 'You can't be worse than me. Cheating on my boyfriend with someone he thinks is his friend? I'm sure whatever you're about to say is no worse.'

'All right then.' He cleared his throat. 'I need her dad to like me.'

'Sorry?'

'Ralph Pearce is a very powerful person. If I break up with his daughter, he won't like me. And then he won't hire me. I want a job at his company. Tabitha and I both know our relationship won't last when she goes to university, so we'll naturally break up. That will be much less painful for her then me dumping her now.'

'And less painful for you because you get the job you want and don't look like the bad guy,' Maeve said slowly.

'I obviously don't want to hurt her. It's no fun for anyone. Isn't that why you haven't told your boyfriend what you've done?'

Maeve stared at him. 'Right.'

He took the last drag of his cigarette and put it out. 'It actually feels really good to talk about this. You know how they always say you shouldn't bottle stuff up? Turns out they may be on to something.'

Maeve didn't say anything, putting her cigarette out too. She hadn't thought she'd feel sorry for Tabitha Pearce at any point in this investigation, but right now she had an overwhelming sense of sympathy for her. Stuck in a doomed relationship with someone who was out for a favor from her father.

'We should go downstairs,' Casper suggested, closing the window. 'Nice to chat though. Hope things work out with your boyfriend, Ronnie.'

'Roxie. And thanks.'

She realized that there was still a piece of his puzzle that she needed to know. It was now or never. She wasn't going to get the chance to ask him about this again. It wasn't exactly easy to weave into casual conversation. She stopped him as he headed for the door.

'Casper, can I ask you a personal question? You can tell me to piss off if you like.'

He grinned at her. 'I feel like we're in this together now. Ask away.'

'It's just . . . the shoebox under your bed,' she began cautiously. 'I saw it when I was looking for the cigarettes and . . .' She trailed off.

'You want to know what's in it,' he said, tilting his head at her curiously.

'Sorry.' She looked down at the ground, realizing how awful it sounded now she'd asked out loud. 'I don't know why I asked. I saw it earlier and it was so out of place with nothing else under there, and I just . . . I'm being so nosy. It's none of my business. Sorry. I'm being a dick. I'll go.'

To her surprise, he started laughing.

'It's fine! I mean, you are being nosy, but it's just football stickers.'

She looked up in confusion. 'What?'

He went over to the bed, crouched down and pulled out the old shoebox, lifting the lid to show her the contents.

'I've been collecting them since I was eight,' he explained, gesturing to what looked like hundreds of football stickers in there. 'I have quite a few rare ones actually – Premier League, FIFA, Champions League, World Cup. It's a real passion project. Tabitha thinks I'm an idiot for keeping them but I reckon one day this collection is going to be worth a lot of money. Cool, right?'

Maeve was stumped by this revelation. She didn't know what to say.

'What did you think was in here?' he asked, chuckling at her stunned expression. 'Creepy porn stuff?'

'No,' she said quickly, shaking her head. 'Not exactly.'

'It would be a fair assumption. Anyway' – he shut the box and shoved it back under the bed – 'we should go back to the party. I want to see if Molly is the pool noodle champion. Maybe I'll challenge her to a second round.'

Maeve nodded. This hadn't gone how she'd expected at all.

'Thanks, by the way,' she said, leaving his bedroom and wondering if that conversation had really just happened. 'For the cigarette.'

'No worries.' He tapped the side of his nose, closing the door behind them. 'Your secret is safe with me.'

TWELVE

As soon as they got back to the hotel room, Eric made a beeline for the bathroom, keen to wash his face and start getting ready for the drag show that night. He'd been so distracted by the hilarious chaos of the noodle jousting tournament that he was blissfully unaware of how late it was getting until he happened to glance at his phone. He'd had to urgently round up his friends, stealthily instructing them it was time to go.

'We have enough time to get ready, Eric,' Otis had chuckled as they left the party, Eric speed-walking down the road. 'Don't worry, we're still on schedule.'

'I don't just want *enough* time to get ready, Oatcake,' Eric had replied haughtily. 'I want more than enough time, so that I can get ready in a *leisurely* way. Do you know what happened the last time I rushed around getting dressed? I got my head stuck in my arm sleeve and it was VERY distressing.'

Following Otis and Aimee into the room, Maeve shut the door behind her and leaned back on it, letting out a sigh. That party had not gone the way she'd expected.

'I'm confused,' Aimee declared, dropping her beach bag on the floor. 'Did you just say that Casper was *happy* about Sean shagging his girlfriend?'

'He liked the idea of her having a distraction,' Maeve

explained. 'He said that Sean was doing him a favor.'

Aimee slumped down on the bed. 'That's mad.'

'Did you believe him?' Otis asked Maeve, coming to sit down next to Aimee.

'It sounded like he meant it,' she acknowledged, biting her thumbnail. 'He didn't seem to be out for revenge on Sean or even angry at Tabitha for cheating on him.'

'That makes sense from what Tabitha told me,' Otis said. 'She made out that Casper wasn't jealous at all; he was indifferent. She wants him to be furious about it, but apparently he acts as though he doesn't care.'

'He cheated on her too, with Grace, remember,' Eric pointed out, coming to stand in the doorway of the bathroom, dabbing his face dry with a towel.

'Yeah, I don't think he's framing Sean,' Maeve admitted. 'What would he gain from it? He's not angry enough at him for sleeping with Tabitha, so a revenge plot seems unlikely. And he's desperate to stay in Mr. Pearce's good books because of this job offer, so I don't think he'd risk stealing from his daughter.'

'I really thought it was going to be him,' Aimee said, disappointed. 'He had such a good motive. Even Pharaoh would have suspected him.'

'Poirot,' Maeve corrected instinctively.

'Now it looks like he may have no motive at all,' Otis said thoughtfully. 'But, thanks to Tabitha, we do now know about Noah and his sticky fingers.'

'Ew! Gross!' Aimee grimaced, prompting a huff of exasperation from Eric.

'As in the phrase, meaning he's likely to steal,' Otis explained much to her relief. 'He's stolen in the past; he could have done it again. Tabitha thinks he got a thrill from it, but we also know that he owes Sean quite a bit of money. Maybe he saw the necklace and took the opportunity that was staring him right in the face. And then there's the whole Grace and Casper angle – Eric, you didn't get anything interesting from Grace?'

He shook his head. 'Nothing, but we have the invite to their photography exhibition tomorrow, so we can try to find out something then.'

'And I couldn't work out if Cece was cut up about Sean's rejection or not,' Maeve informed them, biting her lip. 'I need to call him with an update, but it feels like we're not getting anywhere.'

'Hey, I think we've done well,' Otis insisted, Aimee and Eric nodding in agreement. 'This was never going to happen overnight. Whether they purposefully framed Sean or took the necklace and let him take the fall, the thief clearly isn't going to give themselves up easily. But it sounds like we can pretty much rule out Casper. That's progress, right?'

'Yeah,' Maeve mumbled, peering up at the suspect photos stuck on the wall. 'I guess.'

'Come on,' Aimee said, jumping up and going over to Maeve to grab her hands. 'Let's get ready for a fun night out.'

Maeve nodded, forcing a smile. 'I'd better call Sean. I'll be back in a sec. I'll talk to the receptionist too and see if another room is available.'

Otis nodded, his face flushing hot at the memory of the erection incident. 'Yes. Good plan.'

'I quite like us all sharing,' Aimee admitted when Maeve had left. 'It's fun, isn't it! Like a summer camp, but instead of activities, we're solving crime. What are you going to wear tonight, Eric?'

'I've brought something special along for the occasion,' he revealed, holding up a shirt of kente cloth and matching suit trousers. 'With gold accessories and' – he reached for a black silk tie and held it against the colorful fabric – 'also this. Not sure how I'll tie it yet.'

'I'm really good at knots,' she claimed eagerly. 'I've been sailing and everything, so I can help you.'

Eric gave an unenthusiastic smile at this offer, while Aimee inspected the pile of clothes spilling out of her suitcase.

'What are you going to wear?' he asked.

She picked up a black leather skirt and a canary-yellow sequinned top, holding them against her.

'I was thinking these. Unless' – she gasped, looking up from the outfit at Eric – 'do you think I'll look like a bee?'

'Bees are *fierce*,' Eric told her promptly. 'Grace and I were discussing this earlier. Without bees, we'd be screwed. We'd have no food and stuff. Seriously, they're essential.'

'Amazing! Guess I'm happy to look like a bee then.'

When Maeve returned to the room, Eric was helping Aimee with her eyelashes, while Otis sat propped up against the pillows on the bed, watching the process with great amusement.

'Aimee, I love you,' Eric began in a strained tone, holding the tweezers with which he was attempting to carefully place the strip of fake eyelashes across her lash line, 'but you need to stay still when I am *working my magic*.'

'Right. Sorry,' she said. 'I promise I'll be stoned from now on.'

'Stoned?'

'When you don't show any emotion or react or anything.'

'Stony-faced.'

'Yeah, that's what I said.'

Otis and Maeve shared a smile as Eric took a deep breath and then asked Aimee to tilt her head back slightly for better lighting.

'Did you speak to Sean?' Otis asked as Maeve perched on the end of the bed, tossing her phone on to the duvet.

She nodded. 'He was disappointed with my report. I think he was sure it was Casper. He seemed thrown by the idea that any of the others dislike him so much that they'd bother to go to all this trouble to frame him.'

'We still have some strong suspects with Casper out of the picture,' Eric proclaimed, having successfully applied lashes to one of Aimee's eyes. 'You never know what's going on in someone's head. Maybe Sean pissed them off loads without realizing.'

'Or maybe he wasn't framed in the first place,' Maeve muttered under her breath.

Otis frowned at her. 'We haven't given up yet.'

Maeve didn't say anything, chewing her thumbnail and avoiding eye contact with Otis.

'Exactly. It's not over, Maeve,' Eric declared. 'Now, you've earned a fun night out. All this thinking and stressing . . . you need some downtime to rest your brain and feed your soul.' He sat back to check Aimee's eyes. 'OK, Aimee, you're all done. What do you think?'

Aimee jumped up and skipped to the bathroom before gasping at her reflection. 'I love them! How did you get them on so neatly?'

Eric put the lash glue back in its box. 'Practice.'

Aimee fluttered her eyes at her reflection. 'I've never worn lashes this long before.'

'Wait until you see mine,' he chuckled, turning his attention back to Maeve. 'You want me to do yours too? I've got spares.'

'No thanks,' she said, dropping her hands to her lap. 'I was just planning on touching up my lipstick for tonight anyway.'

'You know what you need, babes,' Aimee said, hurrying over to her beach bag. She whipped out a bottle of champagne.

'Where did you get that?' Maeve asked, astounded.

'The pool party! Sneaked one from the bar.'

'Aimee, that's stealing.'

'No, it's not.' She looked offended. 'The barman said I could take it if I wanted, so I did. He didn't say it had to be drunk at the party *specifically*. I thought it might be fun to have some bubbles before the show.'

'Aimee, you are an actual GENIUS!' Eric exclaimed, clapping his hands.

'It's probably a bit warm. I should have brought it out before now, but I forgot,' Aimee considered, wrinkling her nose. 'Oh no, some of my hairs are stuck to the label. They'll be from my hairbrush in my bag, sticking to the bottle because of the consternation.'

'Condensation.'

'Yeah, that's what I said.' She unwrapped the foil and then

put the bottle between her legs to steady it so she could twist out the cork.

'Aimee, wait—' Maeve began, but too late.

There was a loud pop as the cork erupted from the bottle, soaring across the room straight at Otis, hitting him slap bang in the middle of the forehead. He yelped in pain. The champagne poured out from the top, streaming down Aimee's hands and legs on to the carpet. Eric and Maeve gasped, rushing over to check on Otis.

'Whoopsie!' Aimee said, flicking the liquid off one hand and holding up the bottle with another. 'Are you OK, Otis?! I'm so sorry!'

'I'm fine,' he winced, rubbing his head. 'Lucky it didn't get my eye.'

'Really lucky!' Maeve emphasized, watching him in concern. 'Let's take a look.'

He lowered his hands. Maeve desperately tried not to laugh at the red circle on his forehead. Now that she knew he was OK and not badly hurt, it was a little bit funny.

'Is it bad?' he asked Eric.

Eric grimaced, glancing at Maeve uncertainly. 'Um. It's . . . it's not *too* bad. Don't worry, I'm sure among us we have a concealer that matches your skin tone.'

'Have some champers to help with the pain,' Aimee insisted, handing him the bottle to swig from before putting her hands on her hips and beaming at them all proudly. 'Guess you could say our night is already off with a bang!'

*

Eric could not have loved Amit more when they arrived at The Courtyard and saw the huge queue for tickets running down the pavement. Linking his arm through Otis's, he led them to another door where a bouncer was waving through people who'd booked in advance.

As they weaved their way through the room to take their seats at a small round table, Eric felt elated, the excitement tingling down his arms, right through to his fingertips. He had wanted to come to this show ever since he'd read a review about it online, the writer gushing about the dazzling performance and how it was impossible to leave without a skip in your step.

He nervously checked his reflection in the screen of his phone to make sure none of the silver and green eye gems that he'd painstakingly stuck to his skin in a swirled pattern from the side of his eyes up around to his temples had fallen off, before eagerly looking around the room at the other members of the audience. As he gazed in admiration at the bold and glamorous fashion present in that room, he instinctively lifted his chin. Sometimes when he dressed in drag or applied make-up, he felt he had to be brave. But here, he didn't have to feel anything but himself.

The lights began to dim.

Otis leaned in to whisper, 'Here we go,' in his ear. Eric turned to grin at his best friend – whose forehead was now heavily layered in concealer – before gazing up at the stage in anticipation.

A low, sultry voice came through the speakers. 'Welcome one and all to The Courtyard! Please give a warm hand to our first performer of the night, Pamela Violet!'

There was an eruption of applause and cheers from the audience as a spotlight hit the center of the stage. The black curtains at the back opened and Pamela Violet stepped into the spotlight, placing her hands on her hips with great flourish. She was wearing a bright-purple wig and a full-length magenta gown that glittered under the spotlight and had a slit up one side to reveal killer bejeweled heels. Her earrings were long and silver, swinging and catching the light with just the slightest move of her head, and she had long, pointed silver nails.

Feeling like the breath had been knocked out of his body, Eric marveled at her makeup. Her skin was flawless, heavily contoured and with shimmering cheekbones; the bright white eyeshadow across her eyelids blended into heavy lilac, stopping just underneath the highlighter lining her bold, perfectly arched eyebrows. Her eyeliner was strikingly dramatic, expertly smudged along the lower lash, flowing into the thick black wing by the outer corner, and she had on a glossy dark-purple lipstick.

A pop song came through the speakers and she launched into a slick, energetic performance. She was so talented, but what struck Eric the most was her sheer *presence*. She was powerful, charismatic and glamorous. He'd seen drag online and on TV, but he realized now that the camera couldn't possibly capture this feeling of seeing it live. He'd never forget this moment. He couldn't take his eyes off her. And he could have SWORN that at one point she looked directly at him and smiled.

It was a brilliant first act, bursting with celebration and joy. Eric was mesmerized, and by the end he was up on his feet with everyone else in the audience, clapping until his hands hurt, smiling so wide that his jaw ached.

He'd been so consumed by his own euphoric experience, he hadn't thought to check to see how his friends were enjoying it, but just a quick look at their faces during the applause was enough to know they were feeling the same way.

'She was AMAZING!' Aimee cried across the table. This was hands down the coolest thing she'd EVER been to. That included the time she went to a bouncy castle party hosted by a shopping channel presenter.

And that had been WILD.

Maeve was still staring up at the stage in astonishment, despite Pamela Violet having already sashayed off into the wings. Her performance had just been so . . . *happy*. That sounded stupid – there must be a better word to describe it, especially for Maeve, who prided herself on her essay-writing skills – but it was all she could come up with: happy. That's how it made Maeve feel. And maybe because she didn't get to feel it all that often, maybe because she always had so many things to worry about, maybe because everyone always let her down in the end – *happy* felt like a big deal.

Otis knew he'd love the show as soon as Eric told him about it, but what made it for him was watching Eric's face throughout. He couldn't stop glancing over and grinning at his friend's expression of wonder.

They took their seats as the lights went down for the next performer, a cabaret act that was not only spectacular but also made Eric laugh so much he threw his head back and almost took out someone passing behind him.

By the time the show ended and it was time to leave, they were all on a natural high, adrenaline pumping through their veins. Eric wanted to stay at the table and watch it all again, right from the beginning. He walked out feeling elated.

As Eric and Aimee were both in heels, they all agreed to a taxi back to the hotel, and walked down the pavement to a spot where it was a bit quieter to wait for one. Aimee was in the middle of telling them that the group act at the end was so good it made the hairs on the back of her legs stand up, when Eric saw a figure emerge through a side door of a building. He stared at them and then realized who it was.

Leaving Aimee explaining to Otis and Maeve how she only shaved the front of her legs, because there didn't seem much point in shaving the back when no one sees them, Eric walked towards the figure, the clacking of his heels on the tarmac echoing down the alley.

'Excuse me,' he began cautiously, hoping that he had the right person. 'Pamela Violet?'

They looked up, having been searching for their car keys in a bag, and gave Eric a knowing smile.

'Sorry, is that the name I should call you?' Eric checked, now that they weren't in drag.

'You can call me Isaiah. I go by "he/him" when I'm not Pamela,' he said warmly. He was in black jeans, a green-patterned long-sleeved shirt and no makeup, but still had his glittery nails on.

'I just wanted to say, you were incredible,' Eric gushed, completely star struck. 'Such an amazing performance. I felt . . . I don't know . . . It was just amazing.'

Eric wished he could be more eloquent, but Isaiah didn't seem to mind that he was gabbling away. In fact, he was modestly chuckling.

'Thank you. Sorry, I didn't catch your name?'

'Eric.'

'Thank you, Eric. I'm glad you enjoyed the show.'

'It was like nothing I've ever seen. You were . . . it was like you were made to be up there performing. Sorry, that sounds stupid.'

'Nah, it doesn't,' Isaiah said with a shrug. 'You're right. I found my calling.'

'Yeah, you did.' Eric hesitated. 'What does it feel like up there? On the stage, I mean.'

'It feels' – he searched for the right word – 'glowing. Yeah.' He breathed in deeply, his eyes glinting in the street lights. 'Like everything is . . . glowing.'

Eric nodded slowly, gazing at him in admiration. Isaiah turned his attention back to his bag and found his keys, jangling them as he lifted them out.

'It was nice meeting you, Eric. Thanks for coming over to say hi and I hope you have a good night.' He smiled and pointed his finger at Eric's trousers. 'That is a *nice suit.*'

'Thank you!' Eric said, beaming at him. 'And thank you for tonight. I mean, congratulations. You were FIERCE.'

Isaiah gratefully acknowledged the compliment with a nod, and, slinging his bag over his shoulder, walked away down the alley. Eric watched him go.

'Eric!' Otis called out. 'We have a taxi!'

He tore his eyes away from Isaiah and turned to go and join

the others. As he put on his seat belt he filled them in on their conversation. He then sat back as Otis discussed his favorite bits of the show, and looked out of the window at the buzzing city rushing past, feeling a strange, exciting ache in his chest, as though something had sparked within him.

'STOP THE CAR!' Aimee suddenly screamed.

The taxi driver slammed on the brakes, bringing the car to a sudden halt.

'What's wrong?!' Maeve gasped.

'Nothing's wrong,' Aimee replied cheerily, pointing out of the window. 'I want to show you all something. We'll get out here, thank you!'

Before they could protest, she'd undone her seat belt, opened the car door and hopped out, leaving them all sitting there, aghast.

'Aimee, wait!' Maeve called out, before addressing the others. 'Come on then.'

Moaning about walking too far in his shoes, Eric reluctantly followed Maeve and Otis out of the car and dismally watched the taxi drive off into the distance. They were on a well-lit road next to a grassy hill.

'Where are we?' he asked, throwing his hands up into the air. 'We're not at the hotel yet!'

'We're not too far,' Aimee cried over her shoulder as she strode up a path through the grass. 'This way!'

They trailed after her, Eric muttering about the hazards of heels sinking into grass, until she stopped at the top of the hill next to a bench.

'What are we doing, Aimee?' Maeve had to ask, putting

her hands on her hips.

'When I got lost looking for the baking convention arena, I came across this bench. And I thought to myself, "I have to bring the others here!"'

'Why?'

'Sit down and look at that view!'

They'd been so focused on working out what Aimee was up to that none of them had bothered to look around them. The top of the hill looked over the entire city, a sea of bright lights. They could hear the rush of the city, the sirens and traffic in the distance, but up here it was quiet and tranquil.

'Wow.' Eric grinned at Aimee. 'I officially forgive you for dragging us up here.'

Managing to all squeeze on the bench, they sat together in a line and stared out in silence at the view, admiring the mass of twinkling lights, which made Maeve feel so small when she thought about how many people were out there. She took a deep breath in, feeling a rush of gratitude to be here in this moment with her friends.

'It's amazing here,' Otis said, sitting back and taking it all in. 'So peaceful.'

'Yeah, it is,' Eric agreed. 'I don't want to leave.'

The others nodded and fell silent again, each enjoying a rare moment of contemplation. Suddenly Aimee spoke, her voice echoing through the warm summer night air.

'I saw two people dry-humping on this bench.'

They all turned their heads slowly to look at her. She nodded vigorously in case they might be in doubt about what they just heard.

'They were really going at it,' she said. 'It was quite sweet. Such a romantic spot.'

'On second thoughts,' Eric said, jumping to his feet, 'I would quite like to leave.'

'Yep,' Maeve and Otis chorused, each standing up immediately.

Aimee shrugged. 'OK. I am quite tired. Anyone know the way back from here?'

Otis opened the map on his phone, and Eric repeatedly asked if anyone had any hand sanitizer as he and Aimee started cautiously making their way back down the hill towards the pavement in their heels. Maeve lagged behind to steal one last glance at the view. She took in the lights, breathed in deeply and smiled to herself.

Maybe everything would be OK.

THIRTEEN

Otis was having a bad day.

It got off to a rocky start, so he should have known it would only get worse. Having woken up, he yawned, stretched, got up from the floor and plodded into the bathroom. As he got a look at his reflection in the mirror, he did a double-take.

Right in the middle of his forehead was a big, cork-shaped bruise.

It was a dark purple-blue and had formed a bump. This was, of course, simply HILARIOUS to everyone else and they all had a jolly good laugh at his expense.

'I'm glad I could provide some light entertainment,' he huffed.

'Don't worry, Oatcake.' Eric laughed. 'Concealer works miracles.'

But even though Eric did his best to cover it up once Otis was showered and dressed, there was still a very obvious bruise. If Eric did the concealer any thicker, it would look like a strange round patch on his forehead. Aimee said she felt really bad about it, but it was hard to believe her when she was saying it through wheezes of laughter.

'Why does it look so much worse today?' Maeve mused, folding her arms. 'It's protruding more, I think.'

'There's no need to *study* it, Maeve,' Otis replied grouchily. 'It's not like I'm growing a horn out of my forehead.'

'To be fair though, Otis,' Aimee began, pointing at the bruise, 'if you were growing a horn out of your forehead, it would probably look a bit like that to begin with.'

'OK, everyone stop looking at it now, please,' he demanded.

'It's hard not to look, Otis,' Eric told him. 'It's right in the middle of your forehead.'

'All right! That's it!' Otis put a hand over it and marched towards the door. 'I'm going to go get some air.'

'Maybe go to reception and ask about another room!' Eric called out after him, before tutting as he looked at the mess of clothes strewn all over the floor. 'This place is getting disgusting. And I want to sleep in a bed.'

After bursting out of the room, Otis had only walked a few paces when he realized Maeve was catching up with him.

'You don't need to worry about checking on me, Maeve,' he huffed.

'I wasn't.'

'Oh.'

'I didn't think you'd ask about another room because you're in a strop, so I thought I'd do it instead.'

'I am not in a strop,' he grumbled.

'Good. Because the receptionist likes you, so she may be more inclined to be helpful. I imagine you're getting a bit of a bad back from sleeping on the floor.'

He couldn't argue with that one. The blankets that Helen had provided were scratchy, and even when layered on top of one another, they didn't exactly form an effective mattress.

It would be nice to sleep in an actual bed.

Helen was on shift and, as usual, was sitting behind reception scrolling through her phone. She glanced up as they came through the door.

'Oh, hello,' she said brightly to Otis, putting down her phone. 'How can I help you?'

'We're looking to book another hotel room, if there's one available,' Maeve explained, deciding not to point out that she'd asked the same query almost every day.

'We haven't got any spare rooms,' she informed her. 'It's so busy because of the bird-watching convention. You can try again tomorrow if you like.' She turned her attention to Otis. 'Thanks so much for your advice about my ex. I blocked him on my Instagram.'

'That's great progress. Well done.'

'And I've only unblocked him and reblocked, like, four times since.'

'Well . . . that's still really good. You're taking the steps you need to move on.'

'Do you think I should let him know that I've blocked him?'

'No need,' Otis assured her. 'You just focus on you.'

'OK.' She frowned, squinting at his face. 'What's that on your forehead?'

'Oh, it's nothing, just a bruise,' he mumbled, looking down at the ground in embarrassment. 'I got it from a cork.'

She looked startled. 'A *what*?'

'A cork,' he repeated, a little clearer this time.

'Ooh,' she said, nervously laughing. 'That makes a LOT more sense! I thought you said . . . never mind.'

'What?' Otis smiled, disarmed by her laugh. 'What did you think I said?'

She brushed the question away with her hand as she giggled. 'Nothing, nothing.'

'What was it?' he persisted, chuckling.

'Cock, Otis,' Maeve said impatiently. 'She thought you said you got that bruise from a cock.'

The room fell silent. Helen didn't know where to look and Otis felt his cheeks burning ferociously.

'Good, then.' Maeve gave Helen a sharp nod. 'We'll see you tomorrow.'

She turned and walked out, Otis giving Helen an awkward wave and hurrying after Maeve. On the walk back to the room, he laughed it off.

'That was awkward,' he said, putting on a jokey voice.

'You should try not to mumble when you talk to her next time,' she advised drily as they got to the room and she pushed open the door. 'Just so there's no cock mishaps.'

'What's that about cock mishaps?' Eric asked from the sofa, looking up with great intrigue as they walked in.

'I have some great stories about those,' Aimee commented, finishing her mascara in the bathroom mirror. 'Eric, can I borrow your sequinned bomber jacket?'

'Course!'

Otis's phone started ringing. He checked the screen, rolled his eyes and then put it back in his pocket without answering.

'Are you still *ignoring* Jean?' Eric asked curiously.

'I'm not ignoring her,' Otis insisted grumpily. 'I'm giving her the space she needs. She has to come to terms with the idea that she cannot control every aspect of my life.'

'I think she's just checking in on you, Oatcake,' Eric reasoned.

'Trust me, she's not just checking in. She's *never* just checking in.' Otis sighed wistfully. 'Things would be a lot simpler if she was, but there's an agenda behind every phone call. She'll want to know what I'm doing, who I'm with—'

'She knows who you're with already though,' Aimee said, admiring her reflection in Eric's jacket.

Otis looked down at the floor guiltily. He had told Jean he was going on the trip with Eric, but had left out Maeve and Aimee. When she'd curiously asked how they were traveling, he'd said 'a friend' was driving them.

If he had told her about Aimee and Maeve, she would have asked a HUNDRED questions, desperate for details on them both and his relationship to them. He'd been in a rush to leave at the time, and, to be honest, the less she knew the better. That was his current mantra when it came to Jean, otherwise everything became a huge deal. It was *exhausting*. He'd learned it was best to keep things vague.

When they later left the hotel room for the art exhibition, Otis felt exasperated from the morning's events, rubbing his bruise and feeling irrationally irritated at his mother for calling yet again, making him feel guilty and look bad for not picking up. Distracted, he didn't look where he was going and stepped in dog poo. Hearing his cry of anguish, Eric glanced back over his shoulder and, realizing what had happened, tutted and said, 'You see, Otis? What was I telling you the other day? Irresponsible dog owners. They are a *menace*!'

By the time they arrived at Grace's photography exhibition,

Otis had accepted that it was just one of those days. He could only hope that by channeling Jem – wearing Eric's black and white checkered trousers, a green short-sleeved shirt and Aimee's sunglasses – things were going to get better.

When they walked in, the others wandered over to the first piece of work, but Otis spotted Grace standing nervously in the corner and decided to go over to say congratulations.

As he approached, Grace stared at him. 'Did you know you have dirt on your forehead? It's smeared in a big circle right there in the middle.'

Bugger it.

'It's not dirt, it's a bruise,' he said haughtily, already wondering why he'd bothered to leave the hotel. 'Aimee popped a champagne cork at me.'

'Who's Aimee?'

'Oh! Oh, no one,' he croaked. 'Just a person. A person you don't know. This other person.'

'OK.' Grace laughed. 'You're Finley's friend, Jem, right? We haven't really spoken. He told me you're an artist too.'

'Did he? How good of him.'

'You'll have to tell me your thoughts on my work. Always interesting to hear what a fellow artist thinks.' They spotted someone over Otis's shoulder. 'Ah, I have to go say hi to my aunt, but I'll find you later so we can chat. Tabitha and everyone are around here somewhere. Enjoy the exhibition!'

'I will! And well done again. I'll make sure I have thoughts. To discuss later.'

OH MY GOD STOP TALKING.

Grace grinned. 'I look forward to that.'

Rolling his eyes at his own stupidity, Otis sought out Maeve, Eric and Aimee. He went to stand next to them, looked up at the photograph and found himself surprised.

'Is that . . . ?'

'A penis, yes,' Maeve replied, her arms folded as she examined the art.

'It's an exhibition of them,' Aimee informed him, gesturing around the gallery.

'All of the photos are of penises.' Otis nodded, stroking his chin.

Eric peered at the sign below the first photo. 'It says here that this exhibition is "the first in a series wherein the artist is hoping to tackle myth and taboo around genitalia, celebrating their diversity and individuality."'

'Grace is so cool,' Aimee whispered in awe.

'Yeah, they really are,' Eric agreed, before saying to Otis, 'Your mum would love this.'

'Whose mum would love this?' Casper appeared at Eric's side and punched his arm playfully. 'By the way, Timothy, you were awesome at the pool party. That foam noodle tournament was an excellent idea.'

'It's Finley.'

'Course. Got it.' Casper tapped the side of his head. 'So what do you all think of the art? Grace is a visionary. You know' – he lowered his voice – 'one of these is mine.'

'One of these penises?' Aimee asked, scanning all the photos around the room.

'Yep.' He puffed out his chest proudly. 'I'm not supposed to say, but if you want my opinion, I think it would be an interesting art experiment to tell people which one is mine.'

Maeve frowned. 'How would that be an experiment?'

'You look at a photo one way and form a subjective opinion; if *then* I tell you it's my penis, wouldn't that affect how you saw it?' He nodded smugly as though he'd just cracked an ancient code. 'Just let me know on the sly if you want any hints.'

'Thank you,' Eric said with a fixed smile.

'I'll leave you to enjoy the experience.'

Casper sauntered over to Tabitha, Cece and Noah, who were clustered together at the back of the room, sipping champagne and taking selfies.

Maeve watched him place a hand on the small of Tabitha's back and kiss her head affectionately. She felt irritated that he was leading Tabitha on, not that it was any of her business. Tearing her eyes away from them, she realized she wasn't the only one watching the display of affection with an expression of disgust. Grace was too.

'What a very odd person,' Eric said about Casper, clearing his throat. 'Anyway, shall we move on to the next photo.'

Aimee nodded. 'I think if you tilt your head from side to side, the image moves. Like the Mona Lisa, but different.'

As Eric and Aimee strolled along to the next artwork, Maeve noticed Grace excuse themselves from the conversation they'd been in, make their way past all the guests milling about admiring their work, and slip through the door out on to the street.

Maeve grabbed Otis's arm. 'Come with me.'

Pushing through the door, she stepped out on to the

164

pavement. She spotted Grace leaning on the wall at the corner of the building, having a cigarette.

'Hey,' Maeve said, approaching them with Otis following behind. 'You all right?'

'Yeah. Just needed a nicotine hit.'

'Your exhibition is great,' Otis chipped in. 'I mean, I've only seen one picture so far, but it was brilliant. I'm sure the others are also fab.'

'Thanks.'

As Grace exhaled, Maeve used her eyes to signal to Otis that he should talk to them properly, but he frowned in confusion at her, shaking his head. The door of the gallery swung open and Tabitha stepped out, looking about for someone.

At the sight of Tabitha, Grace quickly straightened and shoved their cigarette into Otis's hand.

'There you are,' Tabitha said. 'What are you all doing out here? You're not smoking, are you, Grace?'

'No, I was just getting some air,' Grace replied brightly.

'I was smoking,' Otis claimed, the cigarette hanging limply and unnaturally in between his fingers.

For authenticity, he attempted a puff and started coughing and spluttering. Maeve smiled to herself. Tabitha did not seem impressed.

'It's a little thoughtless to smoke around Grace,' she said, giving him a dirty look. 'They quit recently and I've been so proud of their progress. And Casper's too. I'd have thought, Jem, you'd be a bit more sensitive about stuff like that, being a natural therapist.'

'I'm not a therapist, I'm an artist,' Otis corrected her

hurriedly. He dropped the cigarette on the pavement, squashing it with his shoe. 'But you're right about the smoking. Very thoughtless. Sorry, Grace.'

'It's OK, Tabitha, we're just talking about art,' Grace said, gesturing to Otis.

'Fine, but don't stay out here too long.' Tabitha checked her phone. 'We need to go back to my place soon for the after-party. Jem and Roxie, you can come too.'

'Another party,' Otis said, deflated. 'Great.'

Tabitha turned on her heel and went back into the gallery, allowing Grace to lean back against the wall again, their shoulders slumped forward.

'What was that about?' Maeve asked them.

'What do you mean?'

'Come on. Are you scared of Tabitha or something?'

'No!' Grace looked taken aback, their eyebrows knitted together in confusion at the idea. 'I'm not scared of her. I'm not . . . I'm . . .'

They trailed off. As it dawned on Otis what was going on, he took off his sunglasses to look at Grace properly.

'You like her,' he said softly.

Grace lifted their eyes to meet his and nodded slowly.

'Does Tabitha know how you feel?' Otis asked.

'No. I don't think so. It's shit. I'm around her all the time and I have to see her with Casper. He doesn't even care about her. I feel . . . trapped. Sorry. Look, keep this to yourselves, yeah? Pretend I didn't say anything.'

'Your secret is safe with us. But out of curiosity, why do you feel trapped?'

166

'Because!' They threw their hands up in the air in exasperation. 'I don't know what to do. I'm stuck! I'm her best friend who has feelings for her and . . . I did something bad. But I'm not sure if I feel guilty about it, because I did it to prove . . . *Shit*. Never mind.'

Otis waited and when they didn't say anything more, he asked, 'Do you want to talk about what you did?'

'Not exactly.'

Grace got out another cigarette and lit it, while Otis and Maeve stood with them patiently.

'If you wanted to talk about it, it would be in confidence,' Otis said as they took a long drag, watching him suspiciously. 'Guilt eats away at you, warping thoughts and, in some cases, causing unreasonable judgment of yourself. It's a burden but it can also be constructive, and talking about it can help release that weighed-down feeling, make sense of it and help us do better in the future.'

Grace frowned at him. 'Did you memorize a pamphlet or something?'

'He just talks like that,' Maeve informed them, leaning back against the wall herself and crossing her arms. 'It's weird but quite helpful sometimes.'

Otis looked insulted, mouthing, '*Quite?*' at her, but she just shrugged in response.

'That right?' Grace looked dubious. 'Seems weird talking about it with someone I barely know.'

'That might be a good thing. No judgment, no bias' – Otis held up his hands – 'just a good listener.'

Grace took a drag. 'Trust me, you will judge me when you

167

hear what I did. It was . . . it was really bad.'

Otis shook his head. 'This is a safe space.'

Grace let out a long sigh, before admitting quietly, 'I slept with Casper.'

Grace must have been expecting a horrified reaction, but to their surprise nothing happened. Otis didn't flinch, his expression neutral and focused. Maeve didn't even look like she was really listening, looking out across the road and watching passersby.

'We were at this party at Tabitha's and we were all really drunk,' Grace continued, finding Otis's lack of reaction comforting. 'Casper and Tabitha had had a big fight. I don't know what about; I don't even think they can remember. Tabitha was flirting with this other guy to piss Casper off, but Casper couldn't care less. And Casper and I were chatting and he leaned in and I don't know.' They ran a hand through their hair. 'It made sense in my vodka-addled brain. I thought, why not? *Why the hell not?* No one is happy in this situation! In a totally messed-up kind of way I thought it might be a good thing, because then she'd know what a wanker Casper is and she might break up with him. I was so *angry*.'

'What were you angry about?'

'I was angry at Casper for not knowing how lucky he was and for treating Tabitha so badly all the time. I was angry at Tabitha for loving him anyway. And I was angry at myself and my stupid broken heart.'

Maeve watched sadly as Grace's eyes filled with tears.

'We can't help who we love,' Otis pointed out. 'It's not wrong to have feelings. You can't punish yourself or feel angry at yourself for them, because they're real and they're important. You can't control what you feel, but you *can* control what you do about it.'

'I just wish I hadn't fallen for *her*,' Grace said, so quietly they were barely audible.

'I know. But you have. And if you don't address your feelings, you're only making yourself suffer more. Developing romantic feelings for a friend can happen. And it can be painful and horrible, and you feel like you're in this impossible position, because the risk of losing them feels so great. But once you've evaluated your feelings, you have to make the decision as to whether you tell your friend or not.'

Maeve couldn't be certain, but she thought she saw Otis's eyes flicker towards her when he said that. And she felt her stomach somersault at the idea.

'If you decide not to tell Tabitha how you feel, because you want to protect the friendship and you believe the outcome of telling her might jeopardize it, that's OK,' Otis continued. 'But, in that case, you need to protect yourself too. Maybe give yourself a bit of distance from her. And if you decide to tell her how you feel, then that's OK too. Prepare yourself for all the outcomes and let her have time and space to digest it.'

Grace nodded, letting his words sink in. 'I know I can't keep going on like this.'

'No,' he agreed.

'I guess shagging her boyfriend probably isn't the answer to my problems,' Grace said with a weak smile.

He chuckled. 'Probably not the best idea, no.'

Grace nodded and the three of them stood in silence,

digesting it all. After a few minutes, Grace took a deep breath and spoke.

'Sorry to offload on you, I don't have many people to talk to. It may surprise you to hear that Noah isn't the best listener,' they said, rolling their eyes. 'I could tell him straight out that I slept with Casper and it would go in one ear and out the other. He's actually the best person to tell a secret to, you know. He'd forget he was in on it.'

'He knows about you and Casper?' Maeve asked curiously.

'Noah? No,' Grace replied, having been so lost in the conversation with Otis, they'd almost forgotten Maeve was there. 'Only one person knows and he hasn't said anything to anyone. It's someone you haven't met. He doesn't hang out with us any more.'

'Are you worried that he knows about it?'

Grace frowned. 'Not really. Honestly, I know this sounds ridiculous, but part of me wanted him to tell Tabitha. Then she'd know what an arsehole her boyfriend is and break up with him for good. And I truly say that as someone who cares about her, not just someone who wants to be with her. I want her to be happy. Casper makes her miserable.'

'But if this guy told her, she'd also know that you'd betrayed her,' Maeve said, feeling a bit guilty saying it out loud, because she liked Grace.

'Yeah, but the thing is, I *did* betray her,' Grace said, looking down at their feet. 'In the end, maybe she deserves to know the truth. Even if I don't tell her how I feel, maybe I should at least sit her down and tell her what I did. Being trapped in all these lies is killing me. As I said, not one person in this whole situation is happy, and when it comes down to it, it's about doing the right thing.'

Otis nodded his approval.

'Anyway' – Grace checked the time and pushed themselves away from the wall – 'that was a really long cigarette break. I should get back to my exhibition.'

'You should,' Otis encouraged, hanging back with Maeve as Grace started to walk away. 'You should be really proud of yourself for such an achievement. And thank you for talking to me.'

'Are you kidding? Thank you for listening. Seems that Tabitha's right.' Grace stopped at the gallery door, turning back to smile at him. 'You're not really an artist, are you?'

FOURTEEN

Soon after Otis's chat with Grace, Tabitha decided they'd been at the gallery long enough and it was time to head to her family house for the after-party. Grace had to stay at their exhibition launch until the end, but said they'd try to make it later. Otis was standing nearby when Grace and Tabitha were talking and couldn't help but overhear their conversation.

'*Try* to make it?' Tabitha gave them a baffled look. 'That sounds like you might not be able to come.'

'I have some work to do, you know, for the exhibition,' Grace replied.

'The exhibition is already up and launched,' Tabitha pointed out, gesturing around her. 'And you've done so well! Everyone loves it. So now you get to celebrate.'

'We've done a lot of partying recently,' Grace said quietly. 'And there is a lot of admin to do. I should probably skip tonight. But I'll see you at the garden party your dad is throwing for you. It's so nice how proud he is of you for getting your university place.'

Tabitha stared at them, bewildered. 'The garden party isn't for two days. What about the charity gala tomorrow? You need to come over and help me pick my dress. Without my necklace, the whole outfit I'd planned is ruined.'

Grace smiled. 'Casper can help you pick, or Cece. I've just got some things to sort out, Tabitha. Maybe after the garden party we can sit down and have a chat.'

'A chat about what?'

'Babe, can we go?' Casper interrupted, coming over to throw his arm around Tabitha. 'I'm bored. No offense, Grace. This is great stuff, really groundbreaking, but that's enough culture for today, am I right?' He laughed, but the other two didn't. 'Your dad's not in today, yeah? We have the house to ourselves?'

Tabitha nodded, still looking at Grace.

'Great,' he said, clapping his hands loudly and making Grace jump. 'We can let loose. I'll go and tell Noah we're leaving now.'

'Well done for today. I guess I'll see you at the garden party,' Tabitha said to Grace, trying to hide her disappointment.

'See you then. And thanks for being here to support me. It means a lot.'

As Tabitha gave them a hug and turned to leave, Grace caught Otis's eye. They gave him a sad smile and then went to speak to another group of visitors. Otis didn't really know Grace that well, but he felt proud of them all the same.

'So we're going to this after-party then,' Eric said urgently to the group, huddling them together. 'Apparently it's at Tabitha's house. I heard it has a cinema and a gym.'

'Otis and I spoke to Grace and I don't think they would have framed Sean,' Maeve said, keeping her voice low and bringing Eric's focus back to the matter of hand. 'They didn't seem too bothered about him knowing about them and Casper.'

'So who does that leave?' Aimee whispered.

'Noah and Cece,' Maeve said, glancing at the two of them standing awkwardly by the door as Tabitha and Casper argued about the best way of getting back to her house. 'We know that Noah has stolen before and he owed money to Sean.'

'And Sean rejected Cece the night of the party,' Otis pointed out. 'Her pride was hurt and she was embarrassed. She might have acted out of spite.'

'I tried talking to her at the pool party about it,' Maeve admitted. 'But I was useless and she didn't give anything away. Otis, you need to be the one to talk to her.'

'Seems like a nasty way to take revenge on someone turning you down,' Eric said, frowning. 'Framing Sean for a crime that might land him in prison.'

Maeve sighed. 'Yeah well, maybe Sean isn't telling us the whole story.'

'Looks like they're leaving now,' Aimee pointed out, as Tabitha and Casper pushed open the gallery door, Cece and Noah following. 'We'd better stick with them so we know where to go.'

'Come on,' Eric said excitedly, gesturing for the others to join the group of people trickling out of the door. 'Looks like a crowd is going.'

Tabitha's house was a short walk away from the art gallery, so everyone coming from the exhibition arrived at her front door en masse. From the outside it looked like a beautiful old Georgian-style house, but inside it was modern and spacious, with vast open-plan rooms, strange, angled furniture that looked uncomfortable but cool, and huge glass doors at the back so you could see out into the garden. They walked in and stood gaping at the stylish interiors.

Cece was on shoe duty, asking everyone to take off their shoes as they arrived and inviting them to make themselves at home with a smile on her face that Maeve couldn't be sure was genuine or not.

'We do ask you to keep the party downstairs,' she said in a serious tone, leaning in conspiratorially. 'Tabitha doesn't like talking about it, but we had a party recently and a very precious piece of jewelry went missing. So we'd rather no one goes wandering. Anyway, I love how you lot are just our friends now, it's like *who even are you?*'

She cackled with laughter. Eric smiled nervously, as it sounded like an insult.

'I know! It's so strange, but I guess it was fate that we met!'

'Oh my God, I so believe in destiny,' she said solemnly, placing a hand on her heart. 'We were *destined* to meet. I mean, I love music and then I meet Roxie? That's FATE. I've always wanted to be friends with a popstar. And now I am!'

'Absolutely,' Maeve said, slipping her boots off. 'You know who you should also be friends with? Our friend, Jem.'

Maeve threw her arm around Otis just as he was taking his shoe off, causing him to lose his balance. She managed to steady him before he toppled over.

'I feel like you haven't met properly,' Maeve continued, as Otis regained his composure. 'But you two should hang out and chat. I think you'd have a lot to talk about.'

'Oh, that's so sweet,' Cece said, tilting her head and giving Otis a sympathetic look. 'I'm so flattered – and Roxie, you little minx, trying to set us up! – but I'm actually seeing someone. It's only recent, but I think it could be the real deal.' She reached out to stroke Otis's arm. 'I know you'll find someone special someday. Don't give up.'

'What? No, I—'

'Oh my God, Casper,' Cece shrieked, distracted by Casper's exploits down the hall. 'Don't put your beer on there without a coaster! Hello, condensation!' She sighed, turning to the others apologetically. 'Excuse me, I have to go and do some damage control.'

Rolling her eyes and giving them a knowing smile, she hurried off to give Casper a lecture before helping Tabitha, who was raiding the drinks cabinet.

'She's seeing someone?' Eric said, attempting to hide the hole in his sock at the little toe. 'That's new information.'

'She did act coy about it at the pool party,' Maeve recalled. 'She mentioned something might be going on with someone. I did wonder at first if it might be Sean and he was keeping it secret from us.'

'I don't think so.' Otis frowned. 'He wouldn't date someone who might be framing him. He told us that he wasn't interested in her when she hit on him.'

'If you believe him.'

'I do,' Otis told her firmly, irritated by her cynical attitude towards her brother. 'It's more likely that she got angry at his rejecting her, and whoever she's seeing now has nothing to do with it. She's still a suspect.'

'If you say so,' Maeve said bluntly.

Moving away from the door as other party guests arrived, they headed into the kitchen where others were lingering, waiting for Cece to put on some music.

'What's Noah holding?' Aimee said suddenly, spotting him crouched down next to an open cupboard full of cans and tubs. 'Oh my God. That's bicarbonate of soda!'

Before anyone could comment, Aimee had wandered over to Noah and stopped right in front of him. He looked up at her, a little freaked out by her dreamy expression as she appeared.

'Um. Hey? Have we met? Like your sequins.'

'Hello, Noah,' she replied. 'You're holding a tub of bicarbonate of soda.'

'Yeah, it's for my heartburn.' He laughed, patting his chest. 'It gets bad when I drink champagne. Usually I have tablets on me, but not today and Cece says they don't have any here. So thought I'd try this alternative. Apparently half a teaspoon of this in water does the trick.'

'Do you like baking, Noah?'

'Sorry?'

'I like baking. And you seem to know a lot about bicarbonate of soda.'

'Well, that's very kind of you, but I only just found out about this whole antidote to heartburn thing. Not sure I have extensive knowledge. Although, now that you say it, I am pretty good at baking. My mum is amazing at baking, so I guess it's in my genes. Not great for my modeling career though. Have to keep an eye on the figure. Have I told you that I'm a model?'

'Do you want to do a bake-off?'

He blinked at her. 'A bake-off?'

Aimee nodded, her eyes twinkling at him. 'Yes.'

'When?'

'Now.'

'Now? What, here? At the party?'

'It will be so much fun!' Aimee exclaimed, grabbing his arm and squeezing it. 'It would be like that TV show, but instead of a tent it's a really nice kitchen.'

He laughed and found himself nodding, finding Aimee strange but her enthusiasm infectious. 'OK. You're on! What's the task?'

'A cake!' she squealed, getting a hairband out her pocket and tying her hair back. 'And then we'll get all the party guests to judge!'

'A bit of healthy competition never did anyone harm,' Noah said, reaching for an apron with chickens all over it that was hanging up on a peg. He slipped it on over his head and tied it around his waist. 'I've never thought of baking at a party before, but why the hell not? I like being spontaneous.'

'I like being spontaneous too,' Aimee said, taking another apron that had cupcakes on it and putting it on. 'Once, I auditioned for a West End musical, just because I walked past the theater and saw the sign. They literally booed me off the stage. It was such a rush.'

Noah held up his hands. 'OK, before we start, what are the ground rules?'

'Clean game, no trying to sabotage the other baker,' Aimee outlined sternly. 'Sharing is caring. If we need something that the other one has, we work out a way we can both use it.'

Noah snorted. 'That won't be a problem. In case you

forgot, we're in the Pearce household. They have a lot of everything. Look, there's even two ovens. I'll have the left one; you go right.'

'And no outside help. Should we have a time limit?'

'Obviously. No fun without pressure. Forty-five minutes should do it, including baking time.'

They agreed on the rules, then went to wash their hands, before Noah set the timer on his phone and held a finger over the start button.

'Here we go,' he said. 'Ready?'

Aimee narrowed her eyes at him, game face on. 'Oh, I'm ready.'

'Ready, set, BAKE!'

Noah pressed go and the two of them got to work, hurrying around the kitchen, throwing open cupboards as they searched for their ingredients. Aimee opened a fridge to look for butter only to find it full of water bottles. She discovered there were in fact THREE FRIDGES in the kitchen, all with different sections depending on what you were looking for.

'Aimee is baking,' Eric whispered to Otis and Maeve, as they watched the spectacle from the other side of the room. 'At a party.'

'Yeah, it's odd, but it's working,' Maeve said in a hushed response, watching Aimee dart about the kitchen.

'What's working?'

'She's bonding with Noah,' she explained, nodding at him as he laughed with Aimee when they nearly collided. 'This is exactly what we needed. I didn't think we'd have any luck cracking him, but this might just work.'

'She's very good at disarming people, isn't she?' Otis observed.

Maeve smiled. 'I don't even think she knows she's doing it.'

Aimee decided to bake a vanilla sponge cake in the shape of a panda, because she loved pandas, but there was no black food coloring so the panda was going to be pink and white. She was going to make the flavor a bit more exciting by throwing some spices into the sponge mixture, just so that her cake had an edge. Noah decided on a simple but classic chocolate cake and was going to cover it in rainbow sprinkles.

'Excellent technique,' Aimee said, observing him beat the sugar, eggs and butter together in a large bowl, while she weighed out her flour.

'Thanks!' he replied cheerily, scratching his cheek and getting some mixture across it accidentally. 'So are you, like, a really big baking fan then?'

'Yeah,' she said, picking up an egg. 'I'm quite new to it, but I'm invested. I think I'm going to be a baker. Have you always wanted to be a model?' She cracked the egg on the side of the bowl a bit too enthusiastically and it poured out of the shell all over the floor. 'Whoopsie!'

He chuckled, leaving his mixture for a moment as he greased a cake tin. 'No, it all happened recently in a bit of a whirlwind, but now I know it's definitely what I want to do.'

'It's hard, isn't it, deciding on your future. It feels quite scary.'

'I know what you mean. You wonder if you're making the right decision.' He paused, glancing over at her. 'Are you putting paprika in your mixture?'

'Yeah. Got to make your cake stand out, Noah. I don't want

mine to be like every sponge you can buy in a shop willy-nilly.'

Noah nodded thoughtfully. 'You are so right. I might add chilli flakes.' He went to search through the spice rack. 'Are your parents supportive of your baking career?'

Aimee shrugged. 'I don't know. I haven't really talked to them about it. Your parents must be really excited about you being a model.'

'Not exactly,' he said with a sigh. 'My mum doesn't think it's a "smart choice." She always says that, but I know what she means is that I'll probably fail. She clearly doesn't think I have what it takes.'

'I once knew this guy who really wanted to do the zip wire at this adventure camp and his mum didn't want him to do it. But then he did and she was really proud of him.'

Noah looked pensive as he sprinkled chilli flakes in the mixture, letting her words sink in. 'I love zip wires.'

'Me too. Although the harnesses aren't very comfy.'

'So you think my mum is secretly proud of me for going after what I want, but she's scared I'll get hurt? Interesting. Hadn't thought of it that way.' He dipped his little finger in the mix and licked it. 'This needs something else.'

'Pepper?'

'Or mustard seeds maybe.'

'What does your dad think of your modeling?' Aimee asked, as he returned to examining the spices on offer.

Noah shrugged. 'No idea. My parents aren't together and he moved away to be with his new partner and now they have a baby. He prefers his new family. We don't really speak apart from Christmases and birthdays.'

Aimee's face dropped as she stirred her mixture. 'That's so rubbish.'

'It's fine. They divorced three years ago. It was bad at the time. I lost my head a bit. But now I'm handling it better.'

'When my aunt and uncle got divorced, my cousin was so upset, she tried to skateboard to France. She only made it a couple of streets away though, before she hit a rock and had to be taken to hospital with a broken wrist.'

'Whoa.' Noah added some cumin to the bowl and stirred it in. 'I didn't run away or anything. But I did lash out and do stupid stuff. I stole some clothes and shit. My parents were furious, but I didn't care. I wanted to hurt them.' He shook his head. 'I was such an idiot.'

'You were hurting,' Aimee said simply, tasting her mix before splashing in some Cointreau that she found among the bottles on a table nearby.

Noah smiled at her gratefully. 'You know, I was talking to this guy recently and he told me I shouldn't focus on past mistakes, I should just live in the moment. "Escape the past." That's what he kept saying. It really inspired me. So I've started practicing mindfulness.'

Aimee's eyes widened. 'Is that when you learn to read other people's minds?'

'No, although that would be cool! Mindfulness is all about being in the present moment and focusing on your current situation. Sean was right. If I dwell on the past I'm wasting the time I have now. It's a shame he's not here. I think you'd really get on. You know those people who are really fun but nice too?'

'Yeah!' Aimee said, squeezing tomato paste into her mix. 'I know some of those!'

'He's like that.' He hesitated, frowning as though remembering something. 'I owe him.'

'For helping you live in the present?'

'No, I actually owe him,' he explained, opening the oven and sliding the cake tin in. 'As in money. Quite a lot actually. He sold me some really good-quality weed. I have to remember to pay him back. I wonder if he'll accept a bank transfer. Probably not. I don't know how I'll get cash to him though. My friends *cannot* know I'm meeting him. They had this big falling-out and . . .' He waved his hand. 'Never mind.'

'I can always give him the cash,' Aimee said absent-mindedly, reaching for a bowl to start mixing her icing.

'Huh?'

'I can give Sean the cash, or you can give it to Maeve to pass on if you like.' She nodded to Maeve. 'We'll probably be seeing him tonight or tomorrow.'

'How do you know Sean? And who's Maeve?'

Suddenly Aimee realized what she'd done. Gulping, she spun around to look to the others for help. Otis caught her eye across the room and recognized her panicked expression. Leaving Maeve and Eric in the corner where they were trying to pretend they were having fun, Otis made his way towards her.

'Are you all right?' Noah asked Aimee, looking at her quizzically. 'You look like you've just remembered something. Did you forget to put a timer on your cake? Because it went in shortly after mine, so you can take an accurate guess, I reckon.'

'I'm fine. I'm just' – she looked around her frantically, trying to work out a way of getting out of this situation – 'I'm just putting away the flour!'

She grabbed the bag of flour and went to walk across the kitchen, but she stepped right on the egg she'd spilled earlier and forgotten to clean up. Her foot went sliding out from under her, and as she toppled backward the large flour bag flew out of her arms. It soared up in the air, somersaulted, and then came hurtling down again, all its contents pouring out in a great, unstoppable torrent.

And it fell right on top of Otis's head.

FIFTEEN

There was a collective gasp from everyone in the room as they witnessed the spectacle and then waited in great anticipation for the white powdery cloud into which Otis had disappeared to settle and dissipate so that they might see the damage.

Coughing and spluttering, Otis emerged, entirely caked in flour. The party guests fell about laughing, while Noah quickly ran to help Aimee up from the floor.

'Oh MY GOD!' Eric exclaimed, hurrying over to Otis with Maeve. 'Are you OK?'

'No!' he yelped, desperately trying to wipe the flour off his face. 'It's everywhere! ARGH! I can taste it in my mouth! It's in my eyelashes! GET IT OFF ME!'

Eric and Maeve, who was desperately trying not to laugh, began helping him pat it off his clothes, swiping piles of it from his shoulders. The other party guests in the room continued to titter among themselves as they looked on.

'Positive from this,' Eric began, recoiling as Otis wiped his arms, releasing more flour into the air, 'you are going to be a silver fox. The gray look suits you.'

Otis rubbed his hands frantically all over his head, but no matter how much he tried to get it out, there was still a white tinge to his hair. After brushing his fingers through it one more time, he looked to Maeve for help.

'Is it better?'

She tilted her head. 'Yeah. It looks like you've aged twenty years, rather than fifty.'

'This is a nightmare! We have to go home.'

'I agree!' Aimee said, sidling up to him guiltily. 'I'm so sorry, are you all right? If it helps, you look quite good gray.'

'That's what I said.' Eric looked thoughtful, peering at him. 'You know, if I squint, you look a bit like your dad.'

'How is that helping?' Otis hissed.

'Um, hello, your dad is hot?' Eric shrugged. 'I know he's got his issues, but there's no mistaking he's a good-looking older man.'

'OK, let's stop talking about that, please,' Otis instructed, attempting to wipe flour from his forehead with the back of his arm, but to no avail since the back of his arm was also covered in flour. 'Can we go home now? My head is getting itchy. I need a shower.'

'Good idea, let's go home,' Aimee said hurriedly. 'No need to say goodbye I don't think.'

'Hang on, aren't you doing a bake-off?' Maeve pointed out, gesturing to the kitchen where Noah was attempting to wipe the slimy egg off the floor using a tea towel. 'Your cake is still in the oven.'

'It's fine! Someone else can take over. I'll let them have the credit for my creation. Otis's hair scratching is much more important.'

'But it seemed like Noah and you were getting on well.'

'Yeah, we were and it was very helpful,' she said positively.

'I've got what I need now. And I can fill you in later. But I really think now is the perfect time to leave.'

'Wait, are you going?' Noah asked, appearing behind them and making her jump. 'But we're in the middle of the bake-off.'

'I know but this is a bit of an emergency and we need to go now. It's the flour. Otis is . . . allergic. Yeah, really bad. Could die at any second. Literally keel over, no warning,' Aimee said, gesturing at Otis and ushering him towards the door.

'Seriously?' Noah looked unconvinced.

'Yep. Got to go right away.'

'Wait, you said that you would be seeing Sean?'

They stopped in their tracks. Aimee winced, gulping audibly. Maeve's eyes flashed angrily at her friend, while Eric and Otis shared a look of panic.

'Yeah, sorry, I got confused.' Aimee laughed nervously. 'I was talking about a different Sean. But hope you find a way of paying your Sean back. I'll be seeing my Sean, a different Sean, who has nothing to do with anyone here in any way. In fact, he's been out of the country for years. So we're definitely not talking about the same Sean. Nice talking to you, Noah. Bye!'

Before anyone had time to protest, Aimee grabbed Otis and steered him out of the room towards the front door, leaving Maeve and Eric to say goodbye to a very confused Noah and hurry along after them.

'Shoes on, everyone,' Aimee instructed, searching for hers in the pile by the door. 'And let's make it snappy.'

'Oh my God, what happened?' Cece came wandering out of the sitting room holding a glass of wine and stopped in her tracks when she saw the state of Otis. 'You look like you've just had a meeting with Pablo Escobar.'

'It's flour,' Otis informed her grumpily, looking for his shoes.

'Why did you take a shower in it?'

'You know what? I'm going to need to wash my face and hair before I leave,' Otis insisted. 'Cece, where is the toilet?'

She pointed at a door and he slipped through it, locking it behind him.

'I've been meaning to say, we should add each other on social media,' Cece said to the others enthusiastically while they waited, getting her phone out her pocket. 'How do I find you? Oh my God, you HAVE to add me on TikTok. I do all the dance trends.'

'That's really cool,' Eric said, hoping Otis would hurry up. 'But . . . um . . . we're not actually on TikTok.'

'Oh. You should be. It's so much fun. You can, like, go behind the scenes of celebrities' houses. I copied all of Hailey Bieber's indoor plants. What's your Instagram then?'

'We're not on Instagram either.'

She blinked at him in disbelief. 'What? You're not on either? Are you on Snapchat?'

He shook his head. Her jaw dropped.

'But . . . how do you stay in touch with people? What do you do all day? Hang on. *None* of you are on social media? At all?'

'None of us,' Maeve said, jumping in to help Eric out. 'We prefer to stay off the grid.'

Cece raised her eyebrows. 'Off the grid. But aren't you trying to make it as a musician? And, Molly, I thought you wanted to go into acting? You need a social media presence if you're going to build a fan base.' She placed a hand on her heart. 'You lot are SO lucky we met. You have so much to learn. No offense.'

'Ah, here he is!' Eric said through gritted teeth as Otis appeared. 'Come on, chop chop. We have to go.'

'But he's all clean now,' she said, gesturing to Otis. His hair was wet but he'd obviously used the hand towel in the bathroom to attempt to dry it as it was sticking up all over the place. 'Why would you need to go? If you stay, I can set you all up with profiles. Honestly, it's SO weird that none of you have any social media. Like, how is that possible?'

'Maeve!' Noah called out, appearing in the hallway looking delighted with himself. 'It's just come to me! Sean's sister.'

Cece blinked at him. 'What are you talking about, Noah?'

He pointed at Aimee. 'She mentioned Maeve and I couldn't work out why that sounded familiar at first, and I've just remembered! Sean said he had a sister named Maeve. You're not talking about a different Sean at all, are you?'

'Hang on!' Cece held up her hands. 'You lot know Sean?'

'No,' Maeve began, shaking her head. 'No, we—'

'Why did you say you could pass on the cash to him then?' Noah asked, looking at Aimee.

Aimee looked panicked, her eyes darting to Maeve, desperate to come up with an excuse but she couldn't think of anything. Tabitha came wandering into the hallway and stopped on noticing everyone standing tensely. Casper had been following her absent-mindedly and bumped into her back as she halted without warning.

'What's going on?' Tabitha asked, glancing from Cece to Maeve.

'This lot know Sean,' Noah proclaimed.

Tabitha stared at them wide-eyed. 'You do? Why wouldn't you say?'

'No, we—' Maeve began, but Tabitha cut her off.

'Is that why you were asking me all those questions by the pool?' she gasped, pointing accusingly at Otis.

'Hang on.' Casper stepped forward and pointed at Maeve. 'She asked me loads of questions at the pool party as well.'

'And I just baked a cake with her,' Noah added, narrowing his eyes at Aimee and stroking his chin. 'So that could mean something too.'

'It doesn't mean anything,' Maeve said firmly. 'We're just leaving.'

'Not until you explain yourselves,' Tabitha demanded, folding her arms. 'Why didn't you tell us you knew Sean?'

'Is this why you're not on social media?' Cece asked suddenly. 'You don't want us to find out your connection to Sean!'

'Wait.' Noah's jaw dropped. 'Are you *spies*?'

Maeve gave him a strange look. 'No, we're not spies. We just . . .'

She trailed off and clenched her jaw, looking down at the ground. The game was up. Their cover was blown. What was the point in weaving any more lies? They weren't going to tell them anything now.

'I'm Sean's sister, Maeve,' she revealed, before gesturing to the others. 'These are my friends.'

'*Oh my God*,' Tabitha uttered, looking stunned.

'We wanted to talk to you and we didn't think you'd speak to us if you knew who we really were,' Maeve explained, deflated.

190

'What the fuck?' Casper said, disgusted at them. 'Who does that?'

'Sean didn't steal the necklace,' Eric announced, prompting Maeve to scowl at him, but he didn't notice. 'We wanted to help him prove his innocence and find the real thief!'

'We thought that maybe we could find out something about that night at the party that might help Sean,' Otis jumped in, attempting to soften Eric's words with his own. 'We know it wasn't him and we just wanted to find the truth, that's all.'

Maeve looked down at the ground, shaking her head. They were making things worse. Casper cackled loudly.

'I'm sorry,' he said, sneering at them. 'You think Sean didn't steal the necklace and one of us did? Have you met the prick?'

Otis noticed Tabitha flinch at this comment, still clearly instinctively protective of Sean, whether she wanted to be or not.

'You lot need to get out right now,' Casper continued, pointing to the door. 'And stay away from us.'

'We won't stop until we get the truth,' Eric announced heroically.

'Get out of my house,' Tabitha seethed, lifting her eyes to meet Maeve's.

'With pleasure,' Maeve replied.

Under the stunned, silent gaze of Tabitha and her friends, they filed out of the door, slamming it behind them. No one said anything until they were halfway down the road.

'What the hell, Aimee?' Maeve began, throwing her arms up in the air. 'Why did you tell Noah about Sean?'

'It just slipped out!' she whined, burying her face in her

hands. 'I was concentrating on making my cake and I got all distracted and he said he needed to pay Sean back but he didn't know when he'd next see him.'

'He admitted that he owed Sean cash?' Otis asked.

'Yeah. He wanted to pay him back because he liked him,' Aimee said, downcast that she'd ruined everything. 'He said that Sean was really fun and nice, and that he'd helped him to live in the present. He told me about the stealing, but he only did it because he was going through a hard time with his parents. He sounded like he really regretted doing it. I don't think he'd steal anything now. His parents were divorcing; he was upset. He wants to contact Sean so he can pay him back, but I think he's scared that the group will get mad at him if he does.' Aimee turned to face Maeve in distress. 'I'm so sorry, Maeve! I feel terrible for letting it slip that we know Sean!'

'It's OK, Aimee,' Otis said when Maeve didn't reply. 'They were bound to find out somehow.'

'But what are we going to do now?' Aimee wailed. 'We haven't spoken to Cece properly and now none of them will tell us anything!'

'We'll work out a different way of getting through to them,' Otis told her confidently.

'No, we won't,' Maeve declared. 'It's time to give up.'

The others stared at her as she turned on her heel and began marching away.

'What do you mean?' Eric asked, as they followed her in confusion.

'We've done what we can, but we've failed,' Maeve repeated,

looking straight ahead with a stony expression. 'The best thing we can do is leave it.'

'Why?' Otis asked, hurrying to fall into step with her. 'As Aimee said, we haven't spoken to Cece yet and there's still time—'

'Time for what?' Maeve asked, stopping to face him angrily. 'To prove Sean didn't do this?'

'Well, yeah!'

'So after everything, you're still convinced that one of them' – she jabbed her finger back down the road in the direction of Tabitha's house – 'stole the diamond necklace? Really?'

Otis took a deep breath. 'Tabitha looked upset at Casper calling Sean a name. That suggests there was a real connection between her and Sean. Why would Sean do something that would hurt her?'

Maeve laughed loudly, shaking her head. 'You are so blind! You think Sean wouldn't hurt someone he cares about, Otis? Is that what you think? Well, let me put you straight on that one. *He wouldn't think twice.*' She swallowed the lump in her throat, scanning the startled faces of her friends. 'You don't know him. I told you right at the start that he was capable of doing something like this and not one thing that we've found out has suggested otherwise. For all we know, he did take the necklace and then he sold it on, never to be found again. He could have the cash stashed away somewhere secret and he's just waiting for the police to stop sniffing around until he takes it and runs.'

'I don't believe he's done that,' Otis said firmly. 'He wouldn't have asked us to come all this way—'

'He didn't, he asked me,' she corrected him.

'He wouldn't let us go to all this trouble—'

'Look,' she interjected sharply. 'It's better we leave it now and protect ourselves from any further disappointment. Because that's the only way this ends. Trust me on that.'

Eric and Aimee both shifted uncomfortably, not knowing what to say. Otis took a moment to collect himself.

'Maeve,' Otis began quietly, stepping closer to her. 'We're so close to the truth. I'm sorry that Sean's disappointed you in the past. I wish he hadn't ever let you down. I wish no one had.' He paused, noticing her expression soften. 'I think we still have a chance to find out the truth. Remember, we agreed that it would be good to find out either way.'

'We've come this far,' Eric added gently. 'And Otis is right, we're really close. I can feel it in my bones.'

'That's amazing,' Aimee whispered. 'Like a fifth sense?'

'Sixth.'

'Bloody hell!' She gawped at him. 'How many extra ones do you have?'

Maeve couldn't help but smile at Aimee's amazement.

'What do you say?' Otis asked hopefully. 'We just have Cece left to talk to. One more shot?'

'Fine. One more shot.' Maeve sighed, walking on again with Otis beside her, and Eric and Aimee quietly high-fiving behind. 'But when this all goes tits up, don't say I didn't warn you.'

SIXTEEN

'Otis!'

They'd been walking for a while from Tabitha's house when they heard Otis's name being called out. They could have got the bus back to the hotel, but it was such a nice day, and after Maeve and Otis's tense exchange there seemed to be an unspoken, mutual agreement that walking things off might be a good idea. Plus, they had nothing to rush back for. Except Otis, who rather wanted a proper shower to make sure he got all the flour off.

It took Otis a moment to work out who was calling out his name, but then he spotted the hotel receptionist approaching them down the road, waving wildly at him.

'Helen!' Otis said in surprise as the group came to a halt when she got near.

'It is Otis, right?' She smiled up at him, clutching the strap of her shoulder bag.

'That's the one,' he said, giving her a thumbs up. 'You're not at the hotel.'

'Observant,' Maeve muttered under her breath. Otis blushed, trying to ignore her.

'I've finished my shift,' she explained, beaming at him. 'I have a message for you though. Your mum called.'

Otis's face fell. '*What?*'

'Yeah, she called the hotel earlier. She wanted to make sure you were OK.'

'Oh my God.' He ran a hand through his hair, utterly mortified, while Eric winced behind him, feeling his pain. 'I am so sorry. What . . . what did she say?'

'She said that she hadn't heard from you and she was worried,' Helen informed him. 'But don't worry! I told her that I'd seen you this morning, alive and well, and that you were with your friends.'

'Ah.' Otis grimaced. 'Did you say who I was with exactly? Or did you happen to keep that vague?'

'I told her that the four of you were in one room, two girls and two boys. She seemed a bit surprised and then said that if I saw you, to pass on the message that she hopes you're having fun, but being careful.'

Maeve desperately tried not to laugh. Eric clasped a hand over his mouth, while Aimee sniggered next to him. Otis closed his eyes in despair.

'She's nice, your mum,' Helen continued. 'Her voice is very calming.'

'It is, isn't it?' Eric said enthusiastically. 'I've always thought that.'

'Thanks for passing on the message,' Otis said, finally able to speak. 'I'm so sorry she bothered you.'

'It's no problem. Like I said, she was nice and I was really bored. I'd been googling pictures of guinea pigs for, like, an hour when she called.' Helen shrugged, smiling at him. 'Are you on your way back to the hotel?'

'Yeah. It's been a long day.'

She nodded. 'I was just on my way to the arcade to meet a friend. I was going to ask if you wanted to join us.'

'Wait, what?' Eric gasped excitedly. 'There's an arcade here?'

Helen gave him a strange look, pointing over his shoulder. He spun around to see they had walked straight past the arcade, just a few meters away.

'How did I miss it?' He turned to face the others. 'Please can we go in? I love arcades!'

'I don't know,' Otis said, glancing at Maeve. 'We have things to talk through.'

'Does the arcade have those machines with the claws?' Aimee asked Helen. 'I love those. When he was little, this guy I know once got stuck inside one.'

'What, *in* the machine?' Eric checked.

'Yeah.' She nodded. 'I thought maybe they managed to fish him out using the claw, but apparently they had to call out the fire brigade.'

'Yeah, they definitely have those machines,' Helen informed her.

'Could be fun,' Aimee said hopefully to Maeve. 'Blow off some steam.'

Maeve chewed her thumbnail. Going to the arcade wasn't exactly what she'd had in mind for the rest of the day. Although saying that, she hadn't actually thought of anything better to do. If they were going to take one last shot at Cece, then they had to come up with a plan of how they were going to talk to her, now that their cover was blown. But it was still early and the idea of sitting in the hotel room, staring miserably at the grimy walls all night trying to brainstorm, wasn't exactly all that tempting.

'It's completely up to you, Maeve,' Otis said gently, as the others waited for her answer in great anticipation. 'Do you want to go?'

'All right,' she said eventually. 'Why not?'

'Great!' Helen exclaimed, speaking directly to Otis. 'Let's go!'

They naturally fell into step together and Aimee linked her arm through Maeve's. Listening to Aimee and Eric talk excitedly about their love of arcades, Maeve watched Otis as he furiously typed and sent a message on his phone – she assumed to his mum – and then began chatting to Helen. Maeve experienced a stab of irritation as Helen threw her head back and laughed at something he said. Whatever it was, it couldn't have been *that* funny.

As they entered the busy arcade, Maeve knew immediately it was a mistake.

It was huge, with bright lights and colorful, noisy machines everywhere you looked, and techno music blasting through the speakers. She scowled as a kid pushed past her, eager to be next in the queue for a stupid car game, while someone nearby screamed at a pinball machine. Aimee squealed in excitement and she and Eric got to work scanning the room for the best games on offer. Maeve watched Helen say something to Otis, touch him on the arm and then walk off.

Otis watched her go, turned around and caught Maeve staring. Her cheeks flushing, she quickly pretended to be looking at something else. He came to stand next to her.

'Helen's gone to find her friend.'

'Great.'

'So what do you think?' Otis asked, gesturing around them.

Maeve sniffed. 'I hate arcades.'

'Why doesn't that surprise me?' He laughed, joining her in following Aimee and Eric as they moved away. 'Arcades are fun.'

'They're inconsequential,' she muttered. 'Nothing more than a pointless and mind-numbing diversion from the mundane reality we're forced to navigate.'

'And that's not a good thing?'

She rolled her eyes. 'Let me guess, you're about to start a sentence with "studies have shown."'

'Studies have shown that gaming can boost multitasking and decision-making skills,' he said, his lips twitching into a smile. 'It helps muscle memory, hand–eye coordination, and has been known to reduce stress. Not to mention the social connections we make through gaming and the satisfaction that comes from being a part of a group effort. It is also, as you mention, escapism. You know what gaming is a bit like?'

'Hitting your head against the wall repetitively while someone shines a torch in your eyes?'

'It could be compared to books.'

'*What?*'

'Just as books offer stories into which we can escape, stimulating our minds, sharpening our intellect and encouraging imagination, so do video games,' he said enthusiastically, trying not to shudder under her cold, hard stare. 'They have characters, storylines and world-building.' He paused before adding, 'You could even argue that books are also – how did you put it? Oh yeah – a "mind-numbing diversion from the mundane reality we're forced to navigate."'

Maeve scowled. 'You really are a dickhead, Otis.'

He burst out laughing. 'Only sometimes.'

'Shouldn't you be enjoying the company of your new friend Helen?'

'And miss out on passionate debate over the frivolity of mindless entertainment? Nah,' he said with a wave of his hand. 'I'll stick with you. Anyway, I feel a sense of duty.'

'What, towards me?'

'No, towards the arcade,' he emphasized, gesturing to the games they were passing. 'Hardly fair to let you bad-mouth it when you are yet to experience its delights.'

Maeve snorted, rolling her eyes. 'Did you message your mum? I saw you typing something crossly.'

He looked pained. 'I had to tell her how embarrassing it was that she'd called the hotel. Why can't she just take a step back from my life? Other parents seem to manage it.'

'I know it's none of my business, but she means well. I get that she's a bit . . . much.'

'That's an understatement,' he muttered.

'She's looking out for you. When you love someone, that's what you do. You might not think you need it but, trust me, everyone does.'

Otis was slightly taken aback by her sincerity, not knowing what to say. She smiled at him and then they were both distracted by Eric and Aimee, who announced their mutual decision to start with a dance game, largely because they both claimed to be the best at it. After slotting their coins in the machine, they took their positions side by side.

'Oh yes,' Eric said, getting in the zone, rolling his shoulders and clapping his hands. 'This is my happy place, my friend. I am so ready for this.'

'Me too,' Aimee said, staring at the screen in front of her with steely determination.

Music pumping, the game started and Eric and Aimee launched into it with boundless enthusiasm, matching their steps on the arrows on the dance platform to the cues up on the screen. Otis and Maeve stood aside watching, entertained by their sheer vivacity. As Eric cried out, 'SMASHING IT,' Maeve couldn't help but laugh, looking down at her shoes, trying to hide that she was enjoying this.

'How good are you at car games?' Otis asked, nodding towards a machine that had just become free.

'Better than you probably.'

'Oh yeah? Prove it.'

Otis dragged her over to the game and she plonked herself down in the fake car seat, which was weirdly comfortable, while he put some coins in to start it up. Grabbing the steering wheel jutting out in front of her, she selected the car she wanted and waited for the countdown to the race.

'I hope you're ready, Wiley,' Otis said playfully. 'I'm a demon behind the wheel.'

'Of a fake car in a video game.'

'Downplay it all you want. I'll be the one laughing when you lose.'

Maeve gripped the steering wheel a little tighter, suddenly

set on winning this stupid game and wiping that annoying little smirk off his face. *Oh, it's on, Milburn.*

With a roaring rev of the fake engines through the game speakers, the race started and Maeve slammed her foot down on the pedal. She quickly learned that the wheel was very sensitive and turning it too much left her viewpoint spinning all over the place.

'Fucking hell!' she cried out when she'd gone smashing into the side. 'Why can't you reverse on this thing?'

Otis chuckled at her reactions before throwing his hands up in celebration as his car soared past the finishing line. Maeve came in third.

'Unlucky,' Otis said, giving her a sympathetic look. 'Never mind. I guess car games aren't really your thing.'

She narrowed her eyes at him. 'Cocky little shit. Best of three?'

He pretended to think about it and then broke into a wide grin. 'Deal.'

Otis forgot that Maeve was a fast learner and had no time to laugh during the second race, considering they were neck and neck for most of it. Nailing the last corner, Maeve took the lead and zipped across the finish line with a cry of 'Noooooo!' from her disgruntled opponent.

By the last race, Eric and Aimee had come over to spectate and were standing behind them, cheering them on so loudly that both gamers felt under intense pressure. Maeve was steady and focused; Otis erratic but skilled. It was a nerve-wracking ordeal for everyone, but Maeve crept ahead at the end and took the win.

'YES!' she cried, punching the air and turning to get a high-five from Aimee.

Otis buried his head in his hands. 'How did this happen?' he whimpered.

'Want to have a go at the dance game?' Aimee asked Maeve as she pushed herself up off the car seat.

'I'm not a dancer.'

'You weren't a racing driver until a moment ago,' she pointed out. 'Come on, it will be fun!'

'I shall challenge Otis on the track,' Eric declared, taking Maeve's place behind the wheel before gazing up at Aimee. 'You were a worthy dance adversary. I have never seen anyone use so much arm movement before.'

'Sorry again about hitting you in the face.'

'Never apologize for being passionate,' he said, stolid and serious. 'Right, Oatcake, let's burn some rubber.'

Leaving Otis to claw his driving reputation back from the brink, Maeve reluctantly followed Aimee back over to the dance game, but it was being used by another pair so they stood and waited nearby.

'I thought you didn't like arcades,' Aimee commented, nudging Maeve. 'You were proper smiling then, and don't pretend you weren't because I saw it with my very own eyes.'

'It turns out I needed a bit of mindless escapism.'

Maeve's phone started ringing and the caller ID came up on the screen: 'Idiot Brother.' She quickly silenced it and put her phone away. She knew she'd have to speak to Sean some time and tell him what had happened today. But not right now.

Aimee groaned as one of the girls on the dance machine put

in more coins for another round. 'We're going to be waiting a while now. I don't think that should be allowed, you know. Do you think I should ask her to sod off so we can have a turn?'

Maeve was too distracted to answer, looking over to the car game where Otis and Eric were now talking to Helen and her friend. Otis had stood up and was leaning with one arm on the back of the car seat.

Aimee saw them and glanced in concern at Maeve. 'I'm sure they're just talking about really boring stuff like hotel towels or something.' She hesitated. 'Are you OK?'

'Yeah, course,' Maeve replied. 'Why wouldn't I be?'

Aimee nodded, deciding not to push it. 'Want to go and play another game while we wait for this one? We could try to win something with the claw.'

Maeve tore her eyes away from Helen's smile as her phone started ringing. It was Sean again. When she didn't pick up, it rang off and almost immediately her phone vibrated with a message from him.

> Hey, any updates?
> Police questioned me again today
> I know they think I did it
> Coming to see you at the hotel

'Shit,' she said, reading it. 'He's gone to the hotel. We have to go.'

'But we're not there! Tell him not to come.'

'I can't, Aimee.'

'Why not?'

204

'What am I supposed to say, we're not there because we're having a laugh down the arcade?' Maeve snapped. She ran a hand through her hair. 'Sorry, I didn't mean to be short. I feel guilty, that's all.'

'It's OK.' Aimee gave her a kind smile and took Maeve's hand in hers. 'Let's go back to the hotel to meet him.'

'Thank you.'

As they approached the boys, they found Eric having a great time, now racing Helen's friend, who appeared to be outrageously good at the game, while Otis chatted to Helen. He was in the middle of asking her about her pets when he noticed Maeve behind him.

'Hey! How was the dancing?'

'Nonexistent.'

'Helen was just telling me that she has five hamsters.'

'I'm really into rodents,' Helen said, nodding.

'Wow.' Maeve cleared her throat. 'Look, I have to go back to the hotel. Sean is heading there already, so I should go and meet him.'

'Oh! Right, OK.'

'You should stay here though,' Maeve stated quickly, before he could tell her that he didn't want to go with her. She'd save them all the awkwardness of that exchange. 'There's no point us all going back. We only just got here.'

'No,' Otis began, frowning. 'We should—'

'Honestly, it's fine,' she interrupted. 'You two stay here with Helen and we'll see you back there later.'

Otis was taken aback by her insistence. 'OK then. See you later.'

Maeve nodded and turned on her heel to leave, Aimee rushing after her. Aimee waited until they had left the dark cave of the arcade and had stepped into the warm early-evening air before asking her question.

'Why did you tell them they should stay?'

'I don't need them to come back.'

'Yeah, but we're all in this together, aren't we? They probably wanted to come back and see Sean too. And make sure you're OK.'

'I'm not going to force Otis to leave a date to help me out. And Eric loves arcades; it's not fair for me to deny them any chance of having fun while we're here. It's fine, honestly.'

'OK, but I don't think Otis is on a date,' Aimee asserted. 'She's only just broken up with her boyfriend and she's clearly not over it. She's still checking his social media. She probably just likes Otis because, through his advice, he's helped her feel positive and hopeful and safe again. Isn't that a thing, people developing feelings for their therapist?'

Maeve was looking at her in wonder. What she'd said was so . . . astute.

'I know what it's called!' Aimee continued brightly, oblivious to Maeve's admiration. 'Transformers.'

'Transference,' Maeve corrected quietly.

'That's what I said.' She nodded. 'She's probably projecting her feelings on to her therapist, Otis. You know, I can't believe she has five hamsters. She must have balls all over her house.'

'What?'

'You know, those plastic balls you put hamsters in and then they just roll all over the place?'

'No.'

'We had a class hamster at primary school called Hank, right, and we'd put him in this green plastic ball and let him roam free. He was perfectly safe in there, just rolling about the place in this big green ball.' She paused, frowning in thought. 'I wonder what happened to Hank.'

'I'm sure he's still having a lovely time rolling about in his ball,' Maeve said, patting Aimee's arm.

'I still think you should have given Otis and Eric the chance to come with us. Helen could have come too and then afterwards we could have gone back to hers to meet the five hamsters. I do like animals with whiskers.'

Aimee talked about hamsters for most of the journey back to the hotel, which Maeve felt was really quite impressive, considering there's not that much to say about them. Sean was there when they arrived, sitting on the ground by their room door, his back against the wall. He was smoking weed. They could smell it before they got to him.

'Hey, Frog-face,' he said with a lopsided grin, not bothering to stand. 'Did you lose your phone? I've been trying to reach you, but it would seem you can't be reached.'

'I got your message and came straight here. I didn't want you waiting around.'

'That is most considerate, thank you.' He held out the joint. 'You want some?'

'No,' Maeve said, frowning.

'I'll have some,' Aimee declared, stepping forward and bending down to take it from his fingers. 'Thanks!'

'You're welcome.' He slowly got to his feet. 'Are we going to go in then? Or stand out here and chat?'

'You can't smoke that in the room.'

Sean snorted as Aimee passed the joint back to him. 'What, because it's so classy in there? *Gracias*, Aimee.'

'It's a non-smoking room.'

'Trust me, Froggy, that room needs a powerful scent to mask whatever else the fuck it smells like.' He chuckled. 'Let's bend the rules just this once, eh?'

Maeve didn't say anything, getting out the room key from her bag and brushing past him to unlock the door.

'Did I mention you both look really good?' Sean said, slumping down on the sofa as soon as he was in the room. 'It must be fun dressing up every day to play these characters you've made up. Although, your character isn't too different to you, is it, Froggy? I mean, you're just a heightened version of yourself. Lots of dark colors and angry expressions.'

'You look good too,' Aimee said nervously, slightly worried about how he would react when they told him she'd let the secret slip to Noah. 'I like your jacket. Is that the one the box was found in?'

'The very one,' he nodded. 'You know what, you can have it if I go to prison. Won't have much use for it in there.'

'What did the police say today?' Maeve asked, standing in front of him and crossing her arms.

'The usual.' He brushed off her question with a wave of his hand. 'They're deluded twats who want the case closed. No doubt Tabitha's father is breathing down their necks to get it solved. I'm the only lead they have, but no sign of the necklace. One of the avenues they've decided to go down is that Amit and I could be in it together. So that's great, because now I've dragged him into this mess, and all he did was offer me a place to stay.'

'We never questioned Amit,' Aimee pointed out, propping up the pillows behind her as she sat down on the bed. 'He was at the party too, right?'

'Yeah, but it wasn't him,' Sean said firmly. 'Like I said to Officer What's-his-name, firstly, Amit was only there for all of a few minutes, and Tabitha was wearing the necklace then. She only put it in the box later that night. Secondly, he's my mate. A good mate. He wouldn't put me through all this. So you can cancel him off your suspect list.' He gestured to the pictures of the group still up on the wall. 'Speaking of our dashing suspects, any leads yet, Miss Marple?'

'We've spoken to everyone but Cece,' Maeve said, shifting uncomfortably and dropping her hands to pick at her nails. 'None of them seem to have a motive to get back at you.'

Sean smiled in disbelief before taking a long drag. He exhaled, shaking his head.

'They were all hiding something,' Maeve continued, perching on the edge of the bed to explain, 'but it's not what you think. They were pretty convincing.'

'You talked to them properly?'

Aimee nodded. 'But we still have to talk to Cece. We're going to find a way to—'

'No, it wasn't her,' he said.

'Why not?' Maeve asked, watching him carefully.

He looked up at her as though she was stupid. 'Because hers was the weakest fucking motive. To do all this because I turned her down that night? It was tenuous at best.'

'And that's the truth?'

'Sorry?'

'About you and Cece? I just want to make sure that you're telling us the truth. Were you sleeping with her as well as Tabitha? If you were, you need to tell us now. Because then she would have a motive. She'd want to get back at you and back at Tabitha at the same time.'

'Bloody hell, Froggy, where's this coming from? No, I wasn't. Like I said to you the first time, I wouldn't do that.'

'Wouldn't you?'

His smile faded. 'No.'

'Fine.' Maeve took a deep breath.

'You believe me, right? About Cece. I promise, Maeve, I wasn't—'

'Promises don't mean shit, Sean,' Maeve snapped. 'They're just words.'

'All right.' He held up his hands. 'I came here to see how you were getting on because I could do with some good news. I think I'll leave you to it, because clearly you're not in the mood for a little chat.'

'Just so we're all clear,' Maeve went on, staring him down. 'If we speak to Cece and she doesn't have a convincing reason to frame you, then that leaves . . . no other suspects.'

Sean grimaced, shaking his head. 'We're missing something.'

'We've spoken to all of them, Sean, and none of them had any motive to frame you.'

'Someone isn't being honest. They must have lied to you. That lot are very good at putting on a facade, Froggy, don't forget that. Candor isn't exactly their thing.'

'Are you sure *you're* telling us everything?'

'Yes!' he cried, exasperated. 'I've told you everything I know! One of them' – he pointed his joint in the direction of the pictures up on the wall – 'is lying to you.'

'I don't think they are, Sean. And the only person left is Cece and you've just told us it can't possibly be her!'

'Look,' he said, taking a drag and exhaling a plume of smoke, 'maybe you can talk to them individually again, try to catch them out—'

'We can't,' Maeve snapped. 'They know who we are.'

He frowned. 'What do you mean?'

'It was an accident—' Aimee began quietly, but Maeve spoke over her.

'They found out that I'm your sister,' she explained. 'As you can imagine, they were pretty pissed off.'

'How did they find that out?' Sean said, furious.

'They were always going to find out eventually, Sean,' Maeve replied, refusing to let Aimee get a word in. 'It's a miracle we lasted as those stupid characters as long as we did. And it doesn't matter, because we spoke to all of them when they thought we had nothing to do with you, and they have no motives to land you in jail.'

'What do you mean it doesn't matter?' Sean exploded, leaping to his feet. 'Now that they know who you are, that's it! We're all locked out! How the fuck are we going to find out the truth now? Do you know what this means for me? Do you even care?'

'*Do I even care?*' Maeve repeated, standing up to face him

with her fists clenched, prompting Sean to take a step back, immediately regretting his words. 'My friends have given up their time to help you! We came all this way! We dressed up and we lied, and we pried into people's lives for *you*. Tell me you would do the same for me!'

'Fine, I get it. But I'm about to go to prison for something I didn't do! One of them is lying and now we've fucked up my only chance of finding out who!'

'None of them wanted to frame you, Sean!'

'I didn't steal the necklace, Maeve!'

'I don't believe you!'

Sean stared at her. Maeve didn't flinch. Aimee gulped audibly, the silence deafening and unbearable to her. Sean eventually stepped back and lifted the joint to his lips, taking a long drag and looking Maeve up and down.

'Guess you've proven me right on one thing then,' he said, stepping around her and walking to the door.

Maeve frowned, turning to face him. 'What's that?'

'What I've always told you, Frog-face. In this life, you and me' – he flung open the door and stepped out into the night, leaving a trail of smoke in his wake – 'we'll always be alone.'

SEVENTEEN

'Why does it smell of weed in here?' Otis asked.

Sean had only been gone a few minutes when he and Eric arrived back at the hotel carrying a shopping bag. Aimee had crawled down the bed to sit next to Maeve, who rested her head on Aimee's shoulder.

'You're back!' Aimee exclaimed.

'What are you doing here?' Maeve asked, confused to see them so soon. 'I thought you were staying on at the arcade.'

'As much as you tried to get rid of us, we decided that the arcade wasn't very fun and we'd much rather be hanging out in our gross hotel room with you,' Otis replied. 'Where's Sean? Is he still coming here?'

'He's left,' Maeve said glumly.

'It didn't go well,' Aimee informed them, making a face.

'We had a feeling it might not be very fun for you when you saw him, Maeve,' Eric said solemnly.

'Did you tell him that they know who you are now?' Otis asked cautiously.

Maeve nodded. 'Yep. And I told him I didn't believe that he didn't take the necklace. It was a really heartwarming family moment. You missed out.'

She lifted her hand to her mouth and bit her thumbnail.

Otis and Eric exchanged a look. Aimee put her arm around Maeve and squeezed her close. After a minute or so of no one speaking, Eric cleared his throat.

'When you left, Otis and I were chatting and we realized that you'd done a lot for us on this trip, Maeve,' he began, eager to provide some light relief. 'The drag night, the arcade – all the fun nights we've had this week were *our* idea of fun. Not yours. But you'd gone along with it to make us happy.'

'You've got a lot on your plate right now and you deserve to do what *you* think is fun too,' Otis said. 'We knew that the conversation with Sean probably wouldn't be . . . uh . . . easy, so we thought to ourselves, we need to give Maeve a night off. So what is her "thing"? What's her "scene"? What can we do that is her idea of a fun night?'

Maeve snorted. 'What are you talking about?'

'First, we need sustenance,' Eric declared, reaching into the bag and pulling out pancakes, whipped cream and chocolate chips. 'So we popped to the shop and stocked up on your favorite meal.'

Maeve smiled in spite of herself, catching the pack of pancakes that he threw to her. She felt completely drained after the confrontation with Sean and hadn't realized how hungry she was.

'And second, we thought that your perfect evening would be a night in with a good book,' Otis revealed with a grin. 'That's where Helen came in.'

'Helen?' Aimee wrinkled her nose. 'She helped with the plan?'

Otis nodded. 'Yes, she did. We explained to her that we

wanted to do something that would cheer you up and when we mentioned your love of books, she suggested the perfect idea: book club.'

'Book club!' Aimee repeated excitedly. 'Are we in one?'

'We are now.'

Otis dug into the bag and pulled out four identical printouts of photocopied and stapled book chapters. He passed one to Maeve, one to Aimee, one to Eric and kept the last one for himself, tucking it under his arm.

'Anneke, Helen's friend who we met at the arcade, is studying English and History at uni,' Eric said. 'She had a couple of books in her car from her course. Otis picked this one for you and then when we came back to the hotel, Helen went and photocopied the first few chapters for each of us.'

'So tonight our first official meeting of the Wiley Book Club will consist of delicious pancakes while we read and then discuss chapters one to three of Jane Austen's *Emma*,' Otis announced.

'I've always wanted to be in a book club!' Aimee exclaimed, clutching the chapters to her chest. 'My mum used to be in one and all these women would come to the house, drink wine and bitch about their partners.' She hesitated, pulling a face and adding, 'I learned a lot about my dad those evenings. Anyway, this is going to be so much fun!'

'What do you think, Maeve?' Eric asked hopefully. 'You want to be a part of the Wiley Book Club? Your name is in the title, so it might be a bit awkward if you don't.'

Maeve smiled, looking down at the photocopied first page of chapter one in her lap. She didn't know what to say. Hot tears prickled behind her eyes. She blinked them back before daring to look up at Eric and Otis.

'I would love to be a part of the book club,' she said. 'You really didn't have to do this.'

'Yeah,' Otis said gently, 'we did.'

'Right,' Eric said, putting his hands on his hips. 'Where shall we gather for the first meeting?'

'I reckon we can all fit on the bed,' Aimee suggested, moving back so there was more space. 'Can we have pancakes now or are they to be eaten during the discussion?'

While Eric and Aimee discussed logistics, Maeve caught Otis's eye.

'Thank you,' she mouthed. He smiled at her.

She shuffled to the back of the bed and leaned back against the pillow, sitting cross-legged and balancing the chapters on her legs. Playing with her necklace, she began to read the first lines of one of her favorite novels.

Emma Woodhouse, handsome, clever, and rich, with a comfortable home and happy disposition, seemed to unite some of the best blessings of existence; and had lived nearly twenty-one years in the world with very little to distress or vex her.

As Maeve lost herself in the world of Miss Woodhouse, all the heartache and bitterness of her own disappeared, if just for a while.

And that meant everything.

The next morning Maeve announced a decision that shocked the group.

'Today we're going to find Cece and we're going to talk to her.'

'Really?' Otis paused midway through brushing his teeth.

'I thought after your chat with Sean, you wouldn't want to keep going with the plan,' Aimee admitted, sipping from the polystyrene cup clutched in her hands. She'd been up much earlier than the others again and set off on her usual tea run.

'Yesterday I said we'd give it one more shot, and I'm a woman of my word,' Maeve said firmly.

She didn't feel the need to mention the other reason she'd come to her decision. Despite the calm that the evening book club had presented, as soon as she'd gone to bed her mind had been flooded with images of Sean's face when she told him she didn't believe him. He'd looked so betrayed, so shocked. But it was his parting words that had really affected her:

'*In this life, you and me, we'll always be alone.*'

Maeve didn't want that, for either of them. If they gave up now and went home, he'd be right. He'd be on his own. If she saw this through, then at least she could say she tried, and he could say she'd been there.

'We're going to try to find out the truth, either way,' she continued, 'and we have no option but to do it as ourselves. No more lies; no more pretending. I have a feeling that it might work out for the better that way.'

Otis finished his teeth and came to stand in the doorway of

the bathroom, looking impressed. 'What makes you say that?'

'Emma Woodhouse,' she said, smiling at him. 'Messing with people's lives on the sly got her nowhere, even if she was just trying to help. I think Austen is telling me that it's time to cut the bullshit.'

'That does sound like something Jane Austen would say.' Otis chuckled. 'And I'm not going to mess with her advice. Let's do it.'

As they went to get coffee and breakfast in their usual cafe, they moved on to the next issue: they hadn't made any plans with the group to meet up.

'In the gallery, Tabitha mentioned to Grace about a gala,' Otis recalled, frowning as he did his best to remember their conversation. 'Grace said they couldn't come to the gala today, but they'd be at the garden party tomorrow.'

'What's a gala? Like a ball?' Eric asked.

'It can be. It's more like a fundraising event,' Aimee explained, buttering a crumpet. 'You organize a big, fancy do and then invite loads of people who will donate money to your cause. My parents used to go to them all the time. It's a great place to find out the most up-to-date gossip. At one of them, there was this huge drama because someone found out her friend was having an affair with her husband. She threw red wine in both their faces and then there was a scuffle and the husband had to go to hospital with a broken nose after. They raised a lot of money for the rainforests though.'

'OK, that's . . . intense,' Eric said, as Maeve and Otis shared a smile. 'But I guess a place where you hear gossip is somewhere we want to be right now. Where do you think it will be held? How are we going to find out?'

With an expression of fierce concentration, Aimee whipped out her phone and began typing furiously into it, before her face lit up and she displayed her screen to the table.

'Here you go. A charity gala to raise money to support a number of art and culture programs in the city. It's in the Slade Hotel and starts at two o'clock. There will be a champagne afternoon tea and a silent auction.'

'Whoa, Aimee,' Eric said, amazed. 'That was brilliant! Fast work!'

'I have a talent for tracking things down online. If you ever need to find out who your ex is dating, you can ask me,' she said, putting her phone down on the table and taking a large bite of her crumpet.

'I'll keep that in mind.' Eric laughed, turning to Otis and Maeve, who were both equally astounded by Aimee's efficiency. 'What do you think?'

'Looks like we're going to the Slade Hotel at two o'clock,' Maeve stated, sitting back in her seat.

'Tickets are expensive,' Eric pointed out, scrolling through the event details on Aimee's phone. 'And sold out.'

'We don't need to get into the event, we just need to speak to Cece,' Maeve pointed out. 'We'll go early and wait for her to arrive. We can try to speak to her before she goes in.'

Aimee nodded. 'All right. And we're trying to find out if she was angry at Sean for rejecting her, right?'

'It seems the flimsiest motive of the lot, but it's all we have on her,' Maeve said, biting her lip.

'You never know.' Eric shrugged. 'People can do things in

the heat of the moment. She might have been really mad at the time and done it without thinking.'

'If it wasn't her, she still might tell us something useful,' Otis said in as encouraging a tone as possible. 'And anyway, it's good to have spoken to every witness there. We can always go back over everything once we've ticked the last person off our list.'

'Right.' Maeve sighed. 'Speaking to Cece definitely can't make anything worse.'

They showed up at the Slade Hotel half an hour before the event was due to start, not wanting to risk missing her. They lingered around the corner, watching the door of the hotel and the cars that began to pull up just after two o'clock. As time went on, they got fidgety waiting but it finally paid off as Maeve saw Tabitha, Casper and Cece arrive together. They were a group that certainly caught the eye, with Tabitha in a red cap-sleeve maxi dress and towering heels, Casper in a tailored light-blue suit, and Cece in a stunning high-neck floral dress.

'They're here,' Maeve announced to the group, nodding towards the steps leading up to the hotel entrance. 'How do we get Cece on her own?'

'Doesn't look like it's going to be that much of an issue,' Otis observed, watching Tabitha and Casper having a heated exchange as they made their way up the steps, while Cece hovered behind them, looking uncomfortable.

As Tabitha stormed up ahead, marching into the hotel with a disgruntled Casper following her in, Maeve darted out from behind the corner.

'Cece!'

At the sound of her name Cece stopped and looked around, bewildered, until she spotted Maeve making a beeline for her. Her expression fell.

'What are *you* doing here?'

'We need to talk,' Maeve insisted, as Aimee, Eric and Otis flanked her.

'I don't even know who you are,' Cece pointed out, raising her eyebrows.

'We shouldn't have lied to you,' Otis said. 'But we felt like we didn't have a choice. We just want to talk, that's all. My name is Otis, that's Eric and Aimee, and this is Maeve, Sean's sister. I'm also not an artist.'

'No kidding,' Cece sighed, her eyes flickering to Maeve. 'You're Sean's sister.'

'That's right.'

She nodded, folding her arms across her chest. 'Well, I have to go in so—'

'I love your dress,' Aimee declared, stopping her as she began to turn away. 'It's so pretty. That neckline really suits you.'

Cece's expression softened. 'Thanks. I had to buy it last minute this morning. Tabitha said I could wear her red dress, but then when I put it on she decided she wanted to wear it instead.' She hesitated. 'Look, if you're here to talk to Tabitha, you might as well give up. She's really upset over everything and she won't want to see you.'

Otis frowned. 'We're not here to talk to Tabitha. It's you we want to speak to.'

Cece looked confused. 'Me?'

Before Otis could explain, a man approached them on the

steps. He was tall, broad-shouldered and had an air of confidence that gave him an imposing presence. He was dressed in a tailored navy-blue suit with a crisp white shirt open at the collar and a paisley-patterned pocket square. As he approached, they were hit by a waft of expensive sandalwood cologne mixed with cigar smoke.

'Cecilia,' he said in a stern tone. 'What are you doing loitering on the steps?'

'I wasn't loitering, Dad,' she replied, instantly straightening and plastering on a smile. 'I was just talking to . . . uh . . .' She gestured at the group, now unsure how to describe them. They certainly weren't friends.

'I see,' he said, turning to Maeve and the others.

Ralph Pearce took them in one by one, unwilling to disguise his disapproval at their casual appearance. He acknowledged them with a sharp nod, before turning his attention back to his daughter.

'Is Tabitha in there already?' he asked.

'Yes, she's just gone in with Casper.'

'Very good. Oh, and remember to talk to Hamish today about work experience.'

'Right,' Cece said with a fixed smile. 'Although, I was thinking that I might be able to get some experience with you, like Tabitha and Casper.'

'Let's be realiztic, Cece,' he said with a sigh, noticing someone else arrive and giving them a wave over her shoulder. 'You're not quite there. You know that. But speak to Hamish. I'm sure he can find something for you to do; he owes me a favor. I have to go.'

She opened her mouth to speak, but Ralph had already gone, turning his back on her to greet another guest, escorting them into the hotel.

Cece stood still for a moment, staring at the floor and looking deflated, before she lifted her chin and flicked her hair behind her shoulder.

'I have to go in now.'

'Wait, are you all right?' Otis asked, taking a step towards her.

'Why wouldn't I be all right?' she said defensively. 'I'm fine.'

'You looked . . . disappointed, that's all.'

'It's nothing. Look, I don't know you, and what you did – lying about who you are to hang out with us and trick us – was super creepy, so I'm just going to—'

'Have you asked for work experience with your dad before?' Otis asked, deciding this was no time to beat around the bush. He *had* to get her talking.

'It's none of your business.'

'He let Tabitha and Casper work with his team, and you want to do the same.'

She pursed her lips, not saying anything.

But she didn't leave either.

'That can't be easy,' Otis offered, his tone gentle and understanding. 'When your dad says no to you, I mean. That must be . . . really hard.'

She shook her head, uttering quietly, 'I shouldn't have got my hopes up. It was stupid of me.'

'Why do you say that?' Otis asked, while Maeve, Aimee and Eric slowly moved away from their conversation to give Cece some privacy now that she was starting to engage with Otis.

'I'm not Tabitha.'

She suddenly looked so vulnerable, so unsure and forlorn. Otis nodded in understanding at this glimpse into their dynamic, something he'd picked up on right from the start. Tabitha had always been the Queen Bee, Cece stuck in her shadow.

It was as though Cece suddenly remembered who she was talking to, because she frowned at Otis and cleared her throat. 'Anyway, I need to go.'

'You're your own person, Cece,' Otis blurted out as she made to leave.

She stopped. 'What?'

Otis took a deep breath. 'It's normal to compare yourself to others; we tend to naturally wonder how we measure up to someone else. It can be common with siblings too; it's difficult not to compare your aspirations and achievements to hers. But you're your own person, Cece. You don't need to compare yourself to Tabitha to define who you are. We all have our strengths and weaknesses. You're two different people. If you keep comparing yourself to her, you risk ruining your relationship with misguided resentment. And you shouldn't let your dad dictate who you are either. You have a right to carve out your own path in life.'

She blinked at him.

'When we said we needed to talk just now, you assumed we meant to Tabitha,' he continued. 'Why was that?'

'I don't know.' She looked annoyed at herself, her eyebrows knitted together. 'She's the one people usually want to talk to.'

'Is that why you were mad at Sean at the party? He proved

224

that theory right,' Otis suggested gently.

She looked taken aback. 'I wasn't mad at *him*. OK, maybe I was mad for a second, but I was drunk and it was stupid. Bet he had a great laugh over that one.' Her eyes fell to the ground and she sniffed. 'Tabitha's pathetic little sister throwing herself at him.'

'He wouldn't laugh at you,' Otis assured her. 'Why do you think he would ever refer to you as Tabitha's "pathetic little sister"? Is that how you think he sees you?'

'Not just him,' she admitted quietly, folding her arms across her chest.

'Cece, if you keep perceiving yourself in relation to Tabitha, you'll be miserable.'

'Because she's so perfect and I'm not.'

'No one is perfect, and no one *feels* perfect either. Everyone has doubts, worries and struggles. But by comparing yourself to Tabitha, you're putting all your focus on her, when it should be on you.'

Cece sighed, forcing herself to bring her eyes up to meet his. 'Tell that to my family.'

'I'm telling it to *you*,' Otis reminded her.

She nodded slowly, letting his words sink in, before narrowing her eyes at him. 'What's your name again? Your real one.'

He smiled. 'Otis.'

'Otis,' she repeated. 'Well, thanks, I guess. I still think what you and your friends did was creepy though.'

'I understand.' He shoved his hands in his pockets. 'We were trying to help our friend.'

'Right. Well.' She gestured to the hotel door.

'Cece,' Otis began, stopping her again, 'when you said you were seeing someone, you weren't talking about Sean?'

'No!' she exclaimed, startled by the suggestion. 'I was talking about Noah.'

Otis raised his eyebrows in surprise. 'You and Noah are an item?'

'Very recently. As in, it's not common knowledge,' she informed him, glancing around to make sure no one was listening. 'We're seeing how things go. It happened that night actually, right after Sean rejected me. I was so embarrassed and then Noah walked in, found me hiding away and one thing led to another.' She smiled bashfully. 'I suppose I have Sean to thank. I'm genuinely grateful to him. If he'd gone along with my drunken stupidity, Noah and I might not have recognized the spark between us.'

Otis nodded. 'I guess that's something.'

'Anyway, I *really* have to go now. If Tabitha wonders where I am and comes out here and sees me talking to you, she'll lose her shit.' She hesitated, offering him a small smile. 'It was nice to meet you, Otis.'

'You too, Cece.'

With an awkward wave, Otis watched dismally as she made her way to the top of the steps and disappeared into the hotel, all hopes of helping Sean disappearing along with her.

EIGHTEEN

Maeve had known it was a long shot.

It would have been a dramatic reaction for Cece to be so upset with Sean that she framed him for a serious crime that might have landed him in prison. But part of her had been hoping that she'd got it all wrong about Sean and there was still a sliver of hope.

'Noah didn't tell us that they were dating, so maybe she was lying,' Otis pointed out, noticing Maeve's disheartened expression as he told them what he'd learned. 'Or she still could have been angry enough to take the necklace at the party in between Sean rejecting her and Noah kissing her. She did say she was really embarrassed. Maybe she lashed out then, before Noah came along.'

'Yeah, that's true,' Eric said.

'We could question them all again,' Aimee suggested. 'If we get Noah on his own, we could ask him—'

'They won't let us talk to them again,' Maeve pointed out wearily. 'It's a miracle Otis managed to speak to Cece.'

'But—'

Maeve stopped in the road and turned to face them. They were walking up a hill in the direction of their hotel and it was warm in the sun.

'It's over,' she said firmly, before Aimee could protest. 'We talked to each person there at that party and not one of them has convinced me that they may have taken the necklace and framed Sean. Does anyone feel differently?'

Nobody said anything.

'We're not detectives. We're not miracle workers,' she continued, shaking her head. 'We've done all we can. It's over. It was never going to work.'

'As long as they don't find the necklace on Sean or any proof that he had it, they won't be able to arrest him,' Otis said, trying to find the positives in the situation. 'I don't think.'

'Yeah, but if someone is trying to frame him, Otis, how do we know that they're not going to plant the necklace on him at some later point to finish the job?' Eric said thoughtfully.

As Otis gave Eric a pointed look in response, he went, 'Oh,' and glanced apologetically at Maeve. 'I mean, that probably won't happen though. Sean will be fine. He won't be arrested.'

'We tried to prove his innocence and what do you know?' Maeve threw up her arms in exasperation. 'We couldn't. So there you go. It's like Sean said, he's alone in this. Nothing we can do.'

Aimee felt a wave of sympathy for Maeve, and looked to Otis and Eric for help on what they should say to make her feel better, but they were as stumped as she was.

'It's time to go home,' she stated firmly.

'Maeve,' Otis began, 'what if we—'

'Please stop,' she pleaded, swallowing the lump building in her throat. 'Please, Otis. Please stop. There's no point. There never was.'

'Don't say that,' he said, reaching out to take her hand, but she moved away from him.

'You don't get it; you never did.' She looked down at the ground, shaking her head. 'People like me and Sean . . . we don't win. We never do.'

'So that's it, you're just going to give up,' Otis said, clenching his jaw. 'We're going to drive home and forget about all of this.'

'I told you we'd give it one more shot, and we did just that. You agreed.'

'Yes, but I still think that we can help somehow,' he asserted. 'All this time and effort coming to nothing. We can't just walk away.'

'Yes, we can, Otis. We have to,' Maeve told him stubbornly. 'Sometimes you just can't win. I tried to protect you all from the disappointment, but you wouldn't listen.'

'Cece and I had a good chat, even though she knew who I really was. We could try that with the others too, and you never know, we might—'

Maeve buried her head in her hands, crying out, 'How many times do we have to do this, Otis? I've had enough! I'm done!' She turned and started marching up the grassy hill next to the road. 'I need a minute on my own.'

'So you're walking away?' Otis called out angrily after her. 'Is that what you're doing? Giving up and walking away.'

She stopped, took a deep breath and spun around to look down at him.

'Yes, Otis. That's what we do, me and Sean. When we know we can't win, we run. We get out. Because unlike you, we don't have someone checking in on us every day, making sure that we're all right. Get this into your head. *We are on our own.*'

'No, you're not! We're right here! We're trying to help, Maeve! We want to help you, and we want to help Sean!' Otis cried, his forehead creased in frustration. 'I still believe we can!'

'Why?!' she yelled. 'Why are you so sure he's innocent?'

'Because I don't give up on people like you do!'

They fell into silence, Otis's words hanging in the air. Maeve was too stung to bring herself to speak. Eric dropped his eyes to the ground; Aimee bit her lip. No one knew what to say. Otis felt too angry to feel bad at first, but as the silence went on and he took in her wounded expression, his rage ebbed and the guilt crept in. He hated hurting Maeve. She was really the last person he would ever want to hurt. She just made him so angry sometimes; she simply refused to see what was right in front of her.

Refused to see that, if she let him, he'd make sure she was never alone.

'Maeve . . .' he croaked.

She cut across him, her tone cold. 'I'll see you back at the hotel.'

The others looked on glumly as she turned away and started making her way up the hill towards the bench that Aimee had found at the beginning of the trip.

Aimee sighed. 'I think I should go with her.'

Otis nodded dejectedly. 'She shouldn't be on her own. We'll go back and see you there.'

'OK. Eric, can I borrow your blazer?'

230

'Um, sure. But aren't you warm in the sun?' he asked, handing it over.

'It's not to wear,' she said matter-of-factly. 'It's to sit on. Who knows what else happens on that bench? And I love this skirt.'

'Right.' Eric frowned as Aimee followed Maeve. 'Otis, remind me to burn that jacket when we get home.'

As Otis shoved his hands in his pockets, Eric gave him a comforting pat on the back.

Maeve sat down on the bench, looking out at the view.

'Mind if I join you?' Aimee asked, placing Eric's blazer down on the bench and then sitting down on top of it.

'You didn't have to stay with me.'

'I *wanted* to,' Aimee said, nudging her. 'And if we're going home soon, then we should take in this view one last time. It's amazing how much you can see from here. The whole bloody city. In some places they'd charge you twenty pounds for a ticket to see a view like this.'

'Who needs a viewing tower when you have a shitty old bench?'

'Exactly.'

Maeve folded her arms across her chest. They sat together in silence.

'Part of me actually thought we might be able to find out the truth about the necklace and maybe even help Sean,' Maeve muttered after a while, shaking her head. 'So stupid.'

'It's not stupid.'

'It is. I knew I wouldn't pull this off. I knew I'd mess it up just like everything else.'

'You don't mess everything up. You're brilliant!' Aimee shifted to face Maeve straight on. 'You have the biggest brain ever and you really care. You came all this way to help your brother when he needed you. You have no idea how amazing that is. Otis didn't mean what he said.'

'He's right,' Maeve admitted, looking down at her hands. 'I do give up on people. When they let you down all the time, it's easier that way.'

Aimee reached for her hand, taking it in hers and squeezing it. 'Maeve, I don't think you'll ever give up on me. It's like that really inspirational quote I read once on the back of a toilet door: "Friends are lurking in the shadows." No. Wait, that wasn't it. That sounds well creepy. It was like that though. Maybe: "Friends are hidden in the shadows." That sounds bad too. When I say it out loud, it sounds much worse that when it's in my head. "Friends are there in the shadows"? That still sounds weird.'

Maeve couldn't help but smile at Aimee rambling on.

'OK, I can't remember the quote,' she continued, heaving a sigh. 'But the gist was, I'm going to be here whether your life is all sunshine-y or shadow-y. I won't give up on you; you won't give up on me. I know that whether you say so or not.'

Maeve squeezed her hand back. 'Sunshine-y or shadow-y.'

Aimee smiled, satisfied, sitting back and getting a pack of cigarettes out of her pocket. She offered Maeve one and then got out her lighter. She lit Maeve's, then her own cigarette and exhaled.

'I'm sorry we couldn't help find out the truth about the necklace,' she said, looking out at the city.

232

'Me too. But it's time to go home.'

'Otis's mum will be pleased. I'll miss sleeping in the same room as you though.'

'That's true. It's been nice waking up and seeing you there, raring to go,' Maeve admitted, chuckling. 'I didn't know you were such an early riser.'

'I'm not really,' Aimee said, shrugging. 'It's only recently because I'm finding it so hard to sleep.'

Maeve gave her a strange look. 'You're having trouble sleeping?'

Aimee nodded. 'I can't switch off my brain. As soon as I lie down, all these worries start drifting into my mind and they completely boggle it. I keep waking up really early and then I can't shut them down, so I might as well get up and distract myself.'

'What kind of worries?'

'Nothing important.' She shrugged. 'Stuff like, is my mum right when she says my face is too round for a bob haircut? If I don't become a baker, what will my future look like? Do my parents even care? Stupid things like that.'

Maeve watched her take a drag. 'They're not stupid, Aimee. And you know you can always talk to me about these worries, OK?'

'I know.' Aimee chuckled. 'And there's always Otis too. Our very own therapist. It's funny, you would never look at Otis and think "he must know a lot about sex and relationships." He looks more like someone who would know a lot about recycling. Or chess.'

Maeve laughed. 'Hey, nothing wrong with knowing a lot

about chess. Or recycling, for that matter.'

'Let me guess, *you* know a lot about chess?'

'I dabble.'

'Will you teach me?' Aimee asked.

'You still haven't got the hang of Scabby Queen and I've been trying to teach you that for ages.'

'I think chess is more my thing,' she declared. 'I like that the pieces have cute little names, like Professor Plum and Colonel Mustard.'

'Those aren't chess pieces, Aimee. Those are names from a game called Cluedo.'

'Oh my God, you are so right! I used to love Cluedo. Very apt when we're trying to solve a real-life mystery.'

'When we *tried*,' Maeve said, raising her eyebrows. 'Past tense.'

'Oh yeah. I forgot.' Aimee sighed. 'I was really getting into *Emma* last night. I think I'll read more of that one.'

'I particularly enjoyed your theory that Emma Woodhouse could be a vampire,' Maeve teased, recalling some of Aimee's hilarious comments that had everyone in stitches.

'It's easy for you to laugh at my ideas,' Aimee huffed. 'You've already read it so you know the ending. I'm taking stabs in the dark.'

'Do you really think Jane Austen wrote a book about vampires?'

'Maybe. Why shouldn't she? They knew about vampires back in those days, didn't they?'

Maeve nodded. 'Yeah. They've been around a while.'

'So not *that* crazy then, that Jane Austen might have let her imagination run wild and written a book about a wealthy heiress who wanted people to get married, but also wanted to drink their blood.'

'No, I guess it's not that crazy,' Maeve said, giggling.

'It was a really nice idea from Eric and Otis to do book club.'

'Really nice,' Maeve echoed, adding quietly, 'No one's really done anything like that for me before.'

They fell into silence as they both considered how thoughtful the book club gesture was until Aimee suddenly leaned forward, squinting at something.

'I think those birds are having sex,' she said, pointing at two pigeons on the grass ahead. 'They're really going at it, look. You see? This really is a romantic spot, whether you're a human or a pigeon.'

They agreed the birds were having a moment and then, trying to give the pigeons some privacy by ignoring them, they returned their concentration to the beautiful view. They continued chatting away on the bench about nothing much until the cooling air made them realize the day was fading into evening.

When she started getting goose pimples on her arms, Aimee decided to sacrifice her skirt and put on Eric's blazer instead of sitting on it.

'It's nice and warm from my bum,' she informed Maeve.

'We should probably get back to the hotel and I suppose I have to speak to Sean. Get it over with.' Maeve groaned.

'I'll be here at your side while you call him.'

As Maeve got her phone out, Aimee stuck her hands in her pockets to keep them warm and started pulling out a patterned orange bandana.

'What's that?' Maeve asked, frowning at it.

'It must be Eric's,' Aimee said, wrapping it around her head and tying it into a bow on one side. 'I keep finding his stuff in my pockets.'

'You mean *his* pockets.'

'Right. The other day, when I was wearing another one of his jackets, I found some Haribo in there. I think he stashes it away for later, like a squirrel with nuts. But then he pointed out that he found a stash of sugar packets from the cafe in the pockets, because I took a few from that little pot on the table at breakfast and then forgot they were in there when I gave him it back. I just always think things like that are handy to have on you, don't you?'

Maeve frowned, a niggle in the back of her mind. 'What did you say?'

'I just think that things like little sugar and salt packets are good to keep around, because you never know when you—'

'No, not that,' Maeve said, gripping Aimee's arm. 'You were wearing his jacket.'

'Yeah?'

'And he found the sugar packets in the pocket later.'

'Because I'd put them in there and forgot about them when I gave it back. But I don't think that's as weird as keeping a Haribo fried egg in there, do you?'

'It may have been an accident,' Maeve whispered, a light bulb going on in her head.

'I don't think so. If a Haribo fried egg is in a pocket, it's been put in there purposefully.'

'Not that. The box!' Maeve cried, jumping to her feet.

'Aimee, we have to go. Come on!'

'What?' Aimee pushed herself up off the bench as Maeve started running down the hill towards the road. 'Where are we going?'

'Back to the hotel!' Maeve called out over her shoulder. 'We need to tell the others!'

'Tell them what?'

Maeve turned to yell back up the hill. 'That we've been looking at this all wrong!'

*

Maeve burst through the hotel door, making Eric and Otis jump out of their skins.

'What if it was an accident that the necklace box ended up in Sean's pocket?' she blurted out, catching her breath, having run most of the way. 'Aimee was wearing Eric's jacket and then later he found sugar packets from the cafe in there!'

'He had Haribo in his pocket too!' Aimee wheezed, arriving just behind her and slumping down on the bed, clutching a stitch in her side.

'She forgot she put the packets in there,' Maeve continued, 'and later, Eric, you found them when she gave the jacket back. What if that happened to Sean? What if we've been looking at this wrong?'

'Yes, we were thinking the same thing and—'

'Maybe someone didn't mean for Sean to get into trouble. They took the necklace and put the box in his jacket because they were wearing it. We've seen what it's like at that house, all the shoes mixed up at the door, the coats all hanging on top of each other on the hooks or in a pile somewhere. Sean even said that he left his jacket lying around on the sofa, right? Maybe someone took it thinking it was theirs, because it was similar.'

Eric nodded. 'Definitely easily done.'

'So I'm not being ridiculous and this could be a possibility?' Maeve asked hopefully. 'Shall I call Sean and ask him if anyone wore his jacket that night?'

'No need.'

Maeve blinked at Otis. 'What?'

'OK, so when we got back, Eric had a genius idea,' Otis explained, slightly on edge around Maeve after their fight, not quite able to look her in the eye.

'It was more luck than genius,' Eric said, holding up his phone. 'I went on Instagram and started the usual scrolling. Then I thought I'd look up Tabitha and that lot, and I was scrolling through Tabitha's many, many selfies when I noticed that she was wearing the necklace in a few of them. So they must have been from that night before the necklace went missing, right?'

'Right.' Maeve nodded, thinking back on what Sean had told them. 'She took it off a bit later and put it in the box next to her bed.'

'Otis and I went through all the social media photos from everyone there that night, searching for clues. There are a LOT of photos.'

'Thank goodness that people are addicted to documenting their lives, because we found something,' Otis said. 'We were just about to call you. Or Eric was. You probably wouldn't want to speak to me after what I said.'

'Forget about it,' Maeve said, her eyebrows knitting together. 'What did you find?'

Eric waved for everyone to gather around as he held up a photo.

Maeve peered at it over his shoulder. 'That's—'

'Yeah, but don't focus on his face,' Otis told her. 'Look at the background. The reflection in the mirror. You can just make it out.'

Aimee gasped. 'Sean's jacket!'

'Yes, it is,' Maeve whispered, her heart thudding against her chest. 'But that's not Sean wearing it.'

NINETEEN

Maeve pressed the doorbell of the Pearce family home.

They had already got through the gate of the drive thanks to the catering company, who'd opened it for one of their vans arriving with more ice. When Tabitha and Grace mentioned something about a garden party, Otis had assumed a small gathering of friends and family with a casual barbecue, but from the number of catering vans parked down the road, not to mention the number of very expensive-looking cars parked up next to them, this was a much bigger deal. He should have assumed as much, knowing Tabitha and Cece, but still.

'Don't these people get tired of parties?' Otis muttered, watching bags of ice being unloaded from the van. 'Don't they ever sleep?'

'Not with the quality stuff I supply them,' Sean replied, winking at him.

'Not now, Sean,' Maeve said sharply, giving him a pointed look from the doorstep. 'It's not really the time or place to say shit like that, is it?'

Sean held up his hands in apology. He might be trying to pretend he was at ease, but Maeve knew him better. He'd been fidgeting ever since they'd met him to come here, hardly able to stand still, and he was trying too hard to be funny.

She hadn't been sure he'd pick up when she called him last night, not after their fight and what she'd said. When he didn't pick up the first time, she messaged him saying they had found something that might help prove he was innocent and then called him again. He answered on the first ring.

She had been nervous to meet him today, wondering how he'd act around her. It was hard for him, though, to be stand-offish with her when she was providing him with hope again. He didn't hug her or anything and there was still a tension between them, but they'd both shown up. That was something.

Maeve understood why Sean was so nervous. This had the potential to go well, but it also had a chance of going really badly. They had a good theory as of last night, but they could be wrong. And he hadn't seen any of these people since the whole incident happened, so no wonder his emotions were running high.

Maeve was about to ring the doorbell again when they heard the sound of heels clacking across the floor of the hall towards the door. It swung open and a woman they didn't recognize stood in the doorway. Elegant and sophisticated, she was tall and slender, perhaps in her late thirties, with dyed honey-blond hair and wearing a dazzling white halter-neck jumpsuit, bright-red lipstick and huge gold hoop earrings.

Eric looked down at his outfit, a pink and blue matching short-sleeved shirt and shorts combo with lobsters all over it. 'I feel hideously underdressed.'

The woman's eyes scanned across the group. 'Can I help you?'

'We're here for the garden party for Tabitha. We're her friends,' Maeve lied.

'Really?' The woman's eyebrows lifted in surprise. 'Well, then come on through. I'm Marianne, Ralph's partner.'

'Nice to meet you,' Maeve said, acknowledging her with a nod as she strode in.

They made their way through the house to the back garden, which was filled with guests in bright summer dresses and panama hats, laughing and drinking champagne and pink cocktails while an incredible jazz band played background music from one side of the garden. Staff weaved their way around the crowd, carrying trays of drinks and delicious-looking canapés.

'Are we sure this isn't a wedding?' Eric asked.

'In case you haven't realized, these people don't do anything by halves,' Sean said, leaning into him. 'It's all a big show. They're in competition with each other.'

'Yeah, well, I think the Pearce family win.' Eric sighed. 'This is how I imagine afternoon tea at Buckingham Palace.'

'What's in this?' Aimee asked one of the waiters as he offered her a canapé that looked like a mini cake.

'Coconut-ice marshmallow,' he replied proudly. 'It is flavored with coconut liqueur.'

She took one and popped it in her mouth. Her eyes widened as she chewed.

'That is *delicious*,' she said with her mouth full. 'So . . . coconut-y! I'm going to have to sell those in my bakery.'

'I can't see Tabitha, can you?' Maeve asked, craning her neck to look over the sea of guests.

'I can't see any of them,' Otis remarked, guiding Maeve away from the house and towards the side of the garden where the band was playing.

The jazz band came to the end of a song and Eric burst into enthusiastic applause. There were some polite claps from the other guests, but no one except Eric had really listened.

'That was brilliant,' he told the young guy on the saxophone nearest to him. 'I'm a musician too. I play the French horn and I'm in my school's swing band.'

'French horns have a beautiful mellow tone,' the saxophonist responded, before his eyes darted down to Eric's hands, noticing the shiny amethyst-purple polish he'd applied this morning. 'Wow. Your nails are *amazing*.'

'Oh! Thank you!' Eric held out his hands so they could be properly admired. 'I just bought this color yesterday, inspired by a drag performance I saw at The Courtyard this week.'

'The shows there are so good, aren't they?'

'I'm sorry,' a voice growled as a shadow came looming over them. 'I believe I've paid you to play, not talk.'

Eric jumped at the sound of Ralph's voice and the saxophonist looked mortified, sitting up to attention and preparing for the next song. Ralph turned his attention to Eric and frowned in disapproval.

'Why do I recognize you?' he asked in a booming voice.

'Ah, well, we met yesterday,' Eric said, smiling up at him. 'On the steps of the hotel. We were talking to your daughter Cece.'

'Dad, have you seen where—'

Tabitha appeared behind her father and stopped mid-sentence on seeing Otis, Aimee and Maeve next to Eric, then Sean. She inhaled sharply, caught off guard.

'Hi, Tabitha,' said Sean with an awkward wave. 'It's been too long.'

'What the fuck do you think you're all doing here?' she hissed with a furious expression. 'You need to leave right now!'

'Who is this, Tabitha?' Ralph demanded to know.

'That is Sean! The one who stole my necklace!'

'Allegedly!' Sean proclaimed, holding up his hands.

'You *what*?' Ralph rounded on him. 'Leave my house this instant before I call the police.'

'Actually,' Maeve began, stepping in between him and Sean, 'he didn't steal anything.'

Sean did a double take at his sister, surprised and impressed.

'You need to get out too!' Tabitha seethed, raising her voice.

By now most of the guests were watching the drama unfold, and Casper, Noah, Grace and Cece had all come marching across the garden to work out what was happening.

'What's going on?' Grace asked, before taking in who Tabitha was addressing. '*You*. Apparently you've been lying to us about who you are! You made everything up so you could spy on us.' They paused, looking hurt. 'I trusted you with personal stuff.'

'We all did,' Tabitha huffed. 'They're a bunch of fakes. Wannabe con artists. It's pathetic.'

'You tricked us!' Noah huffed, jabbing his finger at them. 'You . . . tricksters!

'We had to find out what was really going on so that we could stop an innocent person going down for this crime,' Otis explained.

'I said, *get out of my house*,' Ralph growled, furious at the interruption to his party.

'We don't want any trouble,' Otis said, his eyes darting

nervously at the sea of faces turned their way. 'We just need to check something.'

'I didn't steal the necklace,' Sean said firmly, 'but we think we know who did.'

'What? This is ridiculous!' Tabitha cried.

'I would have thought, Tabitha, you'd want to know who the real thief of your diamond necklace is,' Maeve said.

'Who could it be if it wasn't him?' she asked, gesturing to Sean.

'I didn't take anything,' Sean said firmly. 'You have the wrong guy and we can prove it.'

Tabitha hesitated. 'What do you mean?'

'Hang on just one second!' Ralph instructed pompously. 'What is going on here? Are you telling me you've been doing your own investigation? This is a police matter!'

'When the box was found in Sean's coat, they assumed he was the thief,' Aimee told him. 'Which you can understand, to be honest.'

'But it wasn't Sean who took the necklace,' Maeve said, crossing her arms.

'Then who was it?' Ralph asked.

'It was your daughter.'

Tabitha gasped. 'I didn't do anything! And why would I take my own necklace?!'

'Not you, Tabitha,' Maeve said, looking past her. 'It was you, Cece.'

Everyone turned to face Cece, who acted appalled at the accusation, her mouth dropping open, her hand placed on her heart in surprise. Maeve had to give it to her. She was really quite a good actress.

'What are you talking about? I didn't take it!' she claimed.

'We were looking through photos of the party and in one of Noah's many, many, many selfies there's you, in the reflection of the mirror, wearing Sean's jacket,' Maeve explained calmly. 'And you can see the box shape in the pocket.'

'I just want to say, my face is my work, so that's why I take a lot of selfies,' Noah pitched in, but no one was listening to him.

'I left my jacket hanging over the sofa next to the back door,' Sean said. 'You must have thrown it on when you wanted to go outside. Did you mean to frame me, Cece? Or did you just forget that it was the pocket of my jacket you were shoving the evidence into?'

'I . . . you . . . you must have taken the necklace and put it in the pocket before you lent your jacket to me,' she said hurriedly, as the crowd looked on.

'What, he took an expensive diamond necklace, put it in his pocket and then handed around his jacket for anyone to borrow?' Maeve snorted. 'That doesn't sound likely.'

'You know, Tabitha, if you wanted, you could ask Cece if you'd find the necklace in her room if you were to, say, go and have a look around now,' Otis suggested. 'If she has nothing to hide, then that wouldn't be a problem. I'm guessing she didn't sell it, since it was your mother's.'

'If I were you I would look in her bathroom cabinet,' Aimee added knowingly. 'That's always a good spot for stashing stuff.'

Tabitha was staring at her sister in disbelief. 'You . . . you wouldn't.'

Cece didn't say anything. She swallowed audibly.

'This is preposterous!' Ralph spat, aware now that they had the attention of every single person at the party, including the staff and the jazz band, the members of which were sitting with their instruments poised halfway to their mouths, too enraptured by the drama to play. 'Cece would never do anything of the sort!'

'Then we should go and check her room to prove it,' Eric said, shaking his head at Cece in disappointment.

'Fine,' Tabitha said, looking unsure, her fists clenched. 'I'll go and check and then you can all leave us alone.'

As she went to move towards the house, Cece croaked, 'Wait.'

Tabitha froze. The audience held their breath.

'Stop,' Cece said quietly, her body deflating, her eyes dropping to the floor. 'Don't . . . don't go and check.'

'Cece,' Tabitha whispered in shock. 'Please tell me you didn't take it.'

Cece didn't say anything. Tabitha's face fell.

'Why would you do that? How could you do that to me? You know how much I love it! Why would you cause so much pain and drama?'

'Because *you* cause so much pain and drama,' Cece retorted, lifting her eyes to meet Tabitha's. 'Do you have any idea what it's like to live with you?'

'Oh my God, we have a few spats and you decide to *steal* from me?' Tabitha hissed, her voice getting louder as she got angrier. 'If you wanted the necklace, Cecilia, you could have just asked! What the fuck is wrong with you? Sean could have gone to prison!'

'I didn't just want the necklace!' Cece yelled back. 'I wanted Dad to see the real you!'

Ralph's eyes widened in shock. 'What are you talking about, Cece?'

'You think Tabitha is perfect!' she cried, exasperated. 'You act as though I'm a constant disappointment, as though I'll never live up to *her*.' She pointed at her sister. 'You're always comparing me to your perfect Tabitha, and I'm never good enough, am I? I'm never going to be good enough until you see the truth.'

Ralph looked utterly shocked and devastated at his daughter's accusation.

'Cece,' he began, but she spoke over him.

'I was tired of it,' Cece admitted bitterly, turning to Tabitha. 'I wanted Dad to see what really goes on in your life. I didn't plan it. But you'd been horrible to me that night and I wanted to get back at you. You were treating me like I wasn't worthy to hang out with you and your friends, telling me what to do, tearing me down at every chance you got in front of everyone. That's the *real* Tabitha. I thought, "Why am I being compared all the time to this perfect Tabitha who doesn't exist? What if somehow the world could see her for what she really is? Then I would finally get the credit I deserve." The necklace just presented itself.'

'You took it so that she'd be vulnerable,' Otis said, his forehead furrowed as pieces of the puzzle began to fall into place.

Cece nodded. 'I went into her bedroom because someone was in mine and I needed a place to cry after she'd made fun of me, and then Sean had turned me down. I felt so . . . alone. I saw the box sitting there on her bedside table. You know, Dad didn't even talk to us about who would get that necklace. He just gave it to Tabitha when she turned eighteen. He didn't even *consider* me, even though she was my mother too.'

'I'm the eldest,' Tabitha snapped.

'Why does that matter?' Cece replied bitterly. 'You didn't even think of me and how I might feel about you wearing it!' She shook her head in irritation. 'I saw the necklace and I didn't see why I shouldn't have it. So I took it out of its box and put it on under the high-neck top I was wearing that night and then Noah came barging into the room. I guess I just shoved the box in my pocket without thinking before he could see.'

'But you were wearing Sean's jacket,' Maeve emphasized. 'And when you took it off, you left the box in there.'

'There was no way of me getting it out subtly with everyone there! I never meant for you to get into trouble, Sean,' Cece said, looking up at him apologetically. 'I guess I thought if the police never found the necklace on you, then they couldn't do anything and you'd be fine.'

'And it kept you off the hook,' Maeve pointed out, narrowing her eyes at her.

'Look, I know it doesn't sound great.' Cece sighed. 'I wouldn't have gone along with it forever. I would have somehow found a way of making it magically return. But when I took it that night I knew that Dad would get the police involved and they would ask questions and then he'd *finally* see the real Tabitha. Not the perfect one up on a pedestal with the brilliant grades and a bright future. But the one who thinks she's superior to everyone and treats me like dirt. The one who cheats on her boyfriend with some random guy who smokes weed.'

The audience gasped at this scandalous nugget of information.

'I only smoke it occasionally,' Sean pointed out. 'It's not like I—' He paused as Maeve shot him a pointed look, before clearing his throat. 'Not important. Sorry. Carry on, everyone.'

As Cece folded her arms triumphantly at the reaction to her little speech, Tabitha saw red.

'I'm going to KILL YOU!'

With her arms outstretched, she launched herself at her sister. Cece screamed as Tabitha came at her, batting Tabitha's hands away frantically. Casper jumped into the fray, wrapping his arms around Tabitha's waist, attempting to pull her away, while Noah did the same with Cece.

Everyone else looked on in shock, hands clasped over mouths, letting out yelps of surprise as they watched the sisters brawl. Ralph darted in to help, pushing his way into the middle, allowing Noah and Casper to wrench them apart. The two sisters looked frazzled and distressed, shooting daggers at each other.

'That was *harrowing*,' Eric commented under his breath, Aimee nodding in agreement.

'Stop this right now!' Ralph demanded. 'Both of you!'

'*Where is the necklace?*' Tabitha growled at Cece, throwing Casper's arms off her.

Cece ran a hand through her hair, checking it wasn't too out of place. 'It's upstairs.'

'Where?'

She pursed her lips. 'In the washbag with the poodle on it, in my bathroom cabinet.'

'Aha!' Aimee smiled smugly as Eric and Otis shared a look of surprise. 'I knew it.'

Tabitha stormed into the house. Grace hurried after her, calling for her to wait. Ralph cleared his throat and, yanking on his salmon-pink blazer to make it straight, he plastered on a wide smile and spun around to address his guests.

'How unexpected! Families, eh?' He forced out a laugh and there were a few nervous titters in response. 'Please do enjoy the rest of the day; that champagne won't drink itself!' With a fixed smile he turned to the jazz band and hissed, '*Play!* Play something right *now*!'

The musicians quickly collected themselves and launched into the next song of their set, which happened to be 'Diamonds Are a Girl's Best Friend.'

'Wildly inappropriate song,' Eric whispered to Aimee. 'And yet, at the same time, perfection.'

Inhaling deeply through his nose, Ralph turned to Cece, who was trying to explain herself to Noah in desperate whispers. 'Go inside, Cecilia,' he said sternly, interrupting her conversation. 'We need to have a talk.'

Cece did as she was told, leaving the garden under the scrutinizing gaze of all the guests. Before Ralph could follow her in, Maeve stopped him.

'Just to check, Mr. Pearce,' she said confidently, jutting her chin out, 'you will be talking to the police. Or do we need to?'

He sighed and shook his head. 'No, you can leave that side of things to me. Now, if you wouldn't mind showing yourself out.'

'Not at all.'

His jaw twitching, Ralph turned to march away into the house after his daughters.

Sliding his sunglasses on, Sean put his hands on his hips and inhaled deeply. 'Ah, breathing the air as a free man. It feels good.'

'Shut up,' Maeve said, rolling her eyes. 'Let's get out of here.'

'Let's,' Otis agreed.

'Thanks for having us!' Aimee smiled brightly at Marianne, who was still in shock from the public fallout. 'It was so much fun. And those coconut marshmallow things are delicious!'

As they traipsed back through the house they felt elated at what they'd achieved. They had done it. They'd cleared Sean's name.

'Thanks, Froggy,' Sean said, putting his arm around Maeve as they walked out of the front door and on to the drive. 'I knew you'd pull this off.'

'No, you didn't.'

'Yes, I did,' he protested, grinning at her. 'That's why you were my one and only call.'

'There's no one else for you to call, but thanks all the same.' She hesitated, looking up at him guiltily. 'Sorry for not believing you.'

'All's well that ends well.' He shrugged. 'I understand why you didn't.'

'Wait!' a voice called out across the driveway just as they reached the gate.

They turned around to see Tabitha coming towards them. She was now wearing a sparkling diamond necklace.

'You deserve an apology, Sean,' she said, approaching and stopping in front of them, her arms folded across her chest. 'I'm so sorry. For everything.'

He gestured to the diamonds around her neck. 'You got it back then.'

She gave him a small smile. 'Yeah. Probably never going to let it out of my sight again.'

'That seems very wise. What's going to happen now with Cece?'

'I don't know.' She shrugged. 'I guess we have a lot to work out. Not that I can see myself able to be in the same room as her for the foreseeable.' She hesitated, adding with a hint of sadness, 'For her to do something like this, she must really hate me.'

'She doesn't hate you,' Otis said gently. 'You should talk to her. I think that over time, a feeling of resentment has grown and she became consumed by it. You know the saying, "comparison is the thief of joy."'

'Wow.' Eric nodded. 'Who said that? Sounds like Taylor Swift.'

'Theodore Roosevelt,' Otis and Maeve corrected him in chorus.

'The Chipmunk?' Aimee asked, confused.

'The President,' Otis told her.

'Oh.' Aimee frowned. 'Why was he named after one of the Chipmunks?'

'The point is,' Otis said to Tabitha, deciding it best to move on, 'you should talk to your sister.'

'Maybe I haven't been the easiest person to live with,' Tabitha admitted. 'I'll talk to her, I promise. And I really am sorry, Sean. I feel terrible.'

'I'm just glad it's all over,' Sean replied, sliding his sunglasses up his nose. 'Bye, Tabitha.'

He pressed the button to open the gate and strolled out next to Maeve, with Aimee following close behind.

'Good luck with everything,' Otis said to Tabitha, giving her a wave.

'You too, weird teen therapist,' she replied gratefully, watching them go.

'Hey, Oatcake, "Sex Kid" is so last year for your nickname at school. Let's change it to "Weird Teen Therapist,"' Eric suggested as they walked away together.

Otis grinned. 'It has a ring to it.'

'I liked what Noah called you,' Sean opined. 'You bunch of tricksters.'

'Your nickname could be TTT,' Eric said thoughtfully. 'Teen Therapist Trickster.'

'You have to get sex in there somehow. That is what you specialize in,' Maeve pointed out.

'Sex and relationships,' Otis clarified.

'The Sex Trickster,' Aimee put out there.

Eric chuckled. 'I like The Sex Trickster.'

'I do *not* like The Sex Trickster,' Otis informed them. 'It sounds like a bizarre porno super-villain name.'

'All those in favor of Otis being called The Sex Trickster, say "aye",' Maeve pitched.

'Aye,' Eric cried.

'Aye,' Sean seconded.

'Aye,' Aimee concluded.

'Aye. Sorry, Otis, you're overruled. I'll put the word out when we get back to school.' Maeve grinned at him over her shoulder. 'You will now be known as The Sex Trickster.'

The sound of Eric's booming laugh could be heard all the way down the road.

TWENTY

'I'll be sad to leave this place,' Aimee said, leaning on the counter of the hotel reception and pressing the bell for assistance. 'I've grown quite fond of it.'

'Really?' Maeve asked, unconvinced.

'Yeah! It's become a home away from home. And I'll miss my chats with Lewis.'

'Who?' Otis asked.

'You know, Lewis, the local fox.'

Before Maeve or Otis could ask Aimee for further detail on her nightly conversations with the local wildlife, Helen appeared at the desk.

'I wondered if you might be coming in today,' she began, clicking on the mouse for the computer to start up. 'There's a room that's become available. Do you want it?'

'Typical. We're leaving today,' Maeve informed her. 'We're here to check out.'

Helen blinked at her. 'So you *don't* want the room then.'

'No, we don't. Because we're leaving. We'd like to pay though.'

'Oh, right,' Helen said, looking at Otis in disappointment. 'I'll just get your bill for you.'

'Thanks again for helping us with the book club idea. That

was very nice of you,' Otis said.

'Any time. So will you be coming back this way soon, Otis?' she asked him hopefully.

Maeve smirked, looking away from the desk, while Otis blushed furiously.

'Uh well, I don't know,' he croaked, his face on fire from the attention. 'I'm not sure when we'll be back this way. You know how it is. Not sure where the wind will blow.'

She smiled seductively at him. 'You're always welcome here. Even during peak times I'm sure we can manage to *squeeze* you in.'

Maeve attempted to hide a laugh with a coughing fit, pretending to have something stuck in her throat. Aimee thumped her on the back, and Otis had no idea where to look or what to say, so he stood frozen to the spot, wide-eyed, like a rabbit caught in headlights.

Helen slid the bill across to them, fluttering her eyelashes at Otis the whole time, and, after Maeve checked the numbers were correct, Aimee put it on her card. Feeling unnerved by Helen's intense gaze, Otis was grateful when he felt his phone vibrating in his pocket.

'I'd better get this,' he said, showing them the call up on the screen and gesturing to the door.

'Say hi to your mum for me!' Helen called after him as he scurried out, tripping over his own feet. 'Come again!'

'Mum,' Otis said, answering the phone, pleased to be out of there.

'Hello, darling,' Jean replied, audibly relieved at his picking up. 'Are you still cross with me?'

'No, Mum, I've been meaning to call you. I wanted to apologize,' he confessed, watching Eric and Sean over by the car, trying to load Aimee's suitcase, almost buckling under the weight. 'I should have been in touch more often. I'm sorry for shutting you out this trip and for not telling you who I was with. I should have been honest.'

'No, Otis, I'm the one who needs to apologize. I embarrassed you by calling the hotel. I should trust you to be responsible. You can look after yourself now. You don't need your mother checking in on you all the time.'

Otis glanced up as Maeve walked out of reception.

'Actually, I've recently been reminded that everyone needs someone to look out for them, even when we don't think we do.' He took a deep breath. 'I'm really grateful to you for checking in on me, Mum.'

'I love you, darling,' she replied, and Otis could tell she was smiling into the receiver.

'Love you too. I'll be home soon.'

As Otis hung up and wandered over to the car, Maeve was passing Aimee the cash for her share of the bill. She'd have to speak to Cynthia about paying her rent late, but she'd think about that later. For now she was going to enjoy the moment of having solved the mystery and helped her brother clear his name.

'Move Aimee's case over a bit that way,' Eric directed Sean, gesturing at the car boot. 'Then my case can slide in beside it.'

'How long did you all think you were going to be staying here for?' Sean asked, shifting Aimee's case up against the wall of the boot. 'You've got enough clothes to last you a month.'

'If it wasn't for my and Aimee's zealous dedication to our variety of wardrobe, we would not have got very far fooling anyone, Sean,' Eric reminded him.

He laughed. 'That's true. Hey, I'm not complaining. I owe you all big time.'

'I'm glad it's sorted,' Otis said.

'Me too.' Sean grinned at Maeve as she and Aimee approached the car. 'And you'll be pleased to hear that Amit is going to get me a job, so I can get back on track.'

Maeve made a face. 'Not a job at that club. They might still go there and you'll have to see them after everything that's happened. You want a clean break, don't you?'

'I certainly do and that's why it's not a job at the club,' he assured her. 'He knows someone who works behind the bar down the road. Apparently there might be an opening.'

'Great. Well, we should get going,' Maeve said, checking the time. 'It's a long drive home.'

'Thanks for everything,' Sean said as Eric, Otis and Aimee waved to him and climbed into the car. He turned to Maeve and got an envelope out his pocket. 'This is for you.'

She opened it and saw a wad of cash. 'What is this?'

'It's for your rent. I know that you would have spent a bit getting here and I don't want you to be short because of me.'

'Where did you get it?'

He grinned. 'Noah got in touch to pay me what he owed. Come on, Froggy, just take it, would you? It's the least I could do. Like I said, I owe you.'

She closed the envelope and slid it into her bag. 'Thanks, Sean. But please stop selling?'

He held up three fingers. 'Scout's honor.'

She nodded. She wanted to believe him.

'I'll see you soon, Frog-face.'

'Good.'

She gave him a quick hug before pulling away and walking around the front of the car to get in. As Aimee turned the key in the ignition and they pulled away, Maeve watched Sean grow distant in the reflection of the side mirror until they turned the corner and he was gone.

'I feel like we've achieved so much,' Aimee declared to the group. 'This has been a crazy few days. It's gone so fast!'

'I still can't believe it was Cece all along,' Eric mused as he looked out of the window. 'She had the necklace there in the house that whole time. Talk about it being right under Tabitha's nose. What a mess!'

'Do you think Tabitha will press charges?' Aimee asked.

Otis shook his head. 'No, I don't think so. But that family has a lot of issues to talk through.'

Maeve snorted. 'I can sympathize with that.'

'Me too,' Aimee said.

'Me too,' Eric chimed in.

'Me too.' Otis sighed, before they all burst out laughing.

'I know I've said this already,' Maeve began, once the giggling had subsided, 'but I really am grateful that you all came with me on this trip. I couldn't have done it without you.'

'That's what friends are for.' Aimee beamed with excitement. 'And who knew that solving crimes could be so much fun? Do you think someone will write a book about this someday? And it will be like our grand adventure and they'll want to interview us to get all our different viewpoints to make sure it's orthodontic!'

'You mean authentic?'

'Yeah.' She nodded, beeping at a pedestrian to get out of the way. 'That's what I said.'

'Maybe.' Otis chuckled. 'It could go down as one of the great mysteries of our time.'

'We should consider setting up our own detective agency,' Eric pitched. 'We could be like this awesome crime-fighting team and we'd each have our own skills and when we come together we're this unstoppable force. Like Marvel's Avengers but instead of baddies, we're fighting injustice. The Sex Trickster can be the villain.'

Otis rolled his eyes.

'That sounds so much fun!' Aimee exclaimed. 'Maybe instead of a baker, I'll become a detective. Do you think they'll make a movie about us?'

'Yeah, course,' Eric replied. 'It would have a theme tune and everything. Who would you pick to play you in the film, Oatcake?'

Maeve gazed out of the window as they drove away from the city, listening to her friends passionately discuss who would best play the movie version of themselves.

She smiled to herself. Sean was wrong about one thing. Maybe there had been a time in this life when Maeve was alone.

But she wasn't any more.

ON **REPORT**

Someone has got their hands on some of the students' files. What does new Headteacher, Hope, really think of Otis and his friends? Read on . . .

SCHOOL FILES: CONFIDENTIAL

THE NERDY ONE: **OTIS MILBURN**

- ⊗ Ran a sex clinic under the pretence of being helpful – does he just want to find out about other people's sex lives?
- ⊗ Used to blend into the background until he started the sex clinic and brought up all this sex education nonsense.

THE CONFLICTED JOCK: **JACKSON MARCHETTI**

- ⊗ Former Head Boy. Was the pride of Moordale before he "found" himself and went off the rails.
- ⊗ Sensitive but smart. There's still a chance he can be guided back onto the right path.

THE ECCENTRIC ONE: **LILY IGLEHART**

- ⊗ Alien-obsessed and in her own world most of the time.
- ⊗ She was the "brains" behind the school production of *Romeo and Juliet*. Inappropriate!

THE DITZY ONE: **AIMEE GIBBS**

- ⊗ Sweet but spaced out – perhaps not the most academically minded.
- ⊗ Had a horrible sexual assault experience with a man on a bus so extra support may be needed.
  *NB: avoid any home-baked goods.

THE FRIENDLY ONE: **ERIC EFFIONG**

- ⊗ Always happy and appears to be liked by everyone.
- ⊗ Needs to concentrate more on his schoolwork and less on his love life and fashion choices.

THE SUPER SMART ONE: **VIVIENNE ODESANYA**

- ⊗ Far too clever for her own good. Extremely driven and knows what she wants.
- ⊗ Scarily focused but perhaps lacking in self-confidence.

THE DISRUPTIVE ONE: **ADAM GROFF**

- ⊗ Son of former Headteacher, Mr. Groff.
- ⊗ Previously very angry and difficult to deal with.
- ⊗ Appears to finally want to get an education. Time will tell if he goes back to his old ways.

THE CURIOUS ONE: **OLA NYMAN**

- ⊗ Always direct and to the point. Open to new experiences – see relationship with fellow student, Lily.
- ⊗ Very level-headed and hardworking but has had some difficulties adapting to her new living arrangements. May need some extra support at times.

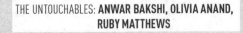

⊗ These three come as a pack – Ruby is a leader while the others follow.

⊗ They are untouchable because they are the popular group and think they are much better than everyone else.

⊗ Ruby's recent relationship with Otis could threaten the group dynamics – keep a close eye on the situation.

THE SCARY ONE: **MAEVE WILEY**

⊗ Can come across as unapproachable, sometimes a bit too smart for her own good.

⊗ Highly intelligent and will go far if she gets the right breaks. Could be the first ex-Moordale student to become Prime Minister?

THE OUTSPOKEN ONE: **CAL BOWMAN**

⊗ Asks to be referred to as they/them. Part of the group of skater kids at Moordale.

⊗ Despite best efforts, will not conform to new uniform rules. Potential to cause trouble.

THE COOL ONE: **RAHIM HARRAK**

⊗ Can come across as petulant and brooding.

⊗ Is always reading poetry, but it would be nice to see him smile a bit more.

LOVE AND RELATIONSHIPS

Love isn't about grand gestures, or the moon and the stars. It's just dumb luck. And sometimes, you meet someone who feels the same way. And then sometimes you're unlucky. But one day, you're going to meet someone who appreciates you for who you are. I mean, there are seven billion people on the planet. I know one of them is going to climb up on a moon for you.

OTIS MILBURN
LOVE GURU AND TEENAGE PHILOSOPHER

YOUR CRUSH IS COMING, **ACT NORMAL**

So there's someone out there that you just can't stop thinking about. Maybe you feel a rush of excitement when you see them, or get butterflies in your stomach every time you think about them. No matter what you do you can't help feeling the feels – you've got a crush.

You can't control who you get a crush on, it's just one of life's great mysteries, like why peanut butter and jelly tastes so good or that a passport photo will always be terrible. Your crush could be a Hollywood superstar or someone you've seen around town – a lot of crushes are a fun, healthy way to discover what you want both from a partner and a relationship. But a crush can also be confusing and a cause of real worry and anxiety.

Maybe you've gone your whole life not thinking about your sexuality and then find you can't stop thinking about someone who is the same gender as you. Does this mean you're gay? Bisexual? (Refer back to chapter two for more on understanding identity.) Having strong feelings for someone of the same gender can be part of growing up. As you learn more about who you are, you may decide you want to identify in a certain way or you might prefer not to label yourself.

There is no right or wrong when it comes to your feelings, but at times it may feel overwhelming. If you feel able to, it can help to speak to a trusted friend, a professional or clinics for help and advice. Some great places are listed at the back of this book.